The New Paltz Town Crier

Murder on Main

Carol Freeman

i

For Bill:

Again, my partner in crime and always my love.

ACKNOWLEDGMENTS

What an extraordinary and challenging year 2020 has been for everyone! I have been fortunate to be able to escape to my writing during this pandemic. My husband, Bill, has provided me with perceptive and honest feedback every step of the way. A very special thank-you, Bill. Your love and enthusiastic support have meant more to me than you could ever imagine.

Carol Brott has, once again, generously offered her invaluable critique and advice as she meticulously combed through my draft. Tom Brott, artist and photographer, has created, yet, another spectacular cover. My heartfelt thanks and love to you both.

I am so grateful that Walter and Cosmo have welcomed Bill and me to their Antique Barn family. They have created an environment filled with outrageous stories, wacky characters and high-spirited laughter. More importantly, they lead with their hearts, as much as they try to pretend otherwise. I wish to thank you both for sharing your humor, your joys, and your frustrations. You've been a source of inspiration and fun at a time when I've needed it the most.

Carol Freeman

Prologue

Monday Afternoon, September 19

New Paltz, NY is an artsy college town located two hours north of Manhattan, in the Hudson Valley region. The village boasts a thriving downtown with cafes and shops, attracting visitors and locals. An added bonus is the vibrant pedestrian area, Water Street Market, featuring an open-air courtyard surrounded by boutiques, cafes, antique shops, and an avant-garde theatre. The Wallkill Valley Rail Trail meanders right behind the market. The backdrop to this picturesque destination is the Shawangunk Ridge, known as "the Gunks". The jagged, vertical cliffs attract hikers and rock-climbers from all over the globe.

On this unseasonably warm September afternoon, Water Street Market was spilling over with free-spirited energy. The courtyard was filled with a diverse cross-section of ages, races, and species, all soaking up a glorious day. This late-summer afternoon appeared to be, simply, an ordinary September day at Water Street Market, but, in reality, today set in motion a series of catastrophic events.

At the Mudd Puddle Cafe, Michelle and James were whipping out lattes and their famous 'huevos wrap' at an impressive rate for the line-up of customers. Across the courtyard from the Mudd Puddle, the Antique Barn, a rambling, two-story, multi dealer shop, was filled with browsers. At the opposite end of Water Street Market, Eddie Siricco, the painter, was precariously balanced on a ladder, meticulously painting the trim around a second story window above Antiques on Main.

Eddie Siricco was in his sixties but had the bravado of a twenty-year-old. He was five feet, six inches tall with a wiry frame and

1

could scramble up a ladder faster than a capuchin monkey. Everyone at Water Street Market knew Eddie. He was a constant presence, either dangling thirty feet from a ladder or strutting around from shop to shop. According to Eddie, even a simple touch-up paint job required his artistic expertise. And Eddie, who claimed to be a direct descendent of Michelangelo, was the man for the job. He operated on Eddie time which included periodic unexplained absences whenever he sneaked off to down a few shots of Jack Daniels. Yet, the eventual results of Eddie's efforts were always indisputably impressive.

In addition, for several decades Eddie had been writing a weekly column for the Daily Freeman. His articles were filled with salacious innuendoes and controversial gossip to which he was privy. The locals referred to Eddie as the Town Crier, his adopted byline. His loyal readers either wanted to catch up on the local gossip or hoped to be featured as the hot topic of the week.

From his perch, Eddie's roving artist's eye caught two attractive young women as they sat at a table below him. "Hey there, ladies! Great day isn't it?" he shouted, tipping his cap without even the slightest wobble.

"Hi, Eddie!" one of the women shouted back. "We're in the middle of reading your latest column." She read aloud, "*And what do you make of the famous babe magnet who strolled around Water Street Market last weekend with his latest eye candy while the wife was home in Brooklyn with their three kids? Hint, hint: Academy Award, 2018! Tune in next week! And remember, always keep your ears open. Your Town Crier.*"

"So, what do you think of it?" asked Eddie who was never shy about fishing for a compliment.

The other woman shouted, "Come on, Eddie. You've gotta tell us! Who is this guy?"

Eddie winked, "Sorry. I've gotta keep you ladies guessing! That's my job!"

"That's so unfair!" the one woman whined. "Oh well, have a great afternoon, Eddie." She smiled and waved up at him.

Eddie chirped, "You know, ladies, I don't think today could get any better. In fact, I think I'm going to quit work early."

Eddie bounced down off the ladder, artfully managing to keep the can of paint from spilling. He whistled his way across the courtyard to the parking lot and loaded his gear into his truck.

Yes, indeed, this late-summer afternoon appeared to be, simply, an ordinary September day at Water Street Market. Yet, in spite of its benign appearance, today was anything but ordinary. Nobody could possibly have imagined that there was never going to be another Town Crier article. And, nobody could possibly have imagined that by the end of this auspicious week, Eddie Siricco, the New Paltz Town Crier, would forever be silenced.

Earlier That Same Day

Eddie Siricco was painting the trim around two windows this morning. He was admiring his work from the top rung of the ladder when his ears perked up as he heard two of the 'regulars' talking at a small cafe table below him.

"You're looking a bit, well, edgy. In fact, you look like hell. What's up Ben?"

Ben Sheppard had a compact build with a prominent beer belly. His thinning gray hair was pulled into a stringy ponytail. Ben showed up in a ripped pair of sweats and a coffee-stained tee shirt. Every one of his sixty-seven years was visible as he slouched down in his chair, sipping his coffee. "Nothing, really. I'm doing great these days," Ben replied unconvincingly. "How about you?"

Phillip Edelstein was six inches taller than Ben and had a neatly trimmed head of salt and pepper hair. From his Prada sunglasses down to his Gucci loafers, he appeared urbane and smug. "Good enough, Ben. So what's going on? This morning you made it sound pretty urgent that we meet." Phillip had been Ben's lawyer and fixer for over twenty years. They had an on-again-off-again friendship, as well, despite their outward differences. Ben was in some sort of jam. Of this, Phillip was certain.

"You know my property out on Milo Road, off 299?" Phillip nodded. "Well, some investors are looking into buying the property and building a hotel/conference center there. And, they're willing to pay big bucks for the property."

"That's crazy!" Phillip insisted. "New Paltz will never allow that. These investors will be run out of town."

4

"Maybe not, Phillip. Oh, I think the town can be persuaded. See, that's where you come in."

"What do you mean?"

Ben spoke out of the side of his mouth, "Let me just say that I've convinced some of the big money behind this investment that I know how to deliver the approvals they're going to need. Look, you've got the political connections. You know how to do this. I know you do, Phillip. They get the approvals, they buy my property. That's the deal. Right now, though, I need cash to make this happen."

"Why do you need cash? The property is yours."

Ben shrugged his shoulders. "Ach, just a couple of liens, some back taxes. That sort of thing. Nothing big. Look, let me level with you, Phillip. I got myself into some online gambling site that, well," Ben sighed, "it didn't work out the way I thought it would. Leave it at that."

"That's a shame, Ben. Guess you're out of luck."

"Not so fast. I need you to lend me the money. I pay off what I owe and you'll get your money as soon as the sale goes through."

"By the way, how much cash are we talking about?"

"Oh, five hundred grand should do it," Ben casually replied.

"You think I'm Bill-fucking-Gates! Here's the way it's going to play out." Phillip shook his finger at Ben. "I lend you the money and get you the approvals. I get paid back in full, plus interest, at the closing."

"Phillip, you've got my word. You'll get your money back," Ben assured him.

Phillip snickered, "Your word is worth crap. Look Ben Sheppard, you try to screw me over and I have enough on you to put you behind bars till you're drooling and in diapers. But, we've got a big problem: Myrna and Joseph Van Dyke. They block every development, every commercial venture I've tried to get in on. You know how they get their groupies to put pressure on the planning board."

"Yeah, yeah, but you'll know how to handle this, Phillip. You know everyone on the planning board. Hell, you and the Mayor are old high school buddies. You told me that. Come on. You must have some dirt on some of them. Use it! And you know I'll take care of you, in return."

Eddie snickered to himself as he mentally entered this conversation into his human hard drive. His eyes were on his painting but his ears continued to zoom-in on the conversation below him.

Phillip knew that Ben was right. He did know all the players and he knew their secrets. Phillip also knew how to leverage that information. "Okay, Ben. We're going to split the selling price. We split this sixty-forty."

Ben gasped,"You're taking forty percent? Hell, it's my land, Edelstein!"

"And without my help, it'll always be your land. You'll never be able to unload it. Besides, I'm the one taking the risk. If I can't do something about the Van Dykes, we won't get the approvals we need and I'm out half a million until you can cough up the cash."

"Well, I may be of some help. Joseph Van Dyke has got himself in a financial swamp that no one is supposed to know about. Van Dyke likes to gamble--big time."

"How do you know about it?"

Ben smirked and raised his eyebrows. "Look, I heard about it from my bookie. And my bookie doesn't lie."

Phillip did not hesitate. "Okay, let's do it. This sale should bring in big bucks." Ben shook his hand to seal the agreement and left. Phillip remained to make an important call.

Eddie waited until Phillip finished his call and then decided to take a break from painting. He climbed down the ladder and plunked himself in the chair across from Phillip. "Well, Phillip Edelstein! What sleazy deal are you cooking up?"

"Siricco, why don't you get back on your ladder and mind your own business for once," Phillip retorted. "I don't remember inviting you to join me."

"Phillip, if I waited to be invited, I'd get nowhere. Now, tell me more about this deal that you and Ben Sheppard are doing."

"You're out of that marinated mind of yours."

"Come on, Phillip. I wouldn't even lend Ben Sheppard the money to buy a cup of coffee. But five hundred grand? Now tell me, who's lost their mind?" Eddie cackled.

Shaking his finger at Eddie, Phillip warned, "Don't start shooting off your mouth about this, Siricco!"

Eddie stood up and tipped his cap to Phillip in response. He headed to the Mudd Puddle Cafe to grab some coffee. Eddie never worried about running out of material for his column--not with guys like Edelstein and Sheppard around. He ordered a coffee and sat down to wait, pulling a pen and notepad out of his overalls pocket to start drafting his next article.

Eddie meandered across the courtyard, coffee in hand, to shmooze a bit at the Antique Barn. This red barn visually dominates Water Street Market. Walter and Cosmo, a couple in their late fifties, run the shop and have worked hard to earn the distinction of winning the "Best Antique Center" by Hudson Valley Magazine for the last six years. They rent spaces to twenty-five independent antique dealers.

The shop has the feel of an off-beat gathering place for slightly wacky antique dealers and customers. Customers become friends and dealers become extended family. Intimate, personal details are routinely shared at the check-out counter. Customers often show up with entire roasted chicken dinners, key lime pies, and brownies for Walter and Cosmo. Eddie was one of the regulars who came into the Antique Barn to gossip but with no intention of making a purchase.

Cosmo was seated on a stool at the check-out counter near the front door as Eddie strolled in. "So, Eddie, honey, what juicy story have you got for me today?" Cosmo asked, raising his eyebrows in anticipation. The more lurid the rumor, the more fired up he became.

"Actually, Cosmo, a pretty juicy one for you," Eddie replied leaning in closer to Cosmo. "You know Ben, Ben Sheppard, right?" Cosmo nodded. "Well, he's trying to sell his property off Route

299, on Milo Road. He wants to sell it to a big developer who's going to build a hotel/conference center. But Ben has to get the town to approve the development or the deal goes south."

"Ach, that'll never happen! He could never convince the town to allow it," Cosmo said dismissively. "Never, never, NEVER! Hah! Ben Sheppard couldn't even convince anyone to buy one of these," he said holding up a two-dollar juice glass. "Who told you that?"

"When I was painting I heard him talking to his buddy, Phillip, Phillip Edelstein. You must know him, Cosmo. Struts around here in his fancy suits like he owns the place."

"Oh, yeah. I know who he is," Cosmo nodded. "Well, go on! Tell me more."

"Now, not a word of this to anyone else," Eddie warned. "So Phillip agreed to lend Ben money to pay off liens on his property, but Phillip gets a share of the sale in return."

"Eddie, come on. You've got to do better than that! Nothing wrong with partners loaning each other money."

"Well, wait till you hear the rest of this! Edelstein is in charge of swaying the planning board and..." Eddie waited while Cosmo took care of a customer. He wanted to be sure to have Cosmo's full attention before he said another word. Unfortunately, Eddie had to get back to work. The rest of the story would have to wait until tomorrow. But, Eddie could not resist dangling an enticing snippet for Cosmo as he walked out the door. "And Cos, I'll bet those two scoundrels would pay me handsomely to keep my mouth shut about what I overheard."

That comment got Cosmo's attention. He was desperate to hear every little detail, but it was too late. Eddie was gone.

By late afternoon, Phillip was waiting for Joseph Van Dyke to arrive at the Clemson Brewery, located across the street from Water Street Market. Clemson Brewery has an open feel to it with a large industrial tap room and an expansive beer garden. They offer craft beers, local wines, and excellent pub fare.

Phillip had insisted that they meet for a beer. With admiration, Phillip watched Joseph approach the bar. Joseph's erect posture and purposeful stride made him appear taller than his actual five-foot, six-inch height and younger than his actual seventy-three years. He had closely-cropped gray hair, glasses, and wore jeans and a tee-shirt. Joseph's slight frame slipped onto a stool next to Phillip. They both ordered a couple of Clemson Pilsners.

"So, what's on your mind, Phillip? I know this isn't a social visit."

Phillip gave a slight nod and explained, "You're right, Joseph. Let's not waste each other's time. I'm here to tell you that developers are looking to buy Ben Sheppard's property out on Milo Road."

"What are they planning to do with it?"

"It seems that they're planning to build a resort hotel and conference center."

"Hell, you know that'll never get traction in New Paltz."

"Hmm, wouldn't be so sure, Joseph. If you and Myrna didn't stand in the way and you gave it your approval, I think the town would go along with it."

"You're out of your mind. We'll do whatever we can to stop it!"

"We don't always have to be adversaries, Joseph. You've cost me thousands over the years but I'm willing to be the bigger person. I just need you to step aside this once. What do you say?"

"Absolutely not, Phillip. You think it's such a good idea, you talk it up. You know everyone. Hell, you and the Mayor are old buddies."

Phillip gave Joseph an icy grin. "Look, I happen to know that you've gambled away all your money. If that gets out, you won't even be able to buy a coffee at the Mudd Puddle without paying up in advance."

"You wouldn't do that," Joseph whispered angrily.

"Ah, but you're wrong, Joseph. I would and I will. Don't you realize that I would love to destroy your reputation? You and Myrna have cost me a fortune with your high and mighty protests. You've blocked every project I've invested in around here. Nothing would please me more, in fact."

"No way, Phillip. I'm not supporting a huge development. No way!"

Phillip smiled, "Bad mistake, Joseph. You may be stubborn but you sure aren't very smart!"

Joseph glared at Phillip. Underneath that Armani suit, Phillip Edelstein was nothing more than a cunning and crooked small-town lawyer.

"And remember Joseph, don't say I didn't warn you," Phillip sneered, giving Joseph a friendly pat on the back.

At the far end of the bar, Eddie Siricco was staring into his draft and pretending not to listen to their muted conversation. He finished his beer and slapped five singles on the bar. He got up and briskly walked out, passing Joseph and Phillip who never even noticed him. Eddie wore a self-satisfied expression. His eavesdropping today was definitely going to pay off and big time.

Tuesday, September 20

This morning, Ellen and Charlie Green arrived at the back door of the Antique Barn to carry a cabinet up the stairs to their booth. They were antique dealers who lived in Montgomery, thirty minutes away, and rented space in the Barn. Although in their early seventies, they each moved like people a decade younger--a necessity for every antique dealer. Charlie's years of hauling around cupboards and throwing concrete statues over his shoulder have kept him in shape. Ellen's years of pulling off the side of the road to load someone's discarded dresser into her car have kept her nimbly scooting around.

"Hi, Ellen and Charlie!" Eddie called as he walked by carrying his ladder and bucket of paint.

"Eddie, good to see you!" Charlie shouted back. "You're doing a great job on that trim. Looks wonderful."

"Thanks, Charlie. Tell that to Harris!"

Ellen yelled, "Hey Eddie, what's the latest scandal? And don't you dare tell me I have to wait to read about it in your column!"

Eddie yelled back, "Here's my tip of the day: check with Cosmo. He'll tell you about it."

"Thanks, Eddie. You're a sweetheart!" Ellen, always eager for the latest gossip, dropped her end of the cabinet halfway through the door, surprising Charlie who managed to withstand the sudden extra weight and keep his balance.

"Ellen!" he groaned, "a warning would have been appreciated."

"Charlie, I'll be right back," she said bounding inside to talk to Cosmo while Charlie lugged the cabinet upstairs by himself. Ellen practically accosted Cosmo. "So, what's the latest scoop? Just saw Eddie and he said I should check with you."

Cosmo leaned across the counter to whisper, "Well Ellen, here's what he told me yesterday. Ben Sheppard is selling his property on Milo Road to a developer who wants to build a big hotel. Ben and his buddy are going in on this together."

"I don't think I know Ben."

With a dismissive flip of his hand Cosmo explained, "Ben Sheppard is about your age. Scraggly gray ponytail. He's a local nobody who probably had to cheat to make it through kindergarten."

Ellen giggled. "And who is his buddy?"

"Phillip Edelstein," Cosmo said shaking his head in disgust. "A nasty, full-of-himself lawyer. Anyhow, Phillip is lending Ben money to pay off liens and Phillip is going to end up with a share of the sale price. But, if Ben can't get the planning board to approve the development, the deal falls apart."

"That'll never happen. So I give that story two out of five stars, Cosmo. I must say, I'm a bit disappointed," Ellen teased.

"Well, here's the interesting part. Eddie wanted to tell me the juicy details but a customer needed to look at a brooch in one of the jewelry cases. Oh, how I wanted to tell her to buzz off! By the time I got back, Eddie was on his way out the door. He shouted to me 'those two scoundrels would pay me handsomely to keep my mouth shut' about what I overheard'. And then he left. I'm dying to know what he meant."

"Eddie never told you?"

"I'll get the rest of the story from him. No worries on that score!" Cosmo assured Ellen.

At a courtyard table near the Mudd Puddle, an intense conversation was unfolding. A well-preserved woman in her early seventies whose lips appeared to be inflated with helium said, "Leonard, you're dead wrong. As soon as I read the script I knew, absolutely knew that I, Dorothy Dawson, am the embodiment of Desdemona!"

"Dorothy, that may have been true forty years ago, but Desdemona needs to exude youth and sensuality. Youth, Dorothy, youth!" Leonard cried out in frustration. Leonard was the director of the Denizen Theatre's upcoming play. He was a lanky man in his mid-thirties, wearing a black turtleneck and skinny black jeans with high-top Converse sneakers.

"You're crazy, Leonard! Desdemona is coming back from the grave and needs to exude strength and passion. Youth cannot play Desdemona like I can. This is a one-woman show and it requires a seasoned woman of substance," Dorothy replied, her eyes piercing right through Leonard's Walgreen's sunglasses. "You are well aware that I've spent years performing Shakespeare with the Royal Shakespeare Company. Do you really think some cutesy little New Paltz theatre major can bring the necessary depth and intensity to this role?"

Leonard removed his glasses and stared at Dorothy. "Some cutesy little New Paltz theatre major is the one who wrote the play, my dear."

"Just give me an audition. That's all I ask. How can you deny me such a small favor?" Dorothy asked batting her overly mascaraed eyelashes at him.

"Alright, Dorothy. You'll get your audition, but if you make a scene you'll be escorted out on your well-seasoned, woman of substance ass. Do I make myself clear?"

Dorothy arose, turned around and looked back over her shoulder at Leonard. "Good-day, Leonard. I'll be sure to give my good friend, Robert, your regards."

"Robert? Who the hell is Robert?"

"Why, De Niro, of course." With a grand sweep of her left hand, she tossed her silk scarf behind her and, head held high, almost stumbled right into Eddie.

Eddie was as stunned as Dorothy by this unexpected encounter. They had not had any contact with one another since their divorce, twenty-five years ago. It was Eddie's drinking and Dorothy's reality show behaviors that had ultimately doomed their relationship. Dorothy snickered, "Well, Eddie, you haven't changed one bit. Still painting people's houses, I see."

"And you, Dorothy Dubinsky, you were sure you'd be the sweetheart of Broadway. Tell me. How has that turned out for you?" Eddie sneered sarcastically.

"I'm Dorothy *Dawson* now and it so happens that the director has begged me to return to the Denizen to do the one-woman 'Desdemona' play. How could I refuse him?" she shrugged, flicking her scarf. "I consider this role my charitable contribution to the Village of New Paltz."

"Hah! And I suppose he fell for your Royal Shakespeare Company bullshit? The only acting you've ever done was with me and even I didn't fall for your lies for very long!"

Dorothy grabbed Eddie by his shirt. "Don't you dare think you can destroy my reputation, Eddie Siricco," she threatened. "You destroyed my life for twenty years. Wasn't that enough for you?"

"Look Dorothy, New Paltz is my town, not yours," he warned, pulling away from her grasp. "As far as I'm concerned, you stopped existing twenty-five years ago. So just keep out of my life and we'll be fine." Eddie strode away and walked into the Mudd Puddle.

Michelle, one of the owners of the Mudd Puddle, was, simultaneously, greeting customers, preparing specialty beverages, and calling out orders to her husband, James, the chef. Without even looking up at Eddie, she knew he was there and she knew exactly what he wanted to order. Before Eddie could open his mouth Michelle said, "Hi Eddie. Coffee, extra milk, no sugar, coming right up."

"Thanks, Michelle."

He took out some cash to pay but Michelle shook her head and held up her hand in refusal. "Next time."

Eddie took a deep sigh, smiled, and thanked her. Michelle confirmed for him that New Paltz was his town and Dorothy was the one who did not belong.

Phillip relished putting Myrna and Joseph in their place after years of bitterness. He was confident that he would have better luck with Myrna than with her husband. Phillip took a chance that Myrna would be home alone and drove to their townhouse to pay her a friendly visit. She looked through the peephole before answering the door. "Phillip Edelstein, why should I let you in?" Myrna was squarely-built. She had no-nonsense, short, straight, gray hair and wore no make-up.

Phillip answered, "Because, Myrna, I'm here to do you and Joseph a big favor."

Myrna opened the door, placed her hands on her hips, and snarled, "Yeah, right!"

"Myrna, it's time for us to make peace with one another. Joseph around?"

"Lucky for him, no. What are you up to? Out with it!"

"Aren't you going to invite me in?"

Myrna scowled and allowed Phillip to enter. "Tell me what you want."

"Alright. I'll be straight up with you, Myrna. A proposal is in the works for a hotel/conference center out on Milo Road. Ben

Sheppard's property. I want your word that you won't stand in the way of them getting the necessary approvals. That's it."

"That huge acreage on Milo Road is a forest that this project will totally destroy. The land will be completely leveled. I'll do everything I can to stop this from moving forward. Thanks for the heads-up, Phillip." Myrna shot him a cynical smile. "Good-bye."

"Not so fast, Myrna. For the last fifteen years, you and Joseph have managed to block every development opportunity that New Paltz has had."

"What you really mean is every opportunity *you* have had to make money by trying to turn New Paltz into one continuous strip mall!"

"Look, last year you cost me over one hundred grand when you got the Village to pass an injunction against the cluster housing project. And the year before that you organized your little army of agitators and blocked the Amazon warehouse on 299. I won't even tell you what that cost me!"

"Spare me, Edelstein." Myrna rolled her eyes. "And why would I ever support this resort hotel?"

"Because you're smart, Myrna, and a lot smarter than your husband." Shaking his finger at her he warned, "Don't push me. I know how to destroy you and that bumbling lump you live with."

"You're nothing but a schoolyard bully and, let me tell you something, Edelstein," she barked poking him in his Ralph Lauren dress shirt, "I've been bullied by bigger bullies than you! Get out of here!"

Phillip gave a courtly nod as Myrna shoved him out the front door.

Wednesday, September 21

Dorothy Dawson, née Dubinsky, was flying through the courtyard at Water Street Market this morning looking for her ex, Eddie Siricco. She had only a few minutes before her audition at the Denizen Theatre and she was determined to make them count. She spotted him painting the window frames over Antiques on Main. "Eddie, you bastard, get down here. I need to talk with you!" Dorothy barked.

Eddie was tempted to dump the entire bucket of antique white right on her narcissistic head, but, instead, he climbed down his ladder. "Yeah?"

Hands on her hips, Dorothy warned, "Don't you dare breathe a word to anyone about me or it'll be the last breath you ever take!"

"For someone with so much to hide, you should be a lot nicer to me, Dorothy. You wouldn't want anyone to start digging into your past, would you?" Eddie asked with a malevolent grin. "Wouldn't it be fun to leak a story to the Town Crier about the real Dorothy Dawson and the so-called accident to the leading lady. A razor blade sewn into her dress. My, my! And the young costume assistant who just happened to be able to step in to save the show. And years later there was the story about..."

Shaking her finger at Eddie's nose, Dorothy growled, "I must get this role and don't you spoil it for me." Her eyes flared angrily at him.

Eddie retorted, "And how much is my silence worth to you? Huh?"

Through gritted teeth Dorothy replied, "Don't push me, Eddie Siricco. Do not push me. If I don't get to play Desdemona, I'll know that you're to blame!"

Eddie shook his head dismissively. "Certainly wouldn't have anything to do with your age or the fact that your acting stinks, would it?"

Dorothy shot Eddie a haughty look, threw back her head, and quoted Desdemona. "*I have not deserved this!*" With that comment, she turned her back to Eddie and marched to the Denizen Theatre to prepare for her audition.

After his encounter with Dorothy, Eddie decided that he either needed a shot of whiskey or he needed to write up his next Town Crier column. He opted to do both and went back to his apartment. After a couple of hours, Eddie was satisfied with his closing paragraph.

"Hmm. A little birdie told me that a big tract of forested land is about to turn into--a Hilton, perhaps? I'll bet local businesses will welcome this economic boost to New Paltz or will they? Get ready to laugh when the Van Dykes mobilize their pathetic aging hippies to protest once again! I wonder how they can be stopped? Or do I? Star power has arrived to the Denizen--or has it? Dorothy Dawson will finally end her less than spectacular career. Watch her humiliation erupt. And I say good riddance."

Eddie read over the ending of his latest piece and toasted his muse: Jack Daniels. He drove back to Water Street to work on his painting job.

By late afternoon, Ben Sheppard called Phillip. "So tell me, is Van Dyke going to give us any trouble?"

Phillip sighed, "Ben, Van Dyke isn't cooperating, but don't worry. I'll come up with something."

"Yeah, Phillip, and make it fast! You want a piece of the action, you better take care of Van Dyke or I'll do it myself and to hell with you!" Ben growled and ended the call.

Eddie decided to quit work a little early. Of course, he also started work a little late but, what the hell. He was folding up his ladder and gathering his supplies when he saw Dorothy heading towards him, her scarf and tunic trying to keep up with her.

"Well, Eddie, dahling," she drawled, "just wanted to let you know that I was brilliant today. Absolutely brilliant! I'm sure I nailed this audition." Lowering her eyes she continued, "Leonard practically said as much. He's the director, in case you didn't know. I'll probably find out tomorrow." Dorothy gave Eddie a smug look. "Tada, must be on my way. I'm going to my flat to begin practicing my lines."

"Well, well, Desdemona," Eddie mocked, "not so fast. You realize that I could still humiliate you if word of your bogus career got out. And we both know that would be the least of your problems if I spilled my guts about everything I know. You've accumulated a rap sheet of accidents and supposed lucky breaks, haven't you. You wouldn't want the truth to get out, would you?" Eddie hissed.

Dorothy's eyes narrowed. "You wouldn't dare! Besides, after my audition today, nobody would believe you." Dorothy began fidgeting with her necklace. "So, how much do you want? Just tell me and let's get this over with."

Eddie snickered, "That would be much too easy, Dorothy. I don't want your money. No, what I want is to keep you looking over your shoulder every day as you go to rehearsal. I want you to wonder if today is the day that I'm going to expose you, you shriveled up hag!"

Fuming, Dorothy stood up and inhaled deeply before speaking. "You miserable creature! This role will be the crowning glory of my career while all you have to show for your life is a bucket of paint and a bottle of Jack." She exited in a state of fury and agitation.

Eddie waited for Dorothy to leave before taking off. Now it was time for him to negotiate a fair and equitable settlement with Phillip Edelstein. At Clemson Brewery, Joseph Van Dyke made it very clear to Phillip that he would oppose the development. Eddie wondered how far Phillip would go to destroy the Van Dykes and how much he would be willing to pay Eddie to keep quiet about it. Eddie got into his Chevy pick-up truck and drove to Phillip's house for a friendly chat.

Phillip lived in a small, stone house on a side street, just off Main Street in New Paltz. Eddie got out of the truck and rang the doorbell. "Eddie Siricco. This is a surprise," Phillip said genially. Eyeing Eddie's paint-stained overalls and boots, he cautiously asked, "What brings you here?"

"A business matter, Phillip."

"A business matter? What are you talking about?"

"I'm going to give you an opportunity to protect your own interests and reputation. Consider this a generous offer on my part."

"What the hell are you talking about, Eddie? Have you been drinking?"

"Not yet." Eddie sneered, "But, I'm wondering how far you would go to keep the Van Dykes from interfering with your plans." Eddie enjoyed keeping Phillip off balance. Phillip and Eddie appeared to be polar opposites. Where Phillip was smooth and slick, Eddie was coarse and gruff. However, they were both equally conniving.

"I have no idea what you're talking about."

"Come on, Phillip. Let's stop with the games. You and Ben know the Van Dykes will never let a resort hotel and conference center happen. So you must have a plan to stop the Van Dykes and I'll bet you wouldn't want anyone to know about it."

Phillip reluctantly invited Eddie to come inside. "You're a miserable bastard, Siricco. What do you want from me?"

"Cash. That's what I want," Eddie said simply. "Just a couple hundred a week for one year. That's all I'm demanding. Payment in cash every Friday." Eddie shrugged, palms facing upward, "I'm not going to get greedy, Phillip. This'll just give me spending money for the weekend."

Phillip eyed Eddie with disgust. "And, why the hell would I ever do that?"

"Because I'm onto you and your ugly tricks. You might even earn top billing in my Town Crier column. Do you realize how the locals vie for that kind of exposure?" Eddie taunted Phillip.

"Siricco, that's blackmail."

"Now Phillip, I may be a bit rough around the edges, but I'm an honorable son-of-a-bitch," he grinned slyly.

Phillip grimaced and pulled out his wallet. "Here you go." He threw a few bills at Eddie's face. "Now, get the hell out of here!"

"Ah, just one more detail. I need an advance of five thousand--a show of good faith. And I better have it by Sunday, my friend. You know where I live. I look forward to seeing you very soon."

With that comment Eddie turned to leave and Phillip slammed the door behind him.

Thursday, September 22

This morning, Eddie was on his way to see Ben Sheppard. He and Ben had a lot in common. They both were scrappy, resourceful, and corrupt. Much to Ben's dismay, they seemed to have crossed paths often over the last decade. Ben's family had owned a fair amount of land that Ben sold off in small parcels whenever he was short of funds. Unfortunately for Ben, Eddie knew of Ben's shady real estate transactions and found that they made juicy material for his Town Crier column. There was the property on Libertyville Road that Ben sold off knowing full well that it was all ledge. The Town Crier exposed Ben's gambling losses and bad debts without ever using his name. Eddie never had to name anyone. New Paltz was a tight community and everyone knew everyone. Since Eddie's commentary posed as entertainment and thinly disguised hearsay rather than news, Ben was never prosecuted. However, Ben was intimidated by Eddie's venomous pen and did his best to steer clear of him. Yet, somehow he and Eddie often wound up sitting side by side at one of the local bars where gossip circulated faster than a swarm of bees.

Ben lived off Putt Corners Road, heading east, towards the NY State Thruway. Eddie pulled up in front of a ranch house and walked up the path to the door. Before he could ring the bell, Ben opened the door and stood still, hands placed defiantly on his hips. Obviously, Phillip had already alerted Ben. "You take one step closer and you'll wish you hadn't!" Ben growled at Eddie.

"Now, Ben. I don't know what Phillip told you, but I'm here to work out a friendly deal with you," Eddie replied.

"Beat it, you drunken asshole! I never want to lay eyes on you again!"

"Ben, look, we go way back. You and I have clawed our way out of trouble before and always landed on top. We can do it again. Phillip is the one who has everything to lose."

"Don't mess with me, Siricco! I've got a chance at something big and I'm not letting you screw this up. Beat it!" Ben glared menacingly at Eddie.

"Ben, I'm curious. If Phillip doesn't take care of the Van Dykes, what do you plan to do about them? We're not through," Eddie warned shaking his finger at him as he backed away. "Not by a long shot!"

Charlie pulled into the parking lot at Water Street Market to drop off a couple of pieces of furniture at the Antique Barn before the weekend. He entered through the back door carrying in a table.

Christopher raced to greet him at the door. Christopher was Walter's talented, young protégé who had recently graduated from college with a degree in business management. "Charlie, you need to do something!" he whispered loudly. "Walter's not here right now and..."

"Christopher, take it easy and tell me what's going on," Charlie stated in a steady voice.

"It's Cosmo and Jack. He's the guy who has the space near Wendy. The two of them are going at it and we've got customers everywhere."

"Christopher, you distract the customers. I'll handle Cosmo and Jack," he winked to reassure him.

Charlie casually strolled over to where the drama was escalating. Drama was not an unusual occurrence at the Antique Barn. However, this drama involved an irate dealer and it was playing out in front of a shop full of people.

"Jack, I've told you many times that I am not willing to fight with a customer over a stupid light bulb!" Cosmo declared, stomping his feet. "The bulb goes with the lamp. So shut up!"

"I pay a lot of money for bulbs and I'm not letting you give them away for free!" Jack argued. "I even stuck an 'NFS' sticker on the bulb. See that, huh?"

Charlie quietly intervened, hoping to deescalate the situation. "Look Jack, are you more interested in collecting light bulbs or selling one of your lamps? It seems pretty simple to me."

"Really? Simple, huh?" Turning to one of the bystanders, Jack asked, "So, tell me honestly, wouldn't you still buy this lamp even if I didn't include the bulb?"

Flustered, the customer stammered, "Uh, I might. Maybe. I'm not sure."

"Jack," Cosmo reprimanded, "stop harassing people! Your lamp is butt ugly. You'd be lucky to give it away!"

Heads turned from Cosmo to Jack as if they were watching the U.S. Open tennis finals. "Butt ugly? I'll tell you what's 'butt ugly', Cosmo: you!"

"Jack, you need to cool it and cool it right now. That's enough." Charlie tried to steer Jack towards the door. "Come on. Let's step outside for a minute."

Cosmo, however, wanted to have the last word--and he did. "Well, let me tell you something, Jack. My butt is better looking than your face!"

That did it. Jack lunged at Cosmo. Cosmo shrieked. Charlie was able to grab Jack and shove him out the front door. Christopher bent down to comfort Cosmo. Customers were aghast.

At that moment Walter walked through the back door. "Hey, Cosmo, Christopher, I'm back. Anything happen while I was gone?"

A dazed Cosmo sat up. "You missed out on an electrifying experience, Walter!"

After a late dinner, Eddie had one more person to visit: Joseph Van Dyke. Joseph and Myrna lived in a townhouse in Gardiner, close to the New Paltz border.

Eddie took time to be sure he had the right address. Every one of these damn condos looked alike. When Myrna answered the door, he was almost relieved to know he had the right condo. Almost. Eddie and Myrna had a mutual dislike of each other. Eddie thought of Myrna as a loud-mouthed liberal and Myrna thought of Eddie as a right-winged bigot. Eddie loved featuring the Van Dykes in his column. The more they took themselves seriously, the more he mocked them.

Eddie referred to the Van Dykes as a *'pair of batty bohippians'*. As the Town Crier, Eddie had often purposely sabotaged a protest or demonstration by giving a heads-up to the local authorities. Recently he wrote, "*We can all hope that our resident geriatric hippies never decide to demonstrate by streaking through the Village. That would surely cause permanent blindness, folks!*"

Myrna's hips spread generously across the doorway, blocking Eddie's entrance. She looked at him suspiciously. "My, this is a surprise. What trouble are you in now?"

"Why Myrna, I'm not in any trouble at all. I came to speak with Joseph. Is he here?"

"Maybe."

Joseph came to the door to see what was going on. "Eddie, what is it?" Myrna stepped aside to let Joseph pass by.

"I need to speak with you--privately," Eddie glared at Myrna.

Scowling at Eddie Myrna said, "I'll get dinner ready. Give me a yell if you want me to get rid of this little punk for you!" Of course, Myrna had no intention of missing this private conversation. She had to find out what Eddie was up to. She hid just inside the doorway.

Joseph stood outside the door and put his hands in his pockets. "What's this all about?"

"Well, Joseph, I see that you've got yourself in some trouble--money trouble. Wouldn't it be a shame if word got out about how you gambled away all your money? Your money and Myrna's?"

Joseph began grinding his teeth as he stared back at Eddie. "That's a lie!"

"I heard it from a very reliable source."

"Who told you that?"

"I don't want to reveal my sources, Joseph, that wouldn't be ethical as an upstanding member of the press corps."

That was enough eavesdropping for Myrna. Eddie was a lowlife and a liar. Myrna went to the kitchen to get dinner started.

"So, what do you want from me? If you're looking for money, I don't have any. Go bother someone else."

"Gee, that's too bad, Joseph. If you could come up with, say, seven thousand, I might forget what I overheard."

Joseph shook his head, "I've known you too long, Eddie. You won't ever keep your mouth shut no matter how much I paid you. I'll be reading about myself in your disgusting gossip column."

"Joseph, this is my final offer and it's quite a bargain, if you ask me," Eddie chuckled.

Beads of perspiration appeared on Joseph's forehead, knowing how easily his life could be upended. "Get out of here, Eddie. You'll be sorry that you ever showed up at my door!" Joseph knew that spreading dirt about everyone fed Eddie Siricco's ego. He was totally incapable of keeping a secret. No amount of money or Jack Daniels could replace the high that Eddie experienced when he had a juicy story to pass along, verbally or in writing.

"Joseph, that's too bad, man, 'cause I really like you. Hmm, I wonder if Myrna knows what you've done," Eddie smirked, scratching his head as he strode back to his truck.

Eddie needed to plan his next move carefully and knew better than to head home right away. Once he got home he would start celebrating and the celebration would not stop until he was passed out on the couch. No, he needed to be clear-headed tonight. Therefore, he took a detour and drove around for another hour.

Finally, Eddie drove slowly down Main Street, made a left onto Duzine Road, and turned onto Beekman Road, a sparsely settled area with only a few houses. He glanced to his left and paused, attempting to make sense of what he was seeing. Even though it was dark, Eddie was quite certain that someone was pouring something around the perimeter of a house.

Eddie opened his window to get a better look. When he was sure about what he had witnessed, he drove off, looking forward to making a couple of phone calls tomorrow. "Well, well, well," he mused, "now ain't that interesting!"

Friday, September 23

Dorothy Dawson had been summoned to the Denizen Theatre by Leonard, the director. Dorothy had been anxiously waiting for this moment ever since her audition. She arose early in order to carefully apply her make-up. Dorothy looked in the mirror one last time, puckering her lips very slowly. She was pleased with the results and ready to pose for the press.

Dorothy entered the theatre and was offended that Leonard was not there to greet the new Desdemona. She sat on the stage and waited for him. When Leonard finally showed up, he approached her with outstretched arms and gushed, "Dorothy, my Dorothy, you look simply radiant this morning!"

Stiffly, she replied, "Why, thank-you, Leonard. I may even have to forgive you for keeping me waiting."

"I do beg your forgiveness," Leonard apologized. "But, there is a reason I am late. Dorothy Dawson, I'd like you to meet Alyssa McPherson, from the State University of New York in New Paltz." With an exaggerated sweep of his arm, Leonard presented a waif with a wispy brown ponytail and eyes that were too big for her face. She barely looked old enough to be potty-trained.

Dorothy quickly assessed the competition and felt herself go rigid with rage. She looked from Leonard to this girl/woman standing in front of her and back to Leonard.

Dorothy summoned all of her limited acting skills to maintain an air of superiority in this moment of utter humiliation. In a modulated tone, Dorothy held out her hand and enunciated slowly. "I am charmed to meet you. Now, what was your name again?" Turning

34

to Leonard, Dorothy smiled coyly, "Leonard, is this little girl your daughter?"

Leonard cleared his throat and looked at Dorothy in amusement. "No, Dorothy. Alyssa is not my daughter. She is the playwright and you, Dorothy Dawson, are her Desdemona."

Dorothy began to hyperventilate at this unexpected turn of events. She stammered, "Oh, my dears. I am so sorry! Alyssa, you are a genius and I will make sure that the entire world knows it!"

This morning, Eddie had one hell of a hangover. However, he was on a mission. He was heading to the Antique Barn to give Cosmo an update about Ben, Phillip, and the Van Dykes. He wanted to give out enough information to pique Cosmo's curiosity, but keep a few of the details to himself for his Town Crier piece.

Eddie almost bumped right into his boss, Harris Landau, owner of the entire Water Street Market. Harris was in his early fifties, six feet tall, and wore a Yankees baseball cap, a white tee shirt with Ralph Lauren jeans, and flip-flops. Harris showed up at the Antique Barn with his wife Judith. Whenever Harris entered the Barn, it was for one reason only; he needed to speak with Walter right away. However, it was unusual for him to show up with Judith. Something big was up. Before Harris even had a chance to ask for Walter, Cosmo looked at Harris and pointed upstairs.

Harris caught Eddie out of the corner of his eye and gave a quick, "Eddie, you need to finish those windows today before the rain begins" as he charged up the stairs in search of Walter. Judith followed close behind him.

Walter was chatting with one of the other dealers, Marc, as Harris raced up the stairs two-at-a-time. "Walter! I need to talk to you!" He shouted breathlessly, "It's important!"

Walter sighed. Everything was important to Harris and everything was an emergency that needed to be taken care of immediately. Walter motioned to Harris to take a seat on a bench in one of the nearby booths.

"It's about the fire last night. Walter, a house on Beekman Road was burned to the ground. Gasoline explosion. This was no accident!"

"That's terrible! Anybody hurt?"

Judith answered, "Fortunately, no. The couple is usually around only on weekends." She reached out and gently placed her hand on Walter's back as Harris continued.

Harris leaned towards Walter to whisper quietly, "But here's the scoop. It appears that this was a hate crime." Walter waited for Harris to continue. "That's what the police suspect, anyway. See, the Van Dykes rented the house to a couple of gay guys and the firemen found this on their front lawn." Harris took out his phone to show Walter a photo of a sign: 'GAYS GO AWAY'.

Walter shook his head in disgust. "Do they have any leads?"

"Not sure, but Walter, the couple, they're friends of yours: Matthew and Pablo."

"You better come down with me and tell Cosmo about this." Walter's deadpan expression did not reveal how shocked and disturbed he was feeling.

At the check-out counter, Cosmo appeared to be holding court with half a dozen customers and Eddie. The entire group was laughing and chattering as Harris and Walter solemnly approached. Walter said, "You might as well share this with everyone here. Our customers are all like family to us."

By the time Harris finished his story, a collective gasp spread through the group. Matthew and Pablo were a thirty-something couple who were regulars at the Barn, but, more importantly, they had become friends with many of the antique dealers at the Barn. They lived in Manhattan but spent most weekends visiting New Paltz and always stopped in to say 'hi'. Targeting a gay couple in New Paltz was unheard of. New Paltz is a community that embraces diversity in every form. Huddled together at the counter, the group was stunned to learn of this ugly act.

However, one person standing among them was not the least bit surprised: Eddie Siricco.

At police headquarters, Chief Liberti of the New Paltz Police Department was meeting with the chief of the New Paltz Fire Department to plan their investigation into the house fire out on Beekman Road. Detective Sergeant Adam Jacobson was asked to join the meeting. After handshakes, Liberti asked, "So, what information can you confirm for us?"

The fire chief explained, "My men were able to detect a residue, indicating that an accelerant was poured from space to space along the base of the structure. A vapor test, used at the scene of the fire, identified gasoline as the accelerant." He cleared his throat before adding, "And with the use of our new gas chromatograph, we were able to confirm this preliminary finding."

Nodding in approval, Liberti concluded, "Thanks. Good work, Joe. My team will take over from here. Detective Sergeant Jacobson will be leading the investigation." Adam looked at the Chief in surprise. He was one of the youngest detectives on the force and had never led an investigation before.

Chief Liberti lowered his voice and said, "Now, let's all keep mum about the possibility of this being a hate crime. This town will go nuts! Every resident, visitor, New Paltz college student will be all over this and that'll only get in the way of our investigation. Are we all agreed?"

Unanimous nods followed as the Chief adjourned the meeting. Adam waited in the hallway for Chief Liberti. "Excuse me, Chief. May I have a word with you?"

"Sure can, Detective. What is it?"

"Well, Sir, um," Adam stammered, "you really think it's a good idea for me to lead the investigation?"

Liberti slapped Adam on the back saying, "Sure do!" as he strode ahead and into his office. Liberti knew that Adam was smart and had that air of innocence that made people trust him. The coeds at New Paltz would be eager to spill their guts to this young, good-looking police officer. "Beats me what they see in him, but the girls seem to love him," Liberti chuckled to himself, shaking his head as he closed the door behind him.

After dinner, Myrna and Joseph Van Dyke, the owners of the property, decided to make a Facetime call to tell their tenants, Matthew and Pablo, the terrible news. Myrna and Joseph had recently purchased the house as an investment property. The rental came furnished and decorated with carefully chosen artwork. Joseph informed his tenants that everything had been destroyed in the fire while he and Myrna were sitting in their townhouse watching Columbo reruns on TV.

Her voice quivering, Myrna added, "You boys are welcome to stay with us in our condo at no charge. We are heartbroken over this for you as much as for us."

"Myrna, thanks but we couldn't impose on you. Right now, you take care of yourselves and we'll figure out something," Matthew replied, too shocked to make a decision.

Joseph added, "There's something else you need to know, boys. We suspect that this was a hate crime."

"What do you mean, Joseph?" Pablo asked.

"Police found a sign in the front yard that said 'GAYS GO AWAY'."

Matthew and Pablo were speechless for several seconds. Finally, Matthew blurted, "But Joseph, this is New Paltz! How could something like this happen in New Paltz? That doesn't make any sense."

"I guess it only takes one evil person. Anyhow, you boys have a lot to think about right now. We'll be in touch in a few days. Sorry about all of this."

"Yeah. This is a lot to take in. Joseph and Myrna, hang in there. Bye," Matthew said.

"Bye," Pablo echoed.

For Matthew and Pablo, the New Paltz house had become a welcome respite from their busy weekday life in Manhattan. The one-year lease had been an extravagance but, they considered it well worth the expense. They ended the call and sat in stunned silence until Matthew got up and poured them each a glass of pinot noir.

Saturday, September 24

Chief Liberti was sorely mistaken to think that he could keep talk of an alleged hate crime tamped down. It was already posted on social media. Letters-to-the-editor were streaming into the Daily Freeman. And at Water Street Market, a rally was being planned. Myrna and Joseph were leading the charge. Myrna arranged for a meeting in the courtyard of anyone interested in helping to organize a rally. She was transported back to her glory days of the '60's when she marched for civil rights, burned her bra, and protested the war in Viet Nam. Myrna felt a power surge charge through her body as people lined up to help out. Joseph was the quiet organizer, attempting to keep people filing through in an orderly fashion.

From Eddie's bird's eye view, he watched as Water Street Market came to life this morning. He was exuberant knowing that by tomorrow evening, he would be feeling very flush. Eddie began whistling "If I Were a Rich Man" as he slapped on the final coat of paint.

The courtyard was teeming with action. Myrna, wearing a muumuu and cowboy boots, was seated at a table as people stood in line waiting to sign up to help. She looked around for Joseph but could not see him. Joseph never told Myrna why Eddie Siricco had come to see him on Thursday and Myrna never told Joseph she had eavesdropped. Regardless, it was obvious that Joseph was troubled ever since that pissant, Eddie, had stopped by. Ironically, since the fire Joseph has appeared less distracted. The fire provided Myrna and Joseph with a common enemy and unity of purpose.

Joseph was outside of Rhino Records, at the opposite end of the market. He was talking with Harris Landau who was delighted by the hubbub at Water Street Market. Harris was savvy enough to appreciate what a promotional opportunity this fire had presented: a hate crime coming face-to-face with a protest. And, what better place than Water Street Market, he thought to himself. Aloud he said, "Joseph, Judith and I are devastated by this heinous act. Please let us know whatever you need for tomorrow's rally: tables, chairs, posters..." Harris whispered, "Look, I've already alerted the press and we should have statewide coverage."

"Thanks, Harris. I really appreciate your support. This has been a disturbing time for Myrna and myself."

Harris shook Joseph's hand. "Take care. Gotta run."

Judith gave Joseph a quick hug. "We'll be here tomorrow."

Myrna saw Joseph and waved to him. She had to pass by Eddie on his ladder who was still whistling away. As she looked up, she yelled, "How I'd love to give that ladder a swift kick and send you flying on your bony ass!"

Eddie looked down at Myrna and cheerfully shouted back, "Nice to see you too, Myrna."

This morning, Ellen and Charlie breezed into the Antique Barn to say hello before heading to Gardiner to check out a couple of barn sales.

"Hey, Ellen and Charlie. Wait till you hear this!" Cosmo called to them. Cosmo eagerly told them the shocking news.

Ellen was stunned. "Matthew and Pablo's rental? Burned to the ground?" Ellen and Charlie had become acquainted with Matthew over the last few years because Matthew had amassed an impressive collection of old typewriters, many of which he had purchased from Ellen and Charlie's booth.

Cosmo nodded and added, "And it was a hate crime, Ellen! A frightful hate crime!"

Ellen looked puzzled. "In New Paltz? No way, Cosmo."

Cosmo nodded. "I'm so upset, I couldn't sleep last night. Every time I heard a noise I thought our house was going to be next! I made Walter leave all the lights on. Yes, every one of them."

Charlie asked, "Do you think the police will find the person who did this?"

"Hell no, Charlie!" Cosmo scoffed. "But, let me tell you who will: Eddie Siricco. He knows everything that goes on in this village. And he loves to talk." Cosmo raised his left eyebrow mischievously, "And he always tells me everything! He'll know who did this!"

"Keep in mind, Cosmo, that this person is extremely dangerous. Eddie needs to tell the police whatever he knows. He better not try to be a hero--or you either."

"Pfft! You know me better than that, Charlie," Cosmo said dismissively. "I leave the heroics to my Walter," Cosmo whispered. Pointing to the front door he continued, "Look outside in the courtyard. See that crowd?" Ellen nodded. "Well, Myrna and Joseph, the owners of the property, are organizing a rally."

Ellen walked out the front door to get a closer look and saw a sturdy woman about her age seated at a table talking to an assortment of people waiting in line. Peace earrings the size of Texas completed the visual. Ellen was irresistibly drawn to the scene and worked her way to the line. When it was her turn, she introduced herself. "I'm Ellen Green, a dealer at the Antique Barn. So sorry to hear about the fire."

"Thanks, Ellen. Myrna Van Dyke. The property belonged to me and my husband." The women shook hands and Myrna continued. "I guess you heard about this being a hate crime?"

"Yes. That's why I'm here. What are you planning?"

"Sunday from noon till 2:00, we're holding a rally right here in the courtyard. My husband Joseph and I will be addressing the crowd."

"By the way, I absolutely love your earrings!"

"Thanks, Ellen. They were a birthday gift from Joseph. He bought them from Maglyn's, right here in the Market. See the little diamonds on the peace symbol?" Myrna proudly turned her head for Ellen to see.

"I'm impressed. Joseph knows how to pick out jewelry," Ellen smiled appreciatively. Lowering her voice, she continued, "What is your message going to be?"

"Human rights, Ellen. This act was an abomination! The police need to find the perpetrators and call it what it is: a hate crime."

Ellen nodded in agreement. "Well, count me in, Myrna. What do you need me to do?"

Myrna explained the details of the rally and the petition that was to be signed by participants that day. "Ellen, let's exchange phone numbers just in case there is a change of plans."

Ellen handed Myrna her number and said, "I'll be here by 11:00. Oh, and I'll bring my husband Charlie along with me. I know he would want to help out." She waved and slowly walked back to the Barn trying to figure out how to break this news to Charlie.

Detective Sergeant Adam Jacobson knew exactly where to begin his investigation and with whom. Rather than driving off in his police cruiser, he hopped on his bicycle and rode the short distance to Water Street Market. He walked his bike through the courtyard just as Myrna and Joseph were packing up all their materials from the rally sign-up.

Myrna approached the officer. "Sir, I'm Myrna Van Dyke. My husband and I own the property on Beekman Road that was burned to the ground."

"So sorry, Mrs. Van Dyke. I'm Detective Sergeant Adam Jacobson," he said offering his hand to each of them. "I assure you that our department is going to do everything we can to bring the perpetrator to justice."

"I would expect nothing less, Detective. And, of course, I hope you begin your investigation by calling it what it is: a hate crime."

"Ma'am, at this point, that has not been confirmed but we have confirmed that the cause of the fire was the work of an arsonist."

"Well, you may think about this differently after our rally on Sunday," Myrna shot back, raising one eyebrow.

"A rally? You do know that..."

Myrna interrupted him. "Of course, Joseph and I are obtaining all the proper permits. No need to worry," she retorted, looking Adam up and down. "I was demonstrating long before you were born. Now if you'll excuse us, we have a lot to do."

Joseph interjected, "Sir, I can personally assure you that this rally will be peaceful. You see, Myrna provides the passion. I provide the planning. We really appreciate that your department is on top of this. Thanks, Detective."

"Thank-you, Mr. Van Dyke," Adam nodded as he continued to walk his bicycle to the far end of the market. He knew that he needed to look up in order to find the person he had come to speak with.   There he was, perched on a ladder: Eddie Siricco. "Hey there, Eddie! Come on down for a minute. I'd like to talk with you."

"Sure, Detective." Eddie practically jumped down from the second story, purposely skipping the final three rungs of the ladder. "What can I do for you?"

"Eddie, let's sit over there," Adam suggested pointing to a small table near the waterfall. "Look, I'm investigating the fire over on Beekman Road. You always know everything that goes on here. I need your help, Eddie. Tell me what you know about this."

Eddie replied, "Hardly nothing, Sir. You have no idea how busy I've been. When Harris wants something painted, he, well, he's not the most patient boss I've ever known," he winked at Adam.

"Eddie, come on. Give me some help. Who around here would target a gay couple?"

"Nobody I can think of, Detective. Maybe the gay couple wasn't really the target," Eddie said cryptically.

"What do you mean, Eddie?"

Eddie shrugged. He was not about to reveal anything that could interfere with the various payments he was looking forward to receiving. "Don't really know. Look, what I will do is post something in my next Town Crier piece. Maybe somebody saw something. You never know."

Adam stared at Eddie. He knew Eddie was holding out on him. "Look, Eddie, I won't keep you from your work any longer, but if you hear anything--every the smallest detail-- give me a call." He handed Eddie his card. "See you around."

"Yeah, Detective. See ya!"

By Happy Hour, the bar at Ward's Bridge Inn in Montgomery was already packed. This restaurant is a local favorite. The owners, Pat and Bernie, greet every guest by name as they arrive and give hugs to everyone as they leave. It looked like the receiving line at a bar mitzvah. The hostess was bustling around, escorting diners to tables. There were several couples relaxing in front of the fireplace with their drinks. Barbara, the bartender, was laughing at a joke a customer had just told her while she continued to pour two martinis, open a bottle of cabernet, and take a drink order from a server while remaining cool and unruffled.

Ben Sheppard and Phillip Edelstein were seated at a high-top table. Phillip presented the agreement he had drawn up for them both to sign. He began, "This is a very basic loan agreement saying that I agree to loan you the money to pay off your liens and back taxes on the property on Milo Road. You, in return, will repay the loan in full plus ten percent interest at the time of sale. Some legalese follows regarding the repayment of the loan should the sale not go through. We both need to sign at the bottom of both copies."

Ben nodded and they each signed the document. Phillip continued, "The agreement goes on and, as you see, it specifies that you receive sixty percent of the sale price and I receive the other forty percent." They both signed at the bottom of the final page. Phillip handed Ben his copies and placed his own in his briefcase.

Lifting his martini glass Ben toasted, "To a powerful partnership."

Phillip lifted his glass in return. "And a profitable one." They spoke quietly as they drank their martinis. In keeping with the spirit of their partnership, Phillip suggested they split the check, sixty-forty, and then they left in separate cars.

That evening, Ellen and Charlie were enjoying a glass of sauvignon blanc on their porch as they did most evenings. Ellen knew that as soon as she mentioned volunteering him to help at the rally, their congenial glass of wine would come to an abrupt end. So, she had not, yet, broken the news. However, after decades of marriage to Ellen, Charlie was not fooled. He knew that her agreeable, breezy manner was a diversionary tactic. Something was up.

Charlie tested the waters. "So, that was terrible news about the place Matthew and Pablo rented. But it's hard to believe that in New Paltz someone committed a hate crime."

"I agree, Charlie. New Paltz--go figure! We can't possibly let this go without calling it what it is."

"But, Ellen, the police will investigate it and make that determination. It's not our call."

"Well, Myrna seems very sure and..."

"Myrna? Who the hell is 'Myrna'?" Charlie asked warily.

"Charlie, she and her husband are the owners of the property that was burned. They're planning a rally right at Water Street Market on Sunday to draw attention to the fact that a gay couple had been targeted." Ellen had that gleam in her eye that Charlie had come to dread.

Charlie poured himself another glass of wine, leaned back in his chair and said, "So, I gather that you're planning to participate. Right?"

Ellen nodded. "And, well, there's more."

Charlie took a sip and stared hard at Ellen. "Okay, go on."

"Well, I'm helping them out. I'll be getting people to sign in, helping to get signatures on a petition. That sort of thing," Ellen said casually.

"I guess I shouldn't be surprised by this."

"And Charlie, there's just one more thing you should know."

"Yes, Ellen?"

"Well, Sweetie," Ellen cooed. "Sweetie, I didn't only volunteer myself. I promised that you would be there to help out, as well." Ellen watched as Charlie took a drink of his wine, emptying his entire glass in one huge gulp.

Eddie could not sleep so he took out his notebook and pen. He began working on his next Town Crier piece. It contained the usual shout-outs to local businesses. Those always paid off for him. He knew if he mentioned the zesty Southwestern chicken salad at Lola's, he'd get a free one the next time he stopped by. He wrote about a missing Chihuahua hoping to collect the hundred dollar reward. And, then, he included an oblique reference to an illicit affair between two locals spotted kissing in a booth at P&G's, a local watering hole in New Paltz. At last, Eddie got to the meat of his article.

"So, folks, think about this carefully. When is a hate crime not a hate crime? I'll tell you when. When it happens in New Paltz. That's when! And when is an actor not an actor? When her name is Dorothy Dawson. That's when! There will be lots more to say on these topics in the weeks ahead, but for now, tune in next week! And remember, always keep your ears open. Your Town Crier."

Sunday, September 25

This morning, Myrna and Joseph arrived at Water Street Market carrying tables, a couple of chairs, and copies of the petition they were planning to give to the police after the rally today. The sunny, crisp morning boded well for the rally which was not due to begin until noon. Joseph went back to the car to grab a few of the posters they had made.

Myrna was pushing cafe tables aside to make room for her folding tables when she heard Harris call to her. "Hey, Myrna, what do you think you're doing? Those round tables are for customers. You can't move them out of your way!"

"Harris, you have a choice; you can be part of the solution or part of the problem!" She put her hands on her hips and glared up at him.

"Myrna, I'm all for this rally. You know that, but customers need to be able to eat and move around the market. It's a Sunday, for God's sake! This place is always busy on a Sunday!"

"And our rally is going to make it even busier, so you should be thanking me--not carrying on about it!"

Harris wished he had never given Myrna permission to set up at Water Street. "Put those tables back where they belong."

"Harris, I think your sense of justice got stuck somewhere in those designer jeans you're wearing," Myrna shot back. She picked up the petition and shoved it under Harris' nose. "Here. I want your name to be the first one on this petition!"

Harris did not even bother to read it. He quickly scribbled his signature on line one and shoved it back to Myrna. Joseph returned, partially hidden under all the posters he was carrying. "Harris, thanks for showing up. We really appreciate your support."

"Thanks, Joseph. Glad someone around here appreciates me!"

"Support? Are you kidding? Harris has been nothing but a pain in the butt this morning, Joseph!" Myrna complained.

Harris warned Myrna, "I'll be back later when this thing gets going." Shaking his finger at her Harris said, "You interfere with the customers and I'm shutting you down!" He walked off to grab some coffee and a bagel at the Mudd Puddle.

Ellen and Charlie Green arrived by eleven to help with whatever Myrna and Joseph needed them to do. The parking lot at Water Street was already full by the time they arrived, so they parked in the municipal lot on Main Street and walked to the courtyard. Charlie sighed and tried not to think about the golf game he had to skip today. Right about now, his golf partner, Hugh, would be hitting a drive from the fourth tee at Otterkill Country Club. Instead, Charlie was shlepping around posters and chairs for a rally at Water Street Market. He muttered to himself, "Well, I never expected that marriage to Ellen was going to be easy."

Ellen, on the other hand, was amped up. She had been making posters since dawn and was dressed in jeans and a tee shirt that read, *"This is what a feminist looks like"*. As she and Charlie walked by, Ellen spotted Eddie up on his ladder. "Hi, Eddie!"

Eddie had no intention of actually painting the trim, but this was the perfect vantage point to watch the Myrna and Joseph shit show. From the top of the ladder he yelled down, "Hey, Ellen and Charlie! You're not getting mixed up in this nonsense today, are you?"

"Hah! We wouldn't think of missing it," Ellen answered for both of them. "Hey, Eddie, could you come down here for a minute?"

"Sure," Eddie agreed, happy to have an excuse not to work. "What is it?"

Ellen spoke quietly. "Eddie, who do you think started this fire?"

Eddie gave a noncommittal shrug. "The police will have to figure that out."

"Who are you kidding, Eddie. The police wouldn't know where to begin. What's your gut telling you? Come on. I know you've got your suspicions," Ellen prodded him.

Eddie had to be on guard when Ellen tried to pump him for information. He was very careful not to reveal more than he wanted to. "I'll just say this, Ellen. Don't be too quick to think this is a hate crime."

"What? You can't be serious! If it looks like a hate crime and smells like a hate crime, it is a hate crime!" she retorted.

Eddie gave her an ambiguous smile. "Better get back to work. Behave yourself, Ellen," he teased.

Joseph addressed the small group and explained the plan. "Good morning, everyone. I'm Joseph Van Dyke and this is my wife, Myrna. Thanks for offering to help with the rally. It's all very simple. We need you to please sign this sheet that I'm passing around and include your phone number. We need to keep a record of everyone who has helped us this morning." Myrna started passing around the clipboard and pen. "At noon, Myrna and I will make brief statements and read aloud the petition. After it is read, please take a copy, walk around, and try to obtain signatures from every single adult at Water Street Market. Any questions so far?"

"Will anyone else have a chance to speak?"

"Absolutely! We will need to recognize you and ask you to come forward to speak through this hand-held mic. Please keep your comments brief and to the point. Remember why we are rallying and for whom."

When noon arrived, Myrna took over and knew how to turn up the volume. Myrna had decades of experience and was able to transfer her passion to a crowd of activists. She stood on a chair and, using her hands as a megaphone, welcomed everyone to this rally. She began, "Joseph and I rented out our lovely home to Matthew and Pablo. And it was burned to the ground because Matthew and Pablo are gay. This is a hate crime, plain and simple! The police need to call it what it is!" Whistles and shouts followed. Myrna waited for quiet before continuing. "We stand here today to rally for justice for all! We stand here today to say we have a right to be free to love and free from hate!" The cheering from the crowd brought all the shop owners out to see what was taking place. Customers exited the Antique Barn with Walter and Cosmo right behind them. When they heard all the shouting, Leonard and Dorothy flew out of the Denizen Theatre where they were starting to rehearse.

Always adept at taking center stage, Dorothy elbowed her way to the front where Myrna was mesmerizing the crowd. Dorothy cheered and hooted along, not quite sure what this rally was all about. Her eyes darted around hoping to see photographers from the local news networks. Instead, she was clunked in the back of her head with someone's placard. Turning around, she was face-to-face with Ellen.

"So sorry!" Ellen yelled. "This sign just flopped over. It won't happen again. I promise."

"Not to worry. I think my acting career will survive. I'm Dorothy Dawson, actor. I'm rehearsing for the new play, 'Desdemona'".

Ellen who had always been a bit star-struck stammered, "Dorothy Dawson, I'm delighted to meet you! I'm Ellen Green, antique dealer. I rent space at the Antique Barn right behind us."

"Charmed. What happens next? I've never been to a rally."

"Stick near me. It's bound to get loud and wild but not violent. Nothing to worry about--except watch your head."

The crowd ranged from the college students who had always wished they had lived in the '60's to the octogenarians who had. Signs such as 'HATE IS UNAMERICAN', 'GAY RIGHTS ARE HUMAN RIGHTS', 'STOP HATE CRIMES' were raised in support.

Joseph took the mic. "Friends, before I read the petition aloud, I would like to read a statement from Matthew and Pablo, the target of this hate crime. 'We have chosen not to participate in person today. We do not wish to be tokenized or put on display. This rally is not about us, personally. It is about calling a hate crime by name.

We thank you for your support. Matthew and Pablo.'" An explosion of cheers and applause followed this message.

Next, Joseph read the petition. "*We, the undersigned, support and defend diversity in every form. Therefore, we demand that the police immediately designate the arson on Beekman Road as a hate crime. The definition of a hate crime is the following: a crime that is motivated by prejudice on the basis of race, religion, sexual orientation, or other grounds. Justice and humanity must be served.*"

From the edge of the crowd, chanting began: "CALL IT WHAT IT IS! CALL IT A HATE CRIME! CALL IT WHAT IT IS!" In solidarity, everyone assembled joined in.

Myrna and Joseph quickly abandoned any notion of spontaneous remarks from the crowd. A couple of participants took the mic and attempted to speak but the chanting drowned them out completely. Instead, Myrna and Joseph led the crowd from one end of the market to the other end. They knew that their permit extended only to the boundary of Water Street Market. Therefore, when they arrived at Main Street, Myrna shouted at everyone to turn around, but it was too late. The crowd of activists had become a rowdy mob.

Instead of turning around, the crowd turned right and aggressively marched up Main Street. Much to her surprise, Ellen found herself at the front of this mob with Dorothy Dawson next to her. An elderly man took the lead shouting, "I'M EIGHTY AND GAY AND I'M NOT GOING AWAY!" The crowd loved it and joined him, Ellen included.

By the time the protesters made it to the traffic light, the police had arrived. Detective Sergeant Adam Jacobson had the misfortune of being assigned to contain the rally. He got out of his cruiser and approached the crowd. Calmly but firmly he ordered them to turn around and go back to Water Street Market. Dorothy, not one to miss a photo op, spoke up, "Sir, we are marching peacefully and we refuse to let you stop us!"

Adam replied, "Ma'am, I do appreciate that this is a peaceful protest, but the permit the organizers obtained confines the protest to the Water Street Market, so please..."

The crowd stood aghast as Dorothy shot Adam a haughty look and marched past him. "Ma'am, I'm afraid if you do not return to Water Street, I will have no choice but to arrest you," Adam said politely. "So please cooperate."

Dorothy was ecstatic. As PR opportunities went, this one was perfection! She transformed into her Desdemona persona, placed her wrists together, and dramatically lowered her voice. "Do what you must, Sir. I will never back down."

Ellen looked on and tried to intervene. "Dorothy," she whispered, "let's turn around and join the others. Come."

Dorothy stubbornly refused to budge. Adam tried one more time to reason with her. "Please, Ma'am," he pleaded. When she continued to ignore him, Adam knew he had to follow through. He firmly grasped her by the elbow and steered her towards his police cruiser. Dorothy tried to wriggle out, but it was useless.

Rushing to Dorothy's side, Ellen shouted at Adam, "How can you do this? She's old enough to be your grandmother! This is an outrage!"

A second officer silently took Ellen by the elbow, opened the door to the police car, and placed her in the back seat next to a euphoric Dorothy Dawson.

Detective Jacobson and his partner escorted Dorothy and Ellen into the police station to meet with Chief Liberti in Room A. The Chief barged into the room and burst out laughing. "Jacobson, are you kidding me? These two, these two are the agitators you've arrested?"

Adam reddened, cleared his throat and responded, "Well, Sir. Yes, Sir. I tried..."

"Jacobson," Liberti began, "the press will be all over this and we'll come across as bullies. Look, these women may have gotten a bit carried away," he winked, "but I'm sure they meant no harm." Liberti put his arm around Adam's shoulder. "Now, Adam, you'll be able to fix this. I know you will. Make this go away." He smiled and left the room.

Meanwhile, Charlie figured he might as well make the best of the situation Ellen had roped him into. He certainly knew that Ellen would completely throw herself into this rally. In fact, she probably would wind up in a confrontation with someone before it all ended. And from previous experience, Charlie worried more about the poor sap who was foolish enough to take her on. So, Charlie decided to kick back and get some lunch while Ellen was busy reclaiming her glory days.

Charlie ordered a turkey B.L.T. and a bottle of water from the Mudd Puddle. Next, he found a table in the shade, propped his feet up on the extra chair, and waited for Michelle to bring him his sandwich. Fortunately, the rally had moved to the other end of the

58

Market so Charlie had the courtyard all to himself. He took out his phone and texted his friend Hugh for updates on the golf game he was missing. They exchanged several texts back and forth that elicited a couple of snickers from Charlie.

"Here you are, Charlie. Enjoy it!" Michelle smiled, handing Charlie his order.

"Thanks, Michelle. It looks great!" Charlie was quite pleased with the way the day was unfolding.

Unfortunately, Charlie's respite ended abruptly when Myrna and Joseph returned with the entire herd of protesters. Reporters from the local newspapers and TV channels were interviewing participants with camera crews in tow. Myrna broke away from this flurry of activity and charged, like a bull, at Charlie. "Charlie, Ellen has been arrested! You have to do something!"

"Myrna, please have a seat," Charlie offered. "Now, calm down and tell me what happened."

Myrna frantically spit out what little information she had. "We had already turned back to Water Street, so I really couldn't tell you exactly what took place, but you have to go to the police station because they could be violating her rights to free speech and ..."

"Myrna, I'm really not worried about Ellen. Actually, I'm more worried for the police," Charlie remarked before taking another satisfying bite of his turkey B.L.T.

Adam stared at the two women seated across the table from him. "Well, you're lucky that Chief Liberti was feeling so generous today." He shook his head in amusement and continued, "So, I'm going to drive you, two, rabble-rousers back to Water Street Market and hope that we never meet again. Do I make myself clear?"

"Detective Jacobson, from what we just overheard, it appears that you owe us an apology," Ellen replied with a self-satisfied smile.

Adam cocked his head to the side and grinned. "Touché. Now, ladies, after you." He gave a courtly bow.

The three of them stood up and were about to leave through the back door when the desk sergeant stuck her head in and announced, "Detective Jacobson. A Charlie Green insists on speaking with you."

Ellen closed her eyes, dreading what was about to ensue. Jacobson turned to Ellen. "From the look on your face, I take it that you are acquainted with Charlie Green?"

Ellen sighed and nodded.

"Then, I say, please invite him in, Sergeant."

A moment later, Sergeant O'Riley returned with Charlie.

Adam introduced himself and extended his hand. "I am Detective Sergeant Adam Jacobson."

"Charlie Green, Detective. I understand that you have arrested my wife, Ellen Green?"

"Yes, I have but," looking from Dorothy to Ellen and back to Charlie, "we have decided that since this is a first offense, we would let them off with a warning."

"Sir, excuse me, but a first offense? Really? Gotta say, I see no need for leniency. These women disobeyed and should be held accountable. You were doing your job as a police officer. Good day, Sir," Charlie said cheerfully. "By the way, Ellen, I brought you your toothbrush. Here you are." He winked, handed it to her, and turned to exit.

Adam tried to disguise a laugh as a cough. Ellen was fuming. "I've had it. Let's get out of here!" She grabbed her poster and the two women followed Adam out of the building.

Dorothy was indignant that this arrest had provided nothing more than a couple of belly laughs for the police chief. The photo op for which she had performed never happened. She and Ellen both wore petulant expressions as they sat in the back seat of Adam's cruiser. He politely opened the back door to let them off in the empty parking lot at Water Street Market. The rally had dispersed more than an hour ago.

Charlie was parked and waiting for Ellen to arrive. She saw his van, flung open the passenger door, climbed in, slammed it shut, and folded her arms across her chest. Staring straight ahead, Ellen snarled, "Do not say one word, Charlie Green. Not one word!"

Charlie was relieved that Ellen refused to look in his direction for the entire trip back home to Montgomery. He found it physically impossible to erase the smirk from his face.

The day seemed endless to Eddie. He was eager to return to his apartment on Main Street and reap the rewards for his vigilance and tenacity. He had planned ahead and was prepared for every contingency. Eddie was ready to let the players involved face the consequences of their behavior--for better or for worse. However, as he waited, he began pacing and drinking in an attempt to calm his nerves.

After another hour, steady Eddie was not very steady. Therefore, he plopped himself on the couch, his bottle beside him, and dozed through several episodes of "Forged in Fire". It is unfortunate that Eddie was totally soused. Had he been sober, he might have been able to alter the event that followed. However, Eddie was Eddie. He was too drunk to hear someone climb the steps and approach his door. In fact, he never even heard the first two rounds of knocking. Finally, by the third series of knocks, Eddie got up from the couch, rubbed his eyes, and staggered over to answer the door. He opened the door, allowed the person to enter, and greeted the visitor with a lopsided grin. Eddie Siricco was so sloshed that he swayed in slow motion and collapsed, unconscious, onto the floor in a heap. What happened next was surprisingly easy and painless. The visitor merely took a seat on Eddie's chest, used one hand to cover his nose and mouth and the other to seal shut his jaw. Eddie Siricco spent the next several hours as he often did: smashed and out cold. However, this time was slightly different. He was stone cold. Eddie Siricco was dead.

Monday, September 26

Adam Jacobson was in a deep sleep when a message came blaring through his phone. He squinted as he checked the time. "Shit, it's 2:00 in the morning!" he moaned.

"APB, APB, Code 100. Code 19". The message was repeated. Adam jumped up, splashed water on his face, grabbed his clothes and sped to the police station in response to the codes: dead body found. All officers are to report to the station.

Chief Liberti met with Detective Jacobson prior to the general emergency briefing that was about to take place. The Chief had ordered every unit to be present. Twenty police officers made up of the full time officers, motorcycle unit, and the bike patrol were all assembled and ready to listen to a briefing. "Officers, this is an emergency meeting. Eddie Siricco has been found murdered. We already know that the victim was suffocated and died from compression asphyxia in his apartment at 681 Main Street on Sunday, September 25 between twenty-two and twenty-three hundred hours. I have directed Detective Sergeant Jacobson to lead this investigation. Detective, please continue from here."

Adam cleared his throat and addressed the officers. "Yes, Sir. Good morning, officers. Earlier this morning I read a preliminary report from the chief medical examiner. The report indicates that there was no evidence of a struggle. It also included a toxicology report indicating that the victim had a blood-alcohol level of approximately.30 %." Adam paused before continuing. "Are there questions at this point?'

"Sir, is there any connection between the murder and the arson?"

"Officer, at this time, there appears to be no connection. However, that has not yet been officially determined. We will concurrently investigate both crimes. Other questions before I move on? Yes?"

"How was the body discovered?"

"The door to his apartment had been left open. At one hundred hours today, a neighbor's dog ran in and the neighbor went into the apartment to retrieve her dog. She called 911 immediately."

After several seconds Adam continued. "This investigation must expand to the entire New Paltz community. Eddie Siricco was a well-known local with contacts that we have yet to discover. Water Street Market and every local bar were his regular stomping grounds." A few snickers were heard. "I will begin with Water Street Market. The rest of you please check with Sergeant O'Riley at the front desk for your assignments. Be sure to report your findings directly to me. Before we adjourn, Chief Liberti would like to say a few words."

"Thank-you, Detective Jacobson. Officers, since there is no next-of-kin, no one, I repeat, NO ONE is to know about the murder of Eddie Siricco until tomorrow. We make our inquiries and say he is missing at this time. New Paltz is a small town and I don't want the press or the public to interfere and contaminate this investigation. Let's give ourselves one more day to do some good detective work." Liberti scanned the room of officers and shook his finger at them. "Word gets out that he was murdered and I'll start an internal investigation to find out who is responsible! Understood?" Every officer nodded vigorously in response.

Jacobson concluded the meeting."Remember, our community deserves fairness and compassion, so be kind and be careful. Oh, and one more thing; those of you who have been assigned to barhopping duty for the next few days, well, remember to take it easy," he warned good-naturedly.

This morning, Myrna was sprawled out on her couch wearing her Minnie Mouse slippers and munching on an everything bagel while she watched the local news channel. *"After this commercial break you will see that activism is alive and well in New Paltz. Stay tuned!"*

"Joseph! Joseph! Come in here. You've got to see this! They're going to show the rally!"

"Good afternoon! This is 'Live with Lauren' and I'm at Water Street Market in New Paltz where activism is still a way of life! I'm here with Myrna Van Dyke, whose home was tragically burned to the ground on Thursday. Myrna, please tell the viewers what happened." Lauren aimed the microphone at Myrna.

"Lauren, my husband Joseph and I rented a house to a wonderful gay couple. The house was burned to the ground and a sign was left on the lawn: GAYS GO AWAY."

"Myrna, what a shocking crime!"

"Ah, yes, Lauren, and that is why we are petitioning the police to stop being a bunch of wimps and call it what it is!"

Myrna pumped her fist in the air and the crowd around Myrna chanted, "HATE CRIME, HATE CRIME. CALL IT WHAT IT IS!"

Myrna continued, "*This is, indeed, a hate crime and we never expected this to happen in New Paltz! We are so grateful for all this support and we will not stop until our mission is accomplished. We plan to...*"

Lauren stepped right in front of Myrna, cutting her off, "*Well, folks, you heard it first on 'Live with Lauren'!*" She chirped, "*Have a great day! Now, back to you, Fred.*" With a wink and a wave, 'Live with Lauren' signed off.

Myrna was livid. "The little bitch cut me off! I can't believe she did that!"

"Well, Myrna, you'll feel better when you check this out." Joseph proudly opened up the Daily Freeman and presented the two-page photo montage of yesterday's rally. Myrna moved in close and studied each photo with sheer delight.

"Hah! I love this one!" Myrna cried, pointing to a photo of her leading the parade through Water Street Market. "And what about this, Joseph? Oh! Check this one out! Isn't that one fantastic?" She high-fived Joseph.

The centerfold spread more than placated Myrna's wounded ego.

Ellen needed to return to the Antique Barn this morning to replenish her inventory of typewriters. Cosmo was the first one to see her arrive. "Ellen, our hero!" he called out, both arms raised over his head. "Come, Honey, give me a big hug!"

"Cosmo, what is all this fuss about?" Ellen asked.

"Oh, my God, Ellen! We all heard how you got arrested yesterday and well, you are so brave!" Cosmo theatrically cried, "Did they use tasers? Tear gas? Were you strip-searched?" he asked eagerly. "Walter, Walter, come quickly. It's our Ellen!"

"Cosmo, you don't need to shout. I'm standing right next to you." Walter and Ellen exchanged eye-rolls. "Cosmo, I really don't think the police viewed Ellen as a threat to their safety."

At that moment, Detective Jacobson arrived at Water Street Market to begin his covert investigation. The first stop was the Antique Barn. When Ellen spotted Jacobson entering the shop, she dropped the typewriter and darted behind a primitive cupboard in Joan's booth.

Cosmo greeted him. "Good morning. Welcome to the Antique Barn." Still dying to learn more about Ellen's arrest, he shouted, "Hey, Ellen! Yoo-hoo! Where did you go? I want to hear all about that despicable, beastly cop who arrested you!"

Adam, clearly amused, put his hands in his pockets and silently waited for Ellen Green to come out from her hiding place. However, Ellen was too mortified to do so. She tried to slink around quietly and slip out the back door unnoticed, but to no avail. Stealth was not one of her strong points. Adam watched her head to the back door and met her there before she could escape. "Well, well, Ellen Green, we meet again."

Ellen responded with an imperious glare and bolted out of the building, her typewriter still in the middle of the floor.

Adam walked back to Cosmo and Walter. He reached out to introduce himself. "Good morning, guys. I'm the despicable, beastly cop who arrested Ellen Green. Pleased to meet you."

"And I'm the mean, miserable manager. Pleased to meet you, too." Walter reached out to shake hands with the Detective. "What can we do for you?"

"I'm making some inquiries and wondered if we could talk privately for a few minutes."

"Sure," Walter nodded. "Let's step outside." He led the way out the back door to the parking lot.

"You're acquainted with Eddie Siricco?" Walter nodded. "Have you seen him in the last few days?"

"Sir, you'd be better off talking with Cosmo. He's everybody's best friend. He'll know more about Eddie than I will."

"Okay, thanks. Please ask him to step outside."

"Sure." Walter went into the shop to get Cosmo.

"Walter, I can't talk to him! I'm too embarrassed. Please don't make me do it," Cosmo begged.

Walter silently motioned to the back door and nudged Cosmo along in front of him.

In the parking lot, Cosmo regrouped. "I gather that ole Eddie has got himself in some trouble for a change."

"Well, you could say that, I suppose. Have you spoken with him lately?"

"Detective, he stops in here all the time to talk. Eddie's quite the talker, you know."

"When was the last time you spoke to Eddie?"

"Hmm. Let me see. It was Friday. Eddie wanted to tell me something but that was when we heard about the fire so he never had a chance to say anything," Cosmo explained.

"Did he talk about anything else? Mention any names? It's important, Cosmo."

Cosmo looked up as he tried to recall his recent conversation with Eddie. "Ah, yes. He stopped in last Monday to tell me some gossip he had overheard. It was nothing much, actually not up to his usual standards," Cosmo laughed nervously.

"Yes?"

"Well, Eddie loves to give all the juicy details and I must admit," Cosmo leaned over and whispered in Adam's ear, "I do love to hear the details! The more the merrier, I always say!"

"Please, go on."

"Well, this guy, Ben Sheppard, is planning to sell his land to a development group that wants to build a resort hotel off 299. How crazy is that?" Adam said nothing. Cosmo continued. "Anyhow, his business partner was lending him money to pay off liens. That's really all I know," Cosmo said cautiously. He did not want to find himself embroiled in Eddie's latest scheme. Gossip was gossip, but talking to the police was another matter entirely.

"Who was his business partner?"

"Why, Phillip Edelstein."

"Thank-you, Cosmo. Here's my card in case you think of something else about Eddie." He nodded and started to walk away.

"Oh and, Detective, there's one more thing. A resort hotel? Ben will never get the town to approve! Never! But tell me, what kind of trouble has Eddie Siricco gotten himself into? Come on," Cosmo winked, "Just give me a little hint."

Adam ignored Cosmo and headed to his next appointment to meet with Harris Landau. He sat in a far corner of the courtyard to wait, conspicuous in his conservative khakis and button-down shirt. Harris breathlessly rushed over. "You must be the detective. Sorry I'm late!"

"No problem, Mr. Landau. This is a great place to wait around. Sure beats the police station. I'm Detective Jacobson." They shook hands.

"First, please call me Harris. Now, what can I do for you? Did I forget to obtain a permit or something like that?"

"Mr. Landau, Harris," Adam explained, "I'm here about Eddie Siricco. I understand that he does a lot of work around Water Street Market."

"Well, look, Eddie does a great job, that is, whenever he actually puts in the work." Shaking his finger at the second-floor windows above Antiques on Main, Harris said, "See the trim around those upper windows? Well, Eddie was supposed to finish it all up by last Friday. Here it is Monday. It's still not finished and he's AWOL again!"

Jacobson continued, "So, I gather that Eddie Siricco is not the most dependable employee. When did you last see him?"

"Well, I think it was Sunday morning. Yeah, Sunday. He was up on his ladder so I didn't actually speak to him. I was talking to Myrna and Joseph Van Dyke about the rally. They're the couple whose house was burned down. Anyhow, what's all this about Eddie? He in some kind of trouble again?"

Ignoring the question, Adam asked, "Harris, who are some of the people Eddie talks with? This is very important, so take your time."

"Hard to say, Detective. Eddie will talk to anybody who will listen. That's Eddie."

"Who have you seen him talking to lately?"

"He's always wasting time, going in and out of the shops here, talking to the owners, customers. Everyone. And, he loves to talk to Cosmo at the Barn." Harris motioned with his head in the direction of the Antique Barn. "Oh, and last week he was talking with Dorothy Dawson, the actress playing in the one-woman show, 'Desdemona'. It's going to be opening right here at the Denizen in a few weeks. You would love it." Harris reached for his card.

"Here, call me directly and I'll nab you a couple of front row seats--on me!" Harris winked.

"Why, thanks, Harris. I would love that." Adam added with a smirk, "Hey, is it a musical? I really love musicals." Every now and then Adam liked to play the dumb cop, just for fun.

Harris was about to explain the Shakespearean origins of the play when Adam stepped aside to take a phone call. "Excuse me, Harris." He listened carefully, lowered his voice and whispered into the phone, "Yes, Chief. So now that you've issued a statement to the press, the gag order is lifted?" He nodded and ended the call.

Turning back to Harris, Adam handed him a business card. "Harris, please let me know if you think of anyone who might be in touch with Eddie. A friend of his, maybe. Anyone."

"Sure, Detective." Looking up again at the half-painted trim Harris complained, "Damn Eddie. He's probably at home nursing a hangover from the week-end!"

Jacobson replied matter-of-factly, "Well, Harris, a hangover would be the least of Eddie's problems."

"What do you mean, Detective?"

Staring directly at Harris, Adam calmly stated, "Eddie Siricco is dead. He was murdered on Sunday night."

Jacobson did not wait for a response. He walked to the police cruiser and drove back to the station.

Adam had arranged to follow up with Ben Sheppard. Sergeant O'Riley was escorting Ben to Adam's office. Adam stood up and reached across his desk to shake hands. "Ben Sheppard, I am Detective Sergeant Jacobson. Please have a seat."

"What's this about?" Ben asked suspiciously.

Leaning on his elbows, Adam said simply. "Eddie Siricco. Tell me about your relationship with Eddie."

"Not much to tell."

"How long have you known Eddie?"

Ben snickered, "Eddie and I go way back. We're not friends, but we have a beer together once in a while--that sort of thing. I mostly avoid him," Ben shrugged. "Problem with Eddie is that he likes to run his mouth."

"Well, Ben, he's not going to be running his mouth again."

"What do you mean, Detective?"

"Eddie Siricco is dead. He was murdered Sunday night." Adam stared at Ben, watching carefully as Ben's left eye began to twitch.

"You're serious?"

"Dead serious. So now, why don't you tell me who would want to shut Eddie up badly enough to kill him?"

"No idea."

"When did you last see Eddie?"

Heaving a loud sigh Ben shook his head. "Detective, I really can't remember."

"Try." Adam leaned back in his chair glaring at Ben.

"Well, I was at Water Street Market last week. Can't remember what day. I waved to Eddie. He was up on a ladder painting trim."

"Why were you there?"

"Probably just passing through. Who knows." Ben kept tapping his right leg as he shrugged.

"Now, I'm asking you again. Tell me why you were there and who you were with." Adam leaned forward, not taking his eyes off Ben.

Ben folded his arms across his chest. "Like I said, I don't remember." He glared right back at Adam.

Adam stood up. "Why don't you stop lying and tell me what you and Phillip Edelstein are up to."

"That's none of your damn business. A personal matter."

Adam announced, "We're finished for today but not for good."

Ben got up, turned his back to Adam, walked to the door but stopped abruptly as Adam said, "Hey, Ben. Funny that Eddie

Siricco knew you were trying to sell your property on Milo Road to a big developer. Wonder what else Eddie knew."

Ben did not look back. He slammed the door on his way out.

Tuesday, September 27

The New Paltz Police station was in turmoil. Until one week ago, the most serious crime in the last year involved a couple of college students streaking across campus. Now, a potential hate crime and a murder had Chief Liberti's blood pressure soaring. He was determined not to involve the NY State Police. He had complete confidence in Detective Sergeant Adam Jacobson's ability to lead the investigation.

Jacobson had been in his office for hours this morning, pouring over information about Eddie Siricco. He was hoping to find even one detail that could begin to suggest a motive for murder. Adam sat, elbows on his desk and his head in his hands, when Sergeant O'Riley knocked on his office door. "Sir, sorry to bother you, but Myrna Van Dyke is here to see you."

Adam groaned, "Tell her she'll have to wait a while."

Several minutes later, Myrna was escorted to Adam's office. They shook hands and Adam motioned for her to have a seat across from him.

"So, what can I do for you, Mrs. Van Dyke?"

Myrna replied, "Detective, please call me Myrna. Everybody does, so you might as well, too."

"Okay, Myrna. Now, what brings you here today?"

"You must be joking! There was a monumental protest on Sunday--or have you already forgotten?"

"Myrna," Adam leaned back in his chair, arms behind his head, "I have not forgotten, but intervening events have overtaken the department since your rally."

"That's absurd! You're telling me that the entire New Paltz Police Department drops a hate crime investigation so they can," Myrna glared at Adam before she spewed, "go looking for a lost dog! What incompetence! Where did you all get your badges from? Toys "R" Us?"

Adam scratched his head as Myrna hurled insults at him. When Myrna finished her rant, he stated, "Myrna, perhaps you haven't seen today's paper, but there has been a murder in New Paltz."

Myrna's eyes bulged with the news. "Oh."

"Did you know Eddie Siricco? He was murdered Sunday night."

"Yes, I did know Eddie. And, Detective, you know what I say to that?" Myrna stood up to leave, walked to the door, and turned around. "Good riddance to Eddie!"

Startled by her comment, Adam grabbed his phone and called Sergeant O'Riley. "O'Riley, send Mrs. Van Dyke back to my office. Immediately!"

Myrna walked back into Adam's office and sat down. "You wanted to see me, Detective?"

"Myrna, let me put it this way. Eddie Siricco has been murdered and I've been racking my brain trying to figure out why someone would want to kill him. So tell me, why would someone want to kill Eddie?"

"Just because I'm not grieving over his death doesn't mean I'd want to kill him."

"I didn't say *you* would want to kill Eddie. Why would someone want him dead?"

"Look, Eddie and I have always shared a mutual hostility towards each other. I'm not sorry that Eddie and his big mouth are gone for good."

"When did you last see Eddie?"

"Saturday. The day before the rally. Eddie was on his ladder. We barely spoke. Oh, and I think he was watching from his ladder the day of the rally, too." Myrna had no intention of telling Adam that Eddie had stopped by on Thursday evening or how agitated Joseph had been after Eddie's visit.

"Myrna, you're free to leave but I'm sure we'll meet again soon."

Myrna smiled sweetly, "I'm sure we will. Quite possibly the next rally will take place right at the police station. For your convenience, of course."

Adam's scheduled appointment was escorted to his office. An elderly gray-haired woman wearing a faded blue cardigan and a pair of frumpy polyester pants stood in his doorway. "Hello, Mrs.

Brucker. I'm Detective Sergeant Adam Jacobson. Please have a seat."

"Nice to meet you," Mrs. Brucker said timidly.

"Now, Mrs. Brucker, you live next door to Eddie Siricco and I understand that you discovered his body. Please tell me about what happened around 1:00 this morning."

"Certainly, Sir. My Fifi, well she is getting on in years and often asks to go out to pee in the middle of the night. I always put her on a leash when we get to the street. Last night, well, technically, it was early this morning, she wanted to go out. I put on my slippers and coat over my pajamas and opened the door of my apartment. Before I could stop her, Fifi ran into Mr. Siricco's apartment next door. His door had been left open. Fifi wouldn't come when I called to her so I went in after her and..." Mrs. Brucker began to blow her nose as she recalled the horrific sight she had witnessed.

"That's okay, Mrs. Brucker. You're doing fine. Please continue."

"Well, there he was: Mr. Siricco. He was flat on his back and not moving so I thought he was drunk. That happened quite often with him, you see," she giggled nervously. "When I got closer to him, he looked kinda funny and I was afraid. I called 911 and picked Fifi up to wait outside in the hall."

"Did you happen to notice if he had any visitors on Sunday evening?"

"I assure you, Detective; I'm not one to snoop. If Mr. Siricco had any visitors, that's not my business."

"Of course, I understand. But you might have been going out to walk Fifi and spotted someone heading to Mr. Siricco's apartment."

"No. I'm sorry but I never saw anyone and, well, my hearing isn't what it used to be so I keep my TV pretty loud but Mr. Siricco never complained about it. Are we finished? I don't like to leave Fifi for too long. Like I said, she's a bit incontinent," Mrs. Brucker whispered.

Adam smiled, "Mrs. Brucker, I appreciate your cooperation and I thank you for calling 911 so quickly. If you think of anything else, here is my card. Please feel free to call me."

Mrs. Brucker placed Adam's card in her handbag. "Detective, when the ambulance arrived, they told me Mr. Siricco was already dead! I couldn't believe it. Why would someone do this to him? He was such a nice man. Mr. Siricco was always friendly to me and Fifi and well, I looked forward to reading the Town Crier article every week. I always loved trying to figure out who he was talking about. He had such a way with words, Detective. In fact, it was my favorite... " She sniffled and honked as she blew her nose again at the very thought of poor Eddie Siricco.

After Mrs. Brucker left, Adam sat tapping his head with his pen. One common theme was emerging: Eddie Siricco had a big mouth and a provocative pen.

Joseph deliberately waited until Myrna left for the police station before following up with his insurance agent regarding his homeowner's claim. Now that the report from the fire department had been sent in, the insurance company had the final piece of evidence they required. Therefore, this morning he was able to find out exactly how much he would receive from the fire damage. It turned out that the amount of the settlement would more than clear up the financial mess Joseph had created. As long as Myrna did not know the total amount they would be receiving, Myrna need not ever know that his gambling debts had wiped out their life's savings. The entire week had been extremely stressful, but at last, Joseph received one bit of good news.

Myrna drove into the garage and called out to Joseph as she walked into their condo. "Joseph, Joseph! You won't believe what I just learned."

"I just learned something this morning, too. Sit down and tell me, Myrna."

"No, Joseph, you go first. What did you learn?"

Joseph smiled gently. "You first, dear."

"Joseph, you'll never believe this but Eddie Siricco has been murdered!"

Joseph did not say anything at all in response. However, a faint, barely perceptible smile appeared on his face and disappeared so quickly, one could not be sure that it was ever there at all.

This evening, Ellen was about to pour each of them a glass of wine when Charlie received a brief call from his golf partner, Hugh.

Charlie looked disturbed as he listened. Finally, he said, "I can't believe it." After a pause he added, "Hugh, thanks for letting me know. Speak to you soon," and he ended the call.

He broke the news of Eddie's murder to Ellen and they each took a glass of sauvignon blanc out to their porch where they sat, attempting to process this shocking event.

Eddie Siricco was an iconic figure in New Paltz. His Town Crier column enlivened the Village and united the community under a common set of half-truths. Water Street Market would not be the same without Eddie gossiping away to Cosmo.

Charlie began somberly, "Everyone knew he was a scoundrel, but he was a lovable one."

Ellen added sadly, "And he was New Paltz' very own scoundrel." Her eyes filled with tears.

Charlie lifted his glass. "To Eddie, we will..."

Ellen vowed, "We will find your murderer and bring him to justice!"

Wednesday, September 28

Water Street Market was abuzz as the news of Eddie Siricco's murder spread faster than the house fire on Beekman Road. Harris was on his phone and frazzled trying to find someone else to complete the paint job Eddie had begun. At the Mudd Puddle, Michelle wiped away tears knowing that Eddie would not be stopping in to annoy her ever again. The courtyard was filled with tables of people gasping as they sipped their coffee and read the lead headline in the Daily Freeman:"*New Paltz Town Crier Murdered*".

Nothing fired Ellen up like a juicy murder. Over the last few years, she and Charlie had become embroiled in murder investigations, both, in Cape Coral, Florida, where they spend the winters, and in Brimfield, Massachusetts, home of one of the largest outdoor antique shows in the country. To their credit, every investigation resulted in bringing a murderer to justice. However, their unconventional and reckless methods often put their own lives in jeopardy.

This morning, Ellen drove to New Paltz determined to learn whatever she could about Eddie Siricco's murder. Cosmo, at the Antique Barn, was her first stop. "Good morning, Cosmo," she called to him. "That was shocking news about Eddie Siricco! How did this happen?"

Cosmo motioned Ellen to the check-out counter and spoke softly. "Well, it seems that Eddie was murdered right in his apartment on Main Street. So, I figure it had to be someone he knew, right?" Without waiting for Ellen to respond, Cosmo continued, "I've gotta tell you, Ellen, between the hate crime and Eddie's murder, I don't feel safe around here all by myself." He shimmied in place to demonstrate how frightened he was.

"Cosmo, you're never alone when you're here so I don't think you have a thing to worry about. But I can't believe that someone murdered Eddie. I'll miss him."

"Not as much as I will. Anyhow this happened Sunday night and that cute, young cop came to see me on Monday."

"Yes, I was hiding behind Joan's cupboard at the time, if you recall," Ellen mumbled. "Eddie had already been murdered and we never knew it."

"Well, Eddie knew a lot about everyone and I think that's what got him killed," Cosmo said with certainty. "I told the cop about Ben Sheppard and Phillip Edelstein. Do you think I'll be involved in this --this ugly matter? Please tell me I won't!"

"No, Cosmo. You did the right thing. We have to find Eddie's murderer!"

"Oh, no! Not 'we', Ellen!" Cosmo clarified. "Maybe that's something you want to do, but not me!"

"Cosmo, did you tell the detective everything Eddie told you?"

"Almost," Cosmo replied sheepishly. "I didn't want to mention that Phillip is responsible for swaying the planning board and if the approvals aren't granted, the deal goes south. I don't like talking to the cops. What really troubles me is that Eddie was about to tell me something big about this land sale and a customer needed help and now Eddie's taken the news with him to the grave," Cosmo said wistfully.

Ellen started up the stairs to add a few items to her booth. "Don't be too sure of that, Cosmo. Just keep me posted if you hear anything!" she shouted from the second floor.

As quickly as she could, Ellen left the shop and went to get some coffee at the Mudd Puddle. On her way, she heard someone calling out to her. "Ellen, oh Ellen, my cell mate!"

"Dorothy, hi! How are rehearsals going?"

"Rehearsals? Who cares? You heard about Eddie Siricco?" Ellen nodded. Dorothy grabbed Ellen by the hand. "Get me some coffee, Ellen, black, no sugar, and I'll tell you about Eddie Siricco. I'll wait for you at this table."

Ellen was happy to comply, eager to hear what Dorothy had to say. She returned swiftly."Here you go, Dorothy. Now, tell me everything."

Dorothy fluffed up her frizzy, brass-colored hair and began. "Well, Ellen, Eddie and I go way back, you see. And he was always a scoundrel. Always had a scheme to borrow money that he never planned to pay back or overcharge for a paint job or swindle money from someone."

"When did you meet Eddie?"

"Many, many years ago and, from what I can tell, he hasn't changed one little bit," Dorothy said bitterly. "Oh, he could put on the charm when he wanted something from you. Yes, he knew how to do that very well." Dorothy stopped to sip her coffee.

Ellen asked, "How did you get to know Eddie?"

Dorothy ignored Ellen's question and said, "I do feel bad that Eddie was, you know, murdered," she whispered. "But he made many enemies over the years."

"Yes?"

"Let me just say that Eddie and I did not part without a great deal of drama and turmoil. We knew way too much about each other. Besides, Eddie was an alcoholic--big time. It wouldn't surprise me in the least if he was quite pickled when he was killed." Dorothy shook her head knowingly.

"Dorothy, you need to talk to the police. You may have information that could help them find the murderer."

"Oh, Ellen, I could never go to the police! Of course, I would be willing to share my thoughts with the press. You know, an appearance on 'Live with Lauren', perhaps," she said coyly.

"Look, why not start with that good-looking, young detective who arrested us?" Ellen suggested.

Several sighs later, Dorothy disagreed. "I'm more interested in appealing to a wider audience."

"Ah, I see where you're going with this." Ellen was beginning to think that Dorothy's connection to Eddie was nothing more than a publicity stunt. "Dorothy, you said that Eddie knew too much about you. What do you mean?"

"He was always jealous of me and my successful career."

"Why would he be jealous? Were you and Eddie---well, were you both lovers, Dorothy?" Ellen asked tentatively.

"Oh, for God's sake, Ellen! Why, Eddie Siricco was my ex-husband." Dorothy raised her eyebrows and, with a grand sweep of her left arm, said, "I simply must get back to rehearsal. Tada!"

Dorothy's unexpected announcement left Ellen gagging on her coffee. She stayed to finish it and mull over what Dorothy had disclosed.

Much later that evening, Ellen and Charlie were enjoying a glass of sauvignon blanc on their porch. Charlie was very relaxed after a wonderful day of golf at Otterkill. He and Hugh played a friendly match with a couple of guys half their age and beat them on the eighteenth hole. Recently, Charlie had been feeling frustrated trying to keep up with these young studs who could hit a drive three-hundred yards. Many of his contemporaries enjoyed the advantage of hitting from the senior tees, but not Charlie. He might be seventy-three, but he still had his pride. He stubbornly refused to take the sensible way out.

"So, Ellen, I may not hit the ball as far as I used to, but I've learned to play smarter," Charlie said as he held up his glass to toast himself.

"To you, Charlie Green," Ellen toasted.

"I was smart enough to marry you, wasn't I?" They clinked glassed. "Now, tell me about your day, Sweetie."

"Charlie." Ellen took a deep breath before continuing. She told Charlie about Dorothy's disclosure. When she finished she asked, "So don't you agree that Dorothy could have important information for the police?"

"Probably, but it's not our business. It's up to Dorothy." Charlie enjoyed another sip of wine.

"But Charlie..."

"Ellen, don't go there. Butt out before you butt in," he warned.

Charlie's feeling of relaxation was fast becoming a distant memory. He knew that Ellen's detective gene was twitching and she would not let this go. "Ellen, don't get started. It's none of our business."

"Of course, Charlie," Ellen purred taking a long sip of her wine. "None of our business," she agreed. "But Charlie, when has that ever stopped us in the past?"

"Leonard, I will not abide by these inane directions!" Dorothy complained, flinging the script onto the floor. "Othello's Desdemona was beautiful! What kind of a Desdemona would look in the mirror and be repulsed by the ghastly vision she saw looking back at her?" She turned to Leonard, hands on her hips.

"A dead Desdemona! That's who, Dorothy." Leonard gritted his teeth as he spoke, "Desdemona returns from the grave. She is not on her way to the Met Gala! Now, take it from the top. AGAIN!" He grabbed his water bottle and took a long drink.

Dorothy transformed into Desdemona and put her hands on her heart. She walked slowly across the stage to a small table, sat down, and wistfully stared into the hand-held mirror. "Ah, beauteous wonder!" She tilted her head to the right with a puzzled expression, staring at her reflection. "You are all that...shit, Leonard, give me the next line. I don't remember it." Dorothy grumbled in frustration.

Leonard sighed, "'You are all that is hideous and shunned by the world.' Take it from 'Ah, beauteous wonder.'"

Dorothy lamented, "Ah, beauteous wonder!" She tilted her head to the right with a puzzled expression, staring at her reflection. "You are all that is hideous and shunned by the world!" Dorothy suddenly stood up and violently threw the mirror to the floor. It shattered as she stormed off the stage in anger.

"Brava! Brava!" Leonard clapped and shouted. "Shattering the mirror was brilliant, Dorothy!"

Dorothy was stunned. "Are you serious? That wasn't part of the performance. I'm pissed! This portrayal of Desdemona is appalling! Where is the skinny little twit who came up with this idea?"

"Now, Dorothy, you need to get hold of yourself. This role requires you to pull from the depths of your soul. Desdemona is inwardly beautiful and that must overcome her being outwardly grotesque."

Oozing resentment Dorothy demanded, "Where is she? Alyssa, where are you?" Dorothy scanned the theatre, spreading her fingers across her eyebrows in a searching gesture. "We need to talk!"

Leonard was sick of running interference between Dorothy and the playwright, Alyssa McPherson. Hiring Dorothy was beginning to feel like a bad mistake, but the show was scheduled to open in three weeks so he had no other option. "Dorothy, my dear, take five and then come back on stage. We'll start with scene three, the sleep-walking scene." Maintaining his equilibrium while appeasing this diva was giving him palpitations. Leonard wiped off his forehead with the back of his hand and reached for his water bottle again.

Ellen was making the most of this beautiful fall day by taking a walk in the Mohonk Preserve with her friend, Pat. This spectacular nature preserve protects and manages over 8,000 acres of mountain, lakes, and wildlife. Located just outside the Village of New Paltz, it is the home of the "Gunks", one of the most popular rock-climbing destinations in the country.

Ellen and Pat parked at the Visitor Center and slowly climbed the arduous trail up to Undercliff Road. When they reached the top, they looked at each other, unable to speak and relieved to have made it. At their age, the walk on the carriage road was the reward for their valiant efforts. Finally, Ellen broke the silence and told Pat of her conversation with Dorothy. "So, Dorothy Dawson was actually married to Eddie Siricco years ago!"

Pat shrugged, "Where are you going with this, Ellen?"

"Well, don't you think she needs to speak to the police? She has a history with Eddie."

"Look, Ellen, we all have a history with our exes, but it's exactly that: history."

"But, Pat, your ex wasn't murdered."

"Only because he skipped town before I got my hands on him! Really, though, if I were dead, I sure wouldn't want my ex-husband telling what I was like way back when! Wouldn't exactly paint a pretty picture!"

"I suppose, you're right but..."

"But nothing! Leave Dorothy Dawson with her personal grudges and let it go. That's what I think." Pat picked up her pace a bit and changed the subject. "I'm getting hungry. How about we give this another half hour and then grab something decadent for lunch. Something that includes alcohol."

"Sounds good to me," Ellen agreed heartily and they headed to Lola's Cafe on Main Street.

This afternoon, Joseph and Myrna Van Dyke were driving to their insurance company. Their agent invited them to stop in to pick up the check for the fire damage. Myrna was chattering away about how she wanted to spend this money. "Joseph, I'm thinking like this. Why bother to rebuild the house we weren't living in anyway? We could take one of those riverboat cruises next spring. Estelle and George went and they absolutely raved about it! Or how about a cruise to Alaska? Wouldn't that be romantic?"

Joseph exhibited his usual restraint. "Myrna, those ideas sound good but let's wait until we actually have the check in our hands before we start counting on this money. Besides, there will be expenses. We'll have to clear the land, fill in the foundation. Please, just wait."

"Joseph, what a buzz kill you are! I'm ready to start packing and I'm not letting you spoil it for me."

Joseph patted Myrna on the leg. "Remember, the police still have not called the arson a hate crime and they haven't found the arsonist. We're not through with all of this by a long shot."

"Joseph, I'm well aware of that but I am looking to find joy where I can so why don't you shut up!"

When they arrived at the insurance office, Joseph suggested, "Myrna, wait here and I'll get the check and come right back."

"No way! I wouldn't miss this moment for anything!"

The receptionist greeted them warmly. "Mr. and Mrs. Van Dyke, how good of you to stop by."

Myrna snickered, "Good of us? We're here for our money."

The receptionist gave a polite smile, picked up her phone, and said in a nasal voice, "Mr. Prentiss, the Van Dykes are here to see you." She pointed them to Mr. Prentiss' office.

Joseph knocked on the door. Mr. Prentiss greeted them. "Come on in. Please have a seat. Ahem, well, um, I suppose you are here regarding your insurance claim?"

Myrna muttered to herself, "Well, isn't he some kind of genius." Aloud she said, "That's right, Mr. Prentiss. Just show us what we need to sign and we'll be out of your hair."

Mr. Prentiss inhaled and assumed an officious tone. "I'm afraid it isn't that simple. Let me explain."

Joseph began rubbing his hands together in his lap. Myrna did not dare to breathe.

"You see, there's been a little glitch. Now, I'm sure you'll be able to clear this up quickly but, well, it seems that. You need to understand that these little hiccups happen often, especially when we're talking about a significant settlement. Anyhow..."

Myrna could no longer contain herself. "Out with it, for God's sake! What's going on?"

Mr. Prentiss folded his hands in front of him as if he were praying and stated, "I'm very sorry but our agency is not able to issue you a check. There seems to be a question regarding the nature of the crime."

Joseph asked, "What does that mean?"

"Well, you see, in the case of arson, almost one-third of the fires are started by the homeowner in order to receive a financial settlement from the insurance company."

Joseph explained, "We sent you the report from the fire department and they confirmed that this was an act of arson."

"Oh, we know it was arson." Mr. Prentiss smiled disagreeably at Joseph and Myrna. "However, this morning new information has been brought to our attention."

"This is ridiculous! New information? Our house was burned to the ground by a homophobic arsonist! That has not changed," Myrna retorted.

"Mrs. Van Dyke, I'm quite certain all of this will be straightened out in no time but, for now, I must ask you to leave. This is a police matter. They will handle it from this point."

"The police? And, may I ask, what friggin' new information has been brought to your attention?" Myrna asked indignantly.

"If you insist, Mrs. Van Dyke. The police received an anonymous note from a witness who claims that you, Mr. Van Dyke, set fire to your own house on Thursday, September 22," Mr. Prentiss said, pointing his finger accusingly at Joseph.

Friday, September 30

Adam dreaded making this call but could not put it off any longer. "Hi, Mom. How are you doing?"

"Adam, is that you? My son? It's been so long since I heard from you that I don't even recognize your voice anymore," his mother theatrically sighed.

"I know. I know, Mom. I'm so sorry but I've been working on this murder investigation and haven't had a moment."

"Really? Not a moment? Not a moment to call your mother who stayed up all night with you every time you had croup? Gilda's son is a police officer and she said that he calls her every single day, Adam. Every day and he's just as busy as you!"

Adam sheepishly replied, "What can I say? Gilda got the good kid. You got stuck with me." He whispered playfully, "but I'm a whole lot cuter, Mom."

"Alright, alright. You know I can't stay mad at you! So, don't forget. You're coming for dinner tonight. I'm making a brisket for you. See you later. Six o'clock and don't be late."

"Mom, about dinner tonight..."

"Yes?" she grimaced.

"Well, I won't be able to make it. Have to work late."

"You still have to eat!"

95

"Well, I'll be eating something at my desk. I'm under a lot of pressure right now and..."

"Adam, do I need to come in and talk to your boss about this?" she scolded.

"No, Mom, please do not do that!" Adam did not scare easily, but he knew that this was no idle threat and that scared him, big time. "You know, Mom, actually Mom, let me see what I can do. I'm pretty sure I can get there for dinner. I'll be there. Promise. See you later. Bye."

As soon as Adam ended the call, Chief Liberti strode in without bothering to knock. "Jacobson, we need to talk."

"Please have a seat, Sir."

"It's been several days now and it looks like you've got nothing to show for it: no motive, no weapon, no phone, no suspects. I know you can do better. Don't let me down, Jacobson. I'm counting on you. Hell, the entire town of New Paltz is counting on you!"

"Chief, here's what we know. The victim made it easy for his killer. He was unconscious while he was being suffocated. Cause of death: compression asphyxia. Forensics was able to determine that this was the work of one person. But Sir, good news to report about the arson case. I'll be meeting with Van Dyke later today. We received a typed note from an alleged witness saying that Joseph Van Dyke set the fire and made it look like a hate crime. Here's the note, Sir. *'I saw Joseph Van Dyke pouring what appears to be gasoline around the perimeter of his house on Beekman Road. He set his house on fire.'*"

Stroking his chin, Liberti looked up and mused, "Happens all the time. Interesting. So Van Dyke did the deed." Pounding his fist on the table, Liberti continued, "The truth is I don't give a damn about the arson case right now! I just want us to find the person who murdered Eddie Siricco. That's top priority. If you have to question every resident of this Village, do it. I sure hope you don't have any big plans for tonight because you're going to be working late, Jacobson!" Liberti sauntered out of Adam's office.

Before Adam had a chance to try to figure his way out of this predicament, Sergeant O'Riley called to let him know that his 1:00 appointment had arrived. "Thanks, O'Riley. Please show him to my office."

Joseph Van Dyke and Adam acknowledged one another. Adam motioned to Joseph, "Mr. Van Dyke, please have a seat. You realize that a very serious allegation has been made against you."

Joseph, ordinarily very composed, snapped, "That's a vicious lie! Some anonymous tip is enough to keep me from receiving my settlement?"

"Mr. Van Dyke, I know this is upsetting but we must follow up on this. Until we thoroughly investigate this allegation, you will never receive your settlement."

"And just how do you go about investigating an anonymous note? Tell me. How do you do that?"

"We begin our investigation by asking you questions and looking into your financial status." Joseph began to fidget. Adam watched carefully as Joseph right leg vibrated vigorously. Adam smiled, "If we find nothing that sends up red flags, well, that works in your favor. Of course, we hope that this investigation exonerates you of any wrongdoing, Mr. Van Dyke."

Joseph looked Adam in the eye and declared, "I can assure you that you will find I am an upstanding member of this community. No outstanding bills or shady dealings. In fact, check with the bank. I've been on the board of the bank for over a dozen years now. This allegation is a sham!"

"Sir, I hope you're right. We are already gathering your financial records as well as information about your joint assets with Mrs. Van Dyke and hope to wrap up this matter as quickly as possible. Before we end this meeting, I have a couple of questions." Joseph nodded grudgingly. "Sir, where were you on Thursday evening from 8:00 until 11:00?"

"I was at home with my wife. Not at the Beekman Road house. That house was an investment property."

"You were at home the entire time?"

"Well, almost. I left to go to the convenience store a few miles away. Myrna wanted some ice-cream."

"And what time was that?"

"Maybe about 9:00 or 9:30 I think."

"And what time did you return home?"

"Probably twenty minutes later."

"Mr. Van Dyke, your trip to the convenience store does not help your case, I'm afraid. The fire department confirms that the fire began between 9:30 and 10:30 Thursday evening." Adam stood up to shake Joseph's hand, signaling that the meeting was over. "I'll be in touch."

Joseph left the police station and sat in his car trying to decide what to do. This damn allegation was completely derailing his life. One thing was clear; Myrna must never find out what he had done with their savings. He took out his phone and called his wife.

"Joseph, so how did it go?"

"Myrna, piece of cake," he lied. "Jacobson said that the matter will be cleared up quickly and we'll be able to get that insurance money."

"Wonderful news, Joseph! Shall I start packing?" she teased.

Joseph closed his eyes, shook his head, and gave a half-hearted chuckle. "Well, dear, at least make sure our passports haven't expired."

Adam spent the rest of the afternoon conducting interviews with locals, hoping someone who knew Eddie Siricco could help him uncover a possible motive for murder. Eddie's big mouth as the Town Crier could pose the threat of exposure to a murderer but so far Eddie Siricco seemed to spread harmless gossip around town. Nothing that would incite a murder.

Adam was examining his notes. From the desk in the lobby he heard Sergeant O'Riley say loudly, "I'm sorry but Chief Liberti is very busy and he cannot possibly see you now."

"He's not too busy to see me! I'm going in there. I know where his office is!"

Adam shuddered as he recognized the voice. He called out, "Mom! Do not go into the Chief's office! Please!" He dashed out of his office but was too late. His mother had done the unthinkable: barged in on Chief Liberti.

Adam stood outside the door to Liberti's office trying to decide whether to knock on the door or, simply, slink away and pretend this never happened. Suddenly, Sergeant O'Riley was at his side. "Detective, the Chief wants you in his office. At once."

Adam's shoulders slumped and he thought, "Shit!" as he knocked on the door.

"Come in, Detective Jacobson," Liberti called. "Sit down."

Adam did not even dare to look in his mother's direction as he sat facing Liberti.

"Now, I have to say, Detective, this has been a difficult day and we're all on overload. You know that the very last thing I ever want is to be interrupted." Chief Liberti turned to look at Adam's mother. "But, Mrs. Jacobson," he smiled broadly, "you are always welcome to stop in. Any time at all!"

Adam was totally nonplussed by this reaction. He looked over at his mother and at Chief Liberti and back to his mother. "Will one of you please tell me what just happened here?" Adam asked baffled.

Mrs. Jacobson began, "Adam, dear, it's quite simple. I know you're busy trying to track down a murderer and keep us all safe. I decided that I could help. Since you couldn't come for my brisket, I brought my brisket to you." She patted Adam's knee affectionately. "Here," she said handing him a plastic container filled with brisket, potatoes, carrots, onions, and drowning in gravy. "Just stick it in the microwave for forty-five seconds. Now, get back to work, Adam," she scolded.

Adam held onto the container, stood up, but could not manage to utter a single word.

"Adam," Mrs. Jacobson said, "don't I even get a kiss good-bye?"

Adam leaned over, gave his mother a hug and a kiss. Just when he thought this scene could not get any more bizarre, Chief Liberti held up an even larger container and chimed in, "Mrs. Jacobson, you and your brisket have made my day. My humble thanks. Adam, you need to do as your mother says."

"Yes, Sir." Adam exited Liberti's office and returned to his office with his brisket dinner.

Several officers and tech experts were also working late this evening. They were able to access every financial transaction in which Joseph Van Dyke had engaged, going back ten years. After hours of research, one of the tech experts knocked on Adam's door. "Sir, you need to check this out." He handed Adam a print-out of the findings and sat down while Adam slowly read the information.

Adam asked, "Now, these are all withdrawals, right?"

"Yes, Detective. And, then, be sure to check this other page," he said pointing to the following page.

Adam studied these spreadsheets carefully. Numbers were not his forte and he was the first to admit it. But he was smart enough to ask the right questions. After meticulously perusing this new information, Adam leaned back in his chair, folded his hands behind his head, and said, "Well, I'll be damned!"

Saturday, October 1

Chief Liberti scheduled a briefing regarding new information in the arson case. Detective Jacobson was addressing a small group of officers with the Chief seated on his left. "Officers, thanks for coming in at this early hour on a Saturday. Here's what we know about the arson on Beekman Road since we learned of the anonymous note. A team of specialists, headed up by our own tech team, has been hard at work checking out Joseph Van Dyke's financial portfolio. The result indicates some suspicious transactions that had taken place over a two-year period."

Adam pulled up a one-page summary and projected it onto the screen. "This is an image of the activity in the joint accounts shared by Mr. and Mrs. Van Dyke. The portfolio begins with a value of more than three hundred grand and ends with a net portfolio value of zero. Nada. Note that the assets are made up of low risk mutual funds and money market accounts. All very conservative investments. No withdrawals had been made in previous years until we come to 2016. No deposits were made but dividends had been systematically reinvested until 2016. Now follow the withdrawals carefully. They're marked in red. You will find that increasing sums of money had been withdrawn from the Van Dyke's joint account over a two-year period. And at an increasing frequency." Adam waited while the officers checked out the spread sheet. "By the end of 2018, the entire joint account had been depleted."

"Sir," asked one of the officers, "Mr. and Mrs. Van Dyke have a right to withdraw their own money. Why does that arouse suspicion?"

"You're right. What they have done is perfectly legal. However, this information sheds light on a possible motive. One, Van Dyke repeatedly withdrew from the joint account and deposited large

103

sums of money into Las Atlantis Casino. Van Dyke is on the board of the bank and I would imagine that the bank might not look kindly upon Van Dyke's hobby as a high-stakes gambler. His reputation as an upstanding member of the community would be shot to hell. And two, I'm betting that Mrs. Van Dyke hasn't a clue that her husband has gone through their life's savings," Adam winked. "Look, all of this is total speculation at this point but, plain and simple, it appears that he was desperate for the insurance money."

"Have you confirmed these suspicions?" asked another officer.

"We're on it. I've met with Van Dyke and he has no verifiable alibi at the time of the arson. He, allegedly, was getting ice-cream at a convenience store but that doesn't account for all of his time. Oh, and this morning his computer is being removed from his home. That will tell a story."

Chief Liberti barked, "Look, the truth is that I don't give a rat's ass about nailing Van Dyke on arson charges! We've got a murderer on the loose and unless this morning's update includes a suspect or two, you'll have to excuse me. I have another meeting and don't want to be late." He smirked, "My foursome is waiting for me at the first tee. Meeting adjourned!"

Today was a perfect golf day for Charlie, as well. He was whistling away this morning as he loaded his clubs into the van. He went back inside, gave Ellen a kiss, and took off for Otterkill Country Club.

Charlie and his golf partner, Hugh, enjoyed a lively round with a couple of other guys. A mishap involving a water hazard, unfortunately, left Hugh drenched from the waist down.

Nevertheless, after they finished playing, the foursome made the mandatory stop at the clubhouse patio for drinks. The slate patio was an expansive area that overlooked, both, the first and ninth holes. Tables for four were filled with golfers eating lunch and making the most of this late-in-the-season day. Several other foursomes appeared to have camped out with absolutely no intention of ever leaving. Doug, the server, came to take their orders.

"A round of Stellas, Doug, and they're on me," Hugh announced cheerfully.

"Hah! After we waited for you to go swimming, you owe us," Ralph winked.

"I had to try to hit that ball out of the water. How could I see it and not give it a whack?" Hugh laughed.

Another foursome meandered over with their drinks. Charlie called to them, "Pull up some chairs and join us. How'd it go today?"

Bob teased, "I played great but Pete, here, should have brought a pail and shovel with him. He spent more time playing in the sand than on the fairway!"

Doug arrived with drinks and the two foursomes kicked back and bantered good-naturedly about their golf games. Finally, Pete leaned in toward the center of the table and spoke in a low voice, "Hey, did you hear about the guy in New Paltz whose house was burned down?"

"Pete, that's old news." Hugh taunted, "Where have you been lately? You need to stop burying your head in the sand!" A round of guffaws followed.

"Seriously, listen to this. The owner, Van Dyke, seems to have started the fire to get the insurance money."

"Where the hell did you hear that?" Charlie asked skeptically. "Van Dyke doesn't seem the type."

"My nephew is an officer with the New Paltz Police Department. He just called me about it while I was on my way to Otterkill."

Charlie declared, "But this was a hate crime. That doesn't make any sense, Pete."

"Maybe Van Dyke wanted it to look like a hate crime. The perfect cover."

Hugh signaled to Doug, "Hey Doug. Another round for everyone. And this one's on Charlie!"

On this beautiful day, Water Street Market was filled with shoppers, walkers, and hikers. Every table in the courtyard was occupied with people taking a break to eat lunch. The Mudd Puddle was grilling, serving, mixing, brewing at breakneck speed to keep up with orders.

The Antique Barn had customers lined up waiting to pay for their purchases. Walter was working as swiftly as possible to write up sales and help people check out, while Cosmo was seated on a swivel stool in a booth near the counter providing the entertainment. Everyone knew that the main attraction at the Antique Barn was not the antiques. It was Cosmo. His hugs, his risqué one-liners, his melodramatic stories drew people to him.

At the moment, Cosmo was engaged in an intense conversation with Matthew and Pablo, the couple who had rented the house on Beekman Road. "So, you guys must have heard all about the rally last week, I'm sure."

Matthew answered, "We sent our regrets but thought it best that we not show up."

Cosmo agreed, "Good decision. But hey, did you guys hear about the murder?" he asked quietly.

Matthew and Pablo replied in unison, "No!"

Cosmo began filling them in when, suddenly, all eyes turned to the front door as Dorothy Dawson swooped in, making her entrance. Cosmo muttered, "The old bag who just waltzed in here is doing a one-woman show at the Denizen in a few weeks." In a snippy whisper he added, "She's such a diva! Watch, she's going to come right over to annoy me. Arrgh!"

Dorothy held up her arms as she floated over to greet Cosmo. "Cosmo! My dahling!"

Cosmo responded by holding up his arms and cooing, "Dorothy, Honey! Come give me a big hug!" Matthew and Pablo looked on in amusement as Cosmo greeted her with a grand, insincere embrace.

Dorothy turned to Matthew and Pablo, "Cosmo, you simply must introduce me to these strikingly handsome friends of yours."

"Dorothy Dawson, meet Matthew and Pablo. They're the guys whose rental house was burned to the ground."

"Oh," she shrieked. "You poor dears! How are you managing to stay so calm amidst a vicious hate crime against you?"

Matthew smiled politely. "Thanks for your concern. We can't do anything about it except try to stay calm."

Pablo was a bit star-struck. "Cosmo told us that you're starring in a one-woman show right here at the Denizen, Ms. Dawson!"

"You must call me Dorothy. Please. Yes, Pablo. Leonard, the director, positively begged me to take this on. What can I say? I didn't have the heart to turn him down. He'd have been devastated." She added, "You boys must come for opening night and join me for the after-party."

"We'd love that," Pablo eagerly agreed. "We'll make it a day trip and then return to the City."

Dorothy covered her mouth with both her hands. "We mustn't allow that. Right, Cosmo?"

Cosmo barely answered. He was miffed that Dorothy had taken center stage and he was stuck in the back row. Besides, she had not invited him to the after-party. He seized the opportunity to upstage her. "You boys can always stay with Walter and me."

Dorothy shook her head dismissively. "Absolutely not! You boys can stay right here in New Paltz at my place. I've got an extra bedroom and it's not the least bit inconvenient. In fact, I have a great idea. Why don't you both plan to use my place every weekend until you can make other arrangements."

"Thanks so much for your generous offer but we couldn't," Matthew protested.

"That's ridiculous! Of course you can and you will."

"But..." Matthew began.

"No excuses! You must. I insist."

Walter had taken care of everyone in line and finally had a chance to breathe. He looked up at the threesome and said, "I see you've met Dorothy."

Pablo replied, "Dorothy's been amazing! Yes, we just met but," turning to Dorothy he added, "I feel like I've known you forever."

Dorothy trilled, "I think we met in a previous life, my dear. Two old souls. Anyhow, Walter, I've invited, no I've *insisted* that Pablo and Matthew use my apartment on weekends. It's the least I can do to make up for this vile act that was foisted upon them!"

"Dorothy, you are a saint!" Pablo gushed.

Dorothy giggled, "Ah, a saint? A saint. Hmm, Saint Joan. Yes, Jeanne d'Arc. Why, who knows. That could be my next show. I must get back to rehearsal but I'll meet you in the courtyard at 4:00 and show you my modest accommodations. How does that sound?"

Walter came from behind the counter and as he gave Matthew a hug, he whispered, "Glad you guys can come for weekends from now on, but don't feel that you owe her anything. Remember, she insisted."

Matthew discreetly nodded to Walter. "Dorothy, thanks so much but we cannot accept," he announced firmly.

109

Pablo was terribly disappointed. "Dorothy, you are so generous! I'm overwhelmed by this offer."

Walter was not the least bit impressed. He sized up Dorothy and saw this display of generosity as nothing more than a cheap publicity stunt.

Late that night, Ellen and Charlie enjoyed a glass of sauvignon blanc on their porch. As they sipped their wine Ellen asked, "So, how did you and Hugh do today?"

Charlie regaled Ellen with the story of Hugh wading into the water to try to slap his ball out onto the fairway instead of taking a penalty stroke. "Of course, it never bothered Hugh that his shoes and shorts were soaked." They both knew that Hugh was someone who never got embarrassed even when he managed to embarrass himself.

Charlie took another sip of wine. "Ellen, you know Pete from Otterkill? Well, he told me something disturbing."

Ellen sat up ready to listen. "Go on."

"His nephew is a New Paltz police officer and told Pete that they suspect that Joseph Van Dyke set his own place on fire to get the insurance money. Does that sound believable to you?"

"Not for one minute, Charlie," Ellen stated with conviction. "How terrible for Joseph and Myrna! I'm going to get in touch with them tomorrow and see how I can help. They must be shattered by this accusation!"

"Ellen, before you do anything foolish, remember, we don't know them well. Look, we don't really know them at all."

"Charlie, I've learned to trust my instincts when it comes to people and my instincts tell me this is all a bunch of bullshit!"

"Ellen," he warned, "this is a very serious allegation and it wouldn't be made without some evidence."

"See, you already think they're guilty! That's so unfair."

"Ellen, you and I both know that anyone can be driven to do anything when someone is desperate, that is. It all depends on how desperate they are."

Sunday, October 2

New Paltz residents tend to ease very slowly into a Sunday morning in keeping with its college-town character. Therefore, at 9:00 this morning Main Street Bistro was still fairly quiet. Ben Sheppard and Phillip Edelstein were sitting in a booth drinking coffee as they waited for Harris Landau to show up and join them. Ben was beginning to lose his patience. "Jesus, Phillip, are you sure this is a good idea for us to involve Harris?"

"Don't worry, Ben. This is a smart move. It's a political game and requires some finesse. You'll see."

"I hope you're right. Maybe Harris won't even show up. He's already twenty minutes late. I want to order some breakfast."

"Good idea. We'll order. But you don't get it. Harris always likes to be late. That's a power play. Nothing more."

"If you say so," Ben agreed dubiously. He waved to the server.

Before the server got to their table, Harris arrived. "Phillip, Ben," he greeted them. "Sorry I'm late but..."

"No worries, Harris. Have a seat. We were about to order," Phillip said. "Here's a menu."

Harris slid in next to Phillip. "Thanks, Phillip, but I don't need to look at the menu. You two should try one of their signature breakfasts. They're fantastic!"

Ben grumbled, "No thanks. I had a lot of time to look at the menu while we waited for you to show up. I know what I want."

The server arrived and Harris quickly took over. "I'll have the 'Veggie X" but with egg whites and a whole wheat tortilla. Oh, and an herbal lemon tea. Phillip?"

"Two eggs over easy. Skip the toast. And more coffee when you have a chance. Thanks."

Ben ordered. "Biscuits and gravy with a side of sausage."

Harris shook his head. "My God Ben, you might as well inject concrete right into your heart! You sure you want to clog up your arteries with all that sausage and gravy?"

Ben glared back at Harris. "Yes."

Phillip ignored the hostility. "Harris, we wanted to get together with you to clue you in on a unique business opportunity that is on the horizon. But, this is strictly insider information."

"Well, Phillip, let's hear what this is all about."

"A group of well-heeled investors are looking to buy Ben's acreage out on Milo Road. They want to build a first class resort hotel and conference center."

"Really," Harris responded skeptically.

Phillip nodded and continued. "They're finalizing plans, and now they need to obtain the necessary approvals from the town. Without prior approval for a project of this scope, they'll go somewhere else to build."

"I don't see that happening," Harris replied. "They'll never get past the planning board.

"Well, it will be a challenge, but that's where you come in. You think futuristically. Look what you've done with Water Street Market when everyone said it would never work. And now the Denizen. Harris, you've got imagination and guts. This would be great for New Paltz. The resort would add needed revenue to our town, provide good-paying jobs, and bring in tourists to our retail establishments. A win-win."

"Why are you telling me about this?"

"Because we need your support. You're on the planning board. You can help get this through if you believe it is good for the town."

They stopped speaking as the server placed their breakfast orders in front of them. When she left the table, Harris spoke up. "Ben Sheppard, you really think anyone is going to give you the green light?" Turning to Phillip, Harris asked, "Are you serious? For Ben?"

If Ben did not have a mouth stuffed with biscuits and gravy, he would have yelled back at Harris. Ben had had enough of kissing up to Harris Landau. He lowered his head and continued to shovel in his breakfast without saying another word.

As they ate, Phillip and Harris discussed the various obstacles in the way of obtaining all the necessary permits. Speaking only to Phillip, Harris concluded, "Phillip, I would support exploring the proposal and I might even be willing to convince the other board members to go along with it. But, there's a problem that I have no control over: Myrna and Joseph Van Dyke."

"They're not on the planning board."

"No, but you can be damn sure that they'll mobilize their troops and fight this with everything they've got!"

Phillip gave Harris a smarmy smile. "They may not be the powerhouse they think they are. Don't you worry about the Van Dykes. Let me handle them. Ben and I are counting on your support. That's what matters."

"If you say so. Look, I've got to get going. I'm taking Judith to Mohonk for the day. She bought one of those day passes to the Mountain House. Better keep moving. I want to get my money's worth out of this full day's pass!" Harris smiled as he stood to leave. "Oh, and thanks for the breakfast. See you!"

A few miles away another breakfast was taking place on the screened-in porch at the home of Myrna and Joseph Van Dyke. This breakfast was not even pretending to be cordial. Myrna poured coffee into their BLM coffee mugs and plopped herself in front of her toasted bagel. "Joseph, you said this would all be over quickly and we'd get our insurance money. What the hell is going on?"

Joseph's pallor turned to gray as he sipped his coffee. He did not know how much he dared to tell Myrna. "The police had to confiscate the computer. They call it standard procedure in cases like this."

"Nothing about this seems like 'standard procedure' to me!" Myrna barked back. "Once they look at all the left-wing sites I go to, we'll be blacklisted for good! They'll bug our home and tip-off the F.B.I. I'll be on every airline's 'no fly' list! "

"Myrna, take it easy, dear."

"I don't get any of this. I want to know who wrote that anonymous note so I can stage a protest right in the middle of that little weasel's living room!"

Myrna was interrupted by an incoming text. She stopped to read it aloud. "Myrna, it's Ellen Green. Heard about RIDICULOUS allegation re arson! Meet me @ Water Street tomorrow for coffee. 10AM."

Joseph asked, "Ellen Green? From the rally? The one who was arrested?"

Myrna nodded, "'Fraid so. How the hell does she know about this and why is she sticking her nose into our business?"

"It sounds like she's offering support, at least. It's probably best to meet her."

"Well, if she knows about this, I wonder who else knows. I can't believe this is happening to us, Joseph!"

"Everything will work out fine. Try not to worry about it, Myrna." Joseph attempted a weak smile, but he knew they both had every reason to be worried. Joseph knew exactly what the police would discover.

Monday, October 3

This morning, Ellen arrived at Water Street Market hoping Myrna would show up. She got a cappuccino from the Mudd Puddle and sat at a table in the courtyard. Michelle came out of the cafe to take a break and sat down to join her. "Hi, Ellen. I think this is the first break I've had in, say, a month. Business is great but if I make one more friggin' huevos wrap, I'm going to throw it at someone!"

"You and James can't do all of this yourselves anymore. You're going to burn out."

"No kidding. I think I already have. You're looking at the charred remains," Michelle groaned spreading her arms out to her sides.

"Well, sit down and relax. It's quiet for the moment."

Michelle literally fell into the chair and began sobbing, "You know, Ellen, I miss that bastard, Eddie. He drove me crazy at times but I can't get over someone murdering the guy!"

Ellen reached across the table and rested her hand on Michelle's arm. "You've got a big heart, Michelle. I'm going to find Eddie's murderer. Eddie deserves that."

Michelle looked at Ellen in disbelief. "What are you talking about?"

"Michelle, Charlie and I have solved numerous murders in the last few years," she began impassively. "I won't bore you with the details but suffice it to say that the local authorities were chasing their tails while Charlie and I were chasing down the murderer."

Michelle's mouth hung down to her apron. "Are you serious? You and Charlie?" She began to laugh.

"Absolutely. We've done it before. We can do it for Eddie. Now, about you burning out..."

Michelle blew her nose. "Don't get me wrong, Ellen. I really love our cafe but I just need to change it up. You know, maybe if we added a new special to our menu, I'd feel energized again."

Ellen thought for a moment and then replied, "Michelle, last month Charlie and I stayed at a wonderful B&B in Geneva, NY, The William Smith Inn, and they served the most incredible breakfast: a lemon -ricotta pancake. It was light, zesty, and well, I'm going to get in touch with Maureen and see if she'll give me the recipe."

"I'm willing to give it a try." Michelle winked, "Better get back to the grill before I get fired! And, Ellen, thanks. I feel much better."

"See you later!" Ellen called out.

Although she had not heard back from Myrna, Ellen waited for her to show. She was about to give up when Ellen recognized Myrna's heavy-footed gait coming towards her. On this brisk morning, Myrna was wearing leg warmers and a vest made from crocheted afghan squares.

"Myrna, good to see you. How are you doing?"

"I'll be doing a lot better when I get a caffeine fix. Be right back."

Myrna returned with her coffee and Ellen asked, "What can I do to help you and Joseph?"

"You can butt out of this, Ellen. It's a baseless allegation and is clearly a gross case of mistaken identity!"

"I've been thinking a lot about this, Myrna, and do you think someone could be trying to get back at Joseph?"

"That's not possible. Everyone likes Joseph. He's Mr. Nice Guy. It's me who people hate," Myrna said glibly. "I'm the agitator. I'm the feminist."

"Yeah, like 'feminist' is a dirty word. I do know how it is. Everyone loves Charlie and thinks I'm the pain in the butt! It's hard to believe I know, but it's true. Can you imagine?"

Myrna opened her mouth to comment but changed her mind and drank her coffee, instead. Myrna's phone quacked. She stepped aside to answer it. After a couple of minutes Myrna returned to the table looking flustered. "Ellen, I really must go. Joseph has been called in to the police station. Yesterday they seized our computer and now Detective Jacobson wants to meet with him. He mustn't do this alone." Myrna walked away as quickly as her Birkenstocks would allow.

Ellen sat there slowly drinking her coffee and wondering what she should do next. Despite Myrna's protests, Ellen was sure Myrna needed her support. So Ellen decided to drive to the police station and be where she was needed.

Sergeant O'Riley was escorting Joseph to Detective Jacobson's office when they heard, "Wait up! I'm coming with you, Joseph!" as Myrna clomped down the corridor trying to catch up.

O'Riley stopped walking and turned to face Myrna. "Mrs. Van Dyke, you'll need to wait in the lobby. Detective Jacobson has requested that he and your husband meet, just the two of them."

Myrna protested, "I have a right to be with him!"

Calmly, Joseph explained, "Myrna, let's do as they say. That will be best for all of us."

With a petulant expression Myrna walked back to wait in the lobby. She saw Ellen sitting there and deliberately sat as far away from her as she could, ignoring Ellen completely.

Detective Jacobson heard the commotion and stuck his head out of his office door. "Please come in and have a seat, Mr. Van Dyke. We need to talk about what the tech team found on your computer." Without any show of emotion on his face, Joseph sat down and looked at Adam. "Tell me what you know about Las Atlantis Casino."

"I don't know much about it. It's a reputable online gambling site."

"Over a two-year period, you've systematically transferred large sums of money into their account. Amounts totaling three hundred grand." Adam waited for Joseph to reply. Joseph sat up straight but said nothing. Joseph began to perspire as he took quick, shallow breaths. "You seem agitated, Mr. Van Dyke. No need to be. You'll be glad to know that what you have done is perfectly legal." Adam placed his elbows on the table and looked directly at Joseph. "However, you and I need to talk. The analysis of your computer clearly demonstrates that you wiped out the joint accounts you shared with Mrs. Van Dyke by excessive online gambling."

Joseph finally found his voice. "Sir, I may have gotten carried away, but I've learned my lesson and haven't done this in over two years."

Adam stood up, put his hands in his pockets and paced back and forth in front of Joseph. "Carried away? That's what you call this? Really?" Adam pointed his finger at Joseph. "You have a strong motive to burn down your own house and get back what you lost to a big-time bookie. That's what I think is going on here."

"That's not true. I did not burn down our house! I swear it," Joseph pleaded wiping his forehead with the back of his hand.

Adam stopped pacing, placed his hands firmly on the table, and leaned on his arms. "You had the opportunity and the motive. All I need is to be able to prove this. You can be sure, Mr. Van Dyke, I will! That's all for today. Oh, but there is one more detail I'm curious about. I wonder how much your wife knows of this recreational past-time of yours? I suppose I'll have to ask her myself."

Joseph was badly shaken. He stopped at the men's room to compose himself before facing Myrna who was still waiting for him in the lobby.

Ellen had tried to get Myrna's attention from across the lobby. Myrna refused to acknowledge her so Ellen walked over and sat next to her. "Myrna, I'm sure you've got nothing to worry about. Detective Jacobson seems to be pretty reasonable. A bit impertinent but he's not much of a threat."

"Look, Ellen. Do not say one more word. Can't you see that I'm avoiding you?"

Ellen nodded. "I won't say another word." The two women sat silently side by side until Joseph appeared. Myrna rushed over to him and she and Joseph made a hasty exit.

Adam took out a pen and scribbled a few notes about his meeting with Joseph Van Dyke. Although most of the other officers put notes into their iPads, Adam found that writing out his notes in a notebook helped him process the information.

As Adam thoughtfully chewed on his pen, Sergeant O'Riley knocked on his door. "Sir, Ellen Green is here to see you. She says it's urgent."

"Okay," Adam sighed. "Send her in." Adam left his door open. "Hello, Mrs. Green. The last time we ran into each other you were hiding behind a large antique cupboard. What brings you out of hiding and into the open today?"

"Detective, please call me Ellen and skip the sarcasm. I'm here about a serious matter: the allegation against Joseph Van Dyke. Someone scribbles an anonymous note and Joseph Van Dyke is labeled as an arsonist? I'm sure that Joseph Van Dyke did not burn down his house."

"And you're certain of this because?" Adam looked quizzically at Ellen.

"Instincts and experience. That's how I know." Ellen shot Adam a disdainful look.

Adam leaned back in his chair. "Well, go on. Let me hear your thoughts."

"The homeowner is always the obvious suspect in an arson case. If Joseph set fire to his own house, he would expect that the police would check out his finances to determine a motive. Then, you would examine his computer, phone and personal contacts. And of course, Joseph would do whatever he could to hide any incriminating evidence. Are you following this so far, Detective?"

"Yes, Ellen. I think I can follow this," Adam answered with a wry smile. "Please continue."

"You tell me, Detective. Did Joseph try to destroy or withhold information from you?"

"Doesn't appear that he's done that."

"So big deal, you've found evidence that points to a motive but that leaves you with nothing. Everyone who ever made an insurance claim would be a possible suspect every single time, based on that brilliant bit of logic." Ellen cocked her head and said, "Based on my experience, I have found that everyone has an enemy. Even the nice guys. Yes, even someone like you, Detective," Ellen asserted, eyeing him critically.

"Me? Impossible. Everyone loves me," Adam teased.

"And everyone loves Joseph Van Dyke, too. Everyone except the anonymous note-writer. You need to talk to Joseph and find out who hates him enough to do this to him. Right now, I'd say that you have much more investigating to do before you get to the bottom of this hate crime! I suggest you get to it." Ellen stood up to leave and said, "But, there's something even more important going on: Eddie Siricco's murder."

At that moment, Chief Liberti burst into Adam's office. He was surprised to see Ellen Green sitting there. "Jacobson, are you arresting this lady again?" He looked at Ellen with amusement. "What did she do this time?"

"I think I'm about to find out, Sir."

"Detective, right now you need to follow me to my office. We need to talk. Mrs. Green, you can wait right where you are."

When Adam returned from his meeting with Liberti, he appeared tense and distracted. "Now, where were we?" he asked absently.

Ellen shot him an uppity look. "I was talking to you about the murder of Eddie Siricco, Detective."

"Look, you're right. There is a murderer on the loose. Quite frankly, I don't give a damn about this arson case right now, if you must know. Chief Liberti needs me and my team to find Eddie Siricco's killer. That is our priority. Today, in fact, Mayor Bradley is demanding that we make an arrest. The State Police are itching to take over. And the Chief expects me to solve it so he can take the credit. So, quite honestly, my career is on the line and I'm screwed. The only person who would be happy about this is my mother. She always wanted me to be a doctor," Adam confessed. "So your timing is not the greatest, Ellen. Now, I must..."

Ellen interrupted, "I'm taking a walk on the wild side when I say this, but I imagine you haven't gotten very far with the Eddie Siricco case."

"Perhaps," Adam shrugged noncommittally. "That's really nothing I am at liberty to discuss with you, Ellen."

"Then, don't. Just nod." Adam's tentative nod made Ellen's eyes gleam with delight. "Well, sounds like my timing is perfect, actually." Ellen sat back down and explained, "If it weren't for my--Charlie's and my--shrewd and brilliant detective work, four vicious murderers would still be terrorizing the public!" She gave Adam a smug look. "That about sums it up. So, Detective Jacobson, it's obvious that you need our help and need it desperately."

"Look, Ellen, I do appreciate your generous offer, but," he chuckled, "I think we'll manage just fine without your services."

"Hah! We'll see about that!" Ellen shot back at Adam as she walked towards the door. "I'm beginning to agree with your mother. You'd have been better off becoming a doctor instead of a police detective."

Adam leaned back in his chair and folded his arms across his chest. "Ellen Green is a meddlesome, headstrong woman who marches in here telling me how to do my job. Who does she think she is?" Adam thought to himself in frustration. However, what frustrated him even more was that it was possible she could be right.

"Please, wait a minute. You really have solved murders in the past?"

"Well, let me modestly say that Charlie and I have achieved, you could say, celebrity status in Cape Coral, Florida and up North in Brimfield, Mass. Why?"

Adam began rubbing his eyes as he spoke. "Eddie Siricco's murder investigation has stalled. We can't even find a concrete motive to pursue. So, I'm wondering if maybe you and Charlie would be willing to help us out. Nothing dangerous, of course. More like consultants. Help us brainstorm. That sort of thing."

"Well Adam, and I assume if we're working together I can call you Adam, our strength is doing the groundwork. Getting down and dirty. People open up to us because we appear to be a harmless, old couple. That's our winning strategy whenever we work undercover."

"Hmm. I see. Well, I'll have to run this by Chief Liberti, of course." Adam had no idea how to navigate that slippery slope.

"And, I'll need to run this by Charlie, of course. I couldn't possibly involve us in another murder investigation without Charlie's full cooperation," Ellen lied sweetly. Fumbling in her purse, Ellen retrieved two business cards that she presented to Adam. "I would suggest that you and Chief Liberti check our references. Here. This one is for you. You need to start with a call to Detective Sergeant Raul Swann in Cape Coral," Ellen instructed. "That's his private line. Oh, and this one is for Chief Liberti. He can speak with his counterpart at the Brimfield Police Station: Chief Harris," Ellen said with a condescending tone."

Adam raised his eyebrows and motioned to Ellen to sit back down. "Ellen, why don't you call Charlie and put him on speaker." Ellen got out her phone and placed the call.

"Charlie, this is Detective Jacobson and I'm here with Ellen."

Charlie replied, "Really? So what has she done this time?"

"I want to speak with both of you to see if you would be willing to assist the department with our murder investigation." Adam quickly added, "On an indirect, outside consultant basis. Certainly, not as investigators. Way too dangerous!"

"Ellen, what kind of a sales pitch did you make? Adam, Ellen tends to overstate her achievements. I don't know what she has told you, but I'm sure you don't need us to get involved." Charlie replied definitively.

"Charlie, believe me, if I weren't desperate, I wouldn't be doing this," Adam admitted.

Charlie took a few deep breaths before responding. "So, Adam, you're saying you want us to meet with you to review interviews, help you strategize? That sort of thing?" Charlie asked.

"Charlie, yes. That's exactly what I had in mind."

Charlie shook his head. "Well, then, I see you don't know my wife! There's no way in hell you're going to keep her on the sidelines."

Adam stated, "Well, I plan to try."

"That's what I said several decades ago, too," Charlie replied glibly as he ended the call.

"For starters, I guess I better check out your references." Adam stared at Raul's phone number and began placing the call on his desk phone.

"This is Detective Sergeant Raul Swann. You have reached my private line. Who's calling?" Raul responded guardedly.

"Detective Sergeant Swann, I'm Detective Sergeant Adam Jacobson in New Paltz, NY and I'm here with..."

Ellen interrupted, "Put Raul on 'speaker', Adam!" Adam obeyed. "Raul, it's Ellen and Charlie Green. How are you doing?"

"Ellen? Ellen and Charlie? Everything okay? You two aren't stalking another murderer, are you?" Raul asked with concern.

"Sir," Adam began, "let me explain. We've had a murder here in New Paltz and since I arrested Ellen, I've gotten to know her and think she and Charlie might be able to share their insights, work with us as consultants."

"Wait a minute. Back up. Did you say that you arrested Ellen?" Raul asked incredulously. "What have you been up to, Ellen?"

"Raul," Ellen scolded, "it was nothing. The important thing right now is for us to help with this murder investigation. They need us! I gotta tell you, Raul, we've got our hands full. The New Paltz police don't know what the hell they're doing!"

"Ellen, let me speak with Detective Jacobson."

"Sir?"

"First, please call me Raul and I'll call you Adam. If Ellen and Charlie are involved in your investigation, this will not be the last time we speak together. I can guarantee it."

"So, Raul, the Greens helped you before?"

"These two do some of the best undercover work I've ever seen. They're smart and perceptive and they get results every time. But, I need to warn you."

"Yes?"

"They're two of the most stubborn people I know. Charlie thinks he's still the toughest and strongest guy in the room. And, Ellen is intrusive and bossy and a general pain in the butt."

"Well, thanks so much for your kind words, Raul!" Ellen said caustically.

"Ellen, stop interrupting," Raul admonished. "But, Adam, you're lucky they're willing to help you. You better be sure to protect them. I may need their help again when they get back to Cape Coral!"

Ellen gave Adam an I-told-you-so look.

"Raul, thanks for your input but you don't need to worry. As I said earlier, Ellen and Charlie will not be working as field agents. They'll be strictly brainstorming with us," Adam said reassuringly.

Raul burst out laughing. "Adam, I can see that you really don't know these two at all!" He paused for a moment. "But you will!"

They all said their good-byes and ended the call.

"Well I must admit, Raul thinks very highly of you both." Adam held up the business card for Chief Harris in Brimfield and continued, "I'll be back in a couple of minutes. I need to run this by Chief Liberti."

Chief Liberti invited Adam to have a seat. "So what news have you got for me?"

Adam heaved a heavy sigh and stammered, "Well, Sir, the investigation has not been going as well as I expected. But I've got some good news."

"Let's hear it."

"I've just been on the phone with a Detective Sergeant Raul Swann from Cape Coral, Florida."

"That's odd. Is he offering to help us with our investigation--you know, unofficially, in some way?" Liberti asked hopefully.

"Well, Chief, I suppose, in a way you could say that," Adam shrugged awkwardly.

"Jacobson, stop keeping me in suspense. What did this Detective Swann have to offer us?"

Adam dreaded the way this conversation was playing out. "Well, Sir, he, um, he's endorsing an undercover team that he says is the best."

"Adam, I'm very impressed! Now, tell me about these top-secret assets." Liberti was rubbing his hands together in anticipation.

Adam lowered his head and muttered, "Ellen and Charlie Green."

"What? You can't be serious!" Liberti threw his head back and roared with laughter. When he was able to compose himself he continued, "Adam, you're like a son to me. I really am proud of your skills and integrity. But, what were you thinking? Ellen Green is a total nutcase!"

"Sir, she actually has references."

"Hah! From who? Miss Piggy, I suppose?"

"Seriously. Here, Sir. Please call Chief Harris with the Brimfield Police Department," Adam shrugged reluctantly.

Liberti frowned and took the card Adam handed to him. "Chief Harris here. Who's calling?" Harris answered gruffly.

"Chief Liberti from New Paltz, NY, Sir. We have a situation."

"Go on," Chief Harris said impatiently.

After Liberti explained the nature of the call, Adam heard only occasional 'uh huhs', several 'oh, reallys', and a 'you don't say!' from his Chief. Throughout the call, Liberti remained rather stone-faced.

When the call ended, Liberti announced, "Chief Harris had plenty to say about the Greens, particularly about Ellen Green. He called her an impertinent busybody who drove him crazy. But he said that, together, the Greens demonstrated persistence, boldness, and grit. And, you won't believe this one, Jacobson. He has made them honorary members of the Brimfield Police Department!"

Adam's eyes bulged with surprise at this stunning endorsement.

"Okay, Jacobson. Get them briefed but," Liberti menacingly pointed his finger at Adam, "not a damn word of this to anyone!"

Tuesday, October 4

Walter arrived at the Antique Barn very early today. He had an unpleasant task ahead of him and needed to finish it before the shop opened. The morning drizzle did not make the job easier, but he chose to ignore it.

By the time the shop opened, the rain had stopped. Customers began wandering around browsing and buying. Harris came barging in through the back door yelling to Walter, "Hey, Walter! Where are you?"

Walter was writing up a sale and did not even bother to look up. Harris walked to the front of the shop and marched behind the counter. "Walter, what is going on in the parking lot? It looks like a junkyard!"

Walter quietly mumbled, "Harris, I'll explain all of this in a minute. Please wait."

Harris sat on one of the stools and waited impatiently for Walter to complete the sale. As soon as the customer left, Harris pointed to the parking lot and complained, "What is that mess out there?"

"Harris, all of it belongs to a dealer in the shop who I kicked out over a week ago. He has probably already started loading it into his truck. In an hour you won't even know his stuff had been there."

"Wait. You kicked a dealer out? What happened? Come on. You've got to tell me!" Drama always piqued Harris' interest. Walter described the Cosmo/Jack light bulb showdown, much to

133

Harris' delight. "Hah! That's hysterical! Where's Cosmo? I want to see if he's got a black eye."

Cosmo heard his name mentioned and rushed down the stairs to see who was calling to him. "Oh, Harris, it's you," he commented with disappointment.

Harris eagerly asked, "So you and a dealer went at it? Wish I had seen this. Let me look at your eye."

"Stop it, Harris. I'm fine. I see that Walter told you about our little scuffle. Now you've got to tell me a juicy story in return." Cosmo missed the back-stabbing gossip he heard every week from Eddie Siricco. He was desperate for a scandalous rumor.

Harris' eyebrows danced up and down. He teased, "Well, maybe I do have a story to let you in on."

"Okay. Let's hear it."

"Well," he muttered, "there's talk of a big resort hotel/conference center that a group wants to build on Ben Sheppard's property on Milo Road."

"Oh, Harris, you've got to do better than that!" Cosmo gave a thumbs-down sign to Harris. "Eddie Siricco already told me about it. Ah, poor Eddie. The late Eddie."

"You already knew?"

"Oh yeah. Old news. But it won't get past the planning board."

"Don't be so sure of that, Cosmo. Remember, I'm on the planning board," Harris stated. "But, if the property isn't pre-approved, the sale is dead."

Cosmo shot Harris a look of boredom.

"You knew about that, too?"

Cosmo shook his head and shrugged, "Harris, nobody in this town could top Eddie when it came to dirty little secrets. Shit, I really miss him."

Harris did not like to be outdone, even by a dead man. "Okay, I'm going to tell you something I know you haven't heard."

Cosmo reminded him, "It has to be a real rumor to count. You can't just make it up. Those are the rules, Landau."

"Okay. Here goes. Judith's friend lives next door to Myrna and Joseph Van Dyke. You know, the ones who had the rally. Their house burned down."

"Oh, yeah. Go on."

"Well, Sunday morning she heard them out on their porch and, wait till you hear this! The police seized their computer. Judith's friend didn't mean to eavesdrop but the Van Dykes were getting pretty loud. Anyhow, Judith put two and two together and she thinks that Joseph is accused of burning down his own house to get the insurance money!"

Cosmo gave Harris a high-five. "Wowee, Harris, that's delicious! I gotta hand it to you. You might have even topped Eddie. That's quite a story!"

Harris grinned and placed his index finger over his mouth. "Shhh!" He walked out the door pleased with himself.

Cosmo was dying to share Harris' tidbit with every customer, dealer, and shop owner at Water Street Market. However, he forced himself to resist the temptation--well, at least for a few hours.

Adam Jacobson was waiting for Ben Sheppard to arrive for further questioning. Sergeant O'Riley escorted him to Adam's office and knocked on the door. "Thanks, Sergeant," Adam said as he opened up and faced an unkempt Ben Sheppard. "Please have a seat."

"What's this about, Detective? I already told you everything I know about Eddie Siricco."

"I disagree. You said Eddie, and I quote, 'likes to run his mouth.' So tell me what Eddie had on you to run his mouth about." Adam folded his arms on the table and stared at Ben, waiting for a response.

"Nothin'."

"Really? Tell me, again, about your property on Milo Road."

"I've owned it for years. Looking to sell it to a developer who wants to build a hotel."

"And wouldn't a developer be taking a big risk trying to build a hotel in New Paltz?"

"These developers always take risks," Ben shrugged. "Where are you going with this? It's my land and I can sell it if I want to."

"You're right. But, here's what I'm curious about. On Tuesday, September 27, the title company reports that the liens were paid up and you now own the property free and clear of encumbrances."

"So? Ever hear of getting a loan, Detective?" Ben chuckled.

"I'm wondering why the hell Phillip Edelstein would do that for you." Adam began to slowly chew on his pen. "I think Eddie Siricco knew a lot more than you wanted him to know about the sale of your land." Adam stood up and pointed his finger at Ben. "You found a way to shut him up and for good."

"I think you've got nothing to go on and you're hoping to pin it on me. What, is the Mayor putting pressure on the police to make an arrest? You're pathetic!"

"Where were you on the evening of Sunday, September 25 between 10:00 PM and 11:00PM?"

"How the hell would I remember?" Ben spewed back.

"If you don't remember, I'd say you're going to need one hell of a good attorney!" Adam retorted.

"Are we done?"

"For the moment."

Ben angrily pushed aside his chair and left Adam's office. Adam sat back down at his desk, tapping his pen against the side of his head. What could Eddie Siricco have on Ben Sheppard? Adam thought to himself, "What did Eddie know that got him murdered?"

A few minutes later, Ellen and Charlie headed directly to Adam Jacobson's office after checking in with Sergeant O'Riley. Adam greeted them looking as if he had slept in his car all night.

"You look like hell," Ellen tactfully commented.

Scratching his head, Adam mumbled, "Well, last evening was a rough one."

"Aha! I'll bet this has something to do with a young woman," Charlie teased.

"Believe me, not in the way you think! My mother is determined to marry me off to a nice Jewish girl. Dinner last night at my mother's was torture," Adam moaned. "Another daughter of one of her bridge ladies and this one had the voice of a screech owl."

"Oy vey!" Ellen exclaimed.

"That about sums it up. Anyhow, Eddie Siricco's murder. Let's talk about that. I need to bring you both up to speed and we'll strategize from there."

Ellen and Charlie both nodded.

Adam described the cause of death and Eddie's inebriated state of unconsciousness. "We found no mobile phone, no computer, no contacts, and obviously, no evidence of a struggle. I have talked to several people at Water Street Market hoping to get names or zero-in on a possible motive but there's not much to report. The common theme is that Eddie's big mouth and his noisy pen seemed to get him killed. I questioned a Ben Sheppard who had known Eddie for years. He had a conversation with him the week before his murder. Sheppard is sleazy and is, definitely, holding out on me. Had no alibi for his whereabouts on the night of the murder. Eddie seemed to have something on him but I can't figure out what." Adam went on to explain about the potential sale of Ben's property on Milo Road, now free of all encumbrances.

Ellen was unimpressed. "Adam, everybody knows about Ben's property. Tell us something we haven't already heard."

He concluded his briefing, throwing his hands in the air. "Well, Ellen and Charlie, I'm afraid, that's really about it."

Ellen declared caustically, "Sounds like if you want to get away with murder, move to New Paltz."

"Ellen, that's not helpful," Charlie chided her. "Look Adam, we do want to help. Some murderer is gloating right now, thinking they've gotten away with this." Suddenly, Charlie was all in. "If we assume that Eddie knew something that got him killed, we can also assume that he talked about it to someone. He liked to brag about what he knew. What fun would it be to hear juicy gossip and not have anyone to tell?"

"My team has been talking to all the local bartenders with that in mind, but we've got nothing."

Ellen asked, "Who discovered the body?"

"A neighbor. Mrs. Brucker. She called 911."

Ellen took out a pad of paper. "Mrs. Brucker? Please give me her address, Adam. I'm going to talk with her."

"It won't do you any good. She didn't hear or see anyone. I've already questioned her."

Ellen replied with a condescending smile. "Can't hurt for me to give it a try."

"Look, he spent most of his time at Water Street Market," Charlie surmised. "Ellen, you and I can start there."

Adam interjected, "I've already spoken with Cosmo at the Antique Barn and Harris, the owner. I even spoke with Dorothy Dawson, the actress."

"Then you must know that Eddie was her ex-husband. Right?" Ellen asked.

"What?" Adam replied stunned. "She never told me that. What else did she say?"

"They had been divorced for over twenty-five years. Apparently, they had a tumultuous relationship. Surprise, surprise. She also said that Eddie was always scheming, conniving, and soused. So, she really didn't say anything new. Anyhow, I agree with Charlie. We'll grill everyone at Water Street and they won't even realize they've been questioned."

Charlie asked Adam, "Do you think there's a connection between the hate crime and Eddie's murder?"

"I didn't think so, but I can't rule that out, Charlie. Let's get to work and meet again on Friday. Same time."

After they closed for the day, Walter and Cosmo moved furniture around in the front of the Antique Barn to make room for chairs. Tonight was a meeting of all the dealers in the shop. Several important items were on their agenda. Marc, one of the dealers, had volunteered to pick up the pizzas from Rocco's. He came through the back door buried under several large pizza boxes.

Cosmo ran to greet him. "Come on in, Marc. Thanks so much. Put the boxes on the counter. Don't be shy, everyone! Help yourselves. Beverages are on Walter's big oak table. And don't you dare spill anything on it or you'll own it!"

Dealers were one lively, extended family enjoying a chance to be together. They hugged, chatted, and aggressively attacked the pizza. Clearly, they were in no hurry for the meeting to begin, despite Cosmo's futile attempts. Finally he stood on a stepstool, clapped his hands, and shouted, "Quiet down! Quiet down! I'm thrilled that everyone is having such a good time, aren't we, Walter? We'll have to party together more often but right now, find a seat so we can begin our meeting."

As soon as everyone grabbed an extra piece of pizza and sat down, Walter began. "Glad to see all of you enjoying each other. We have the good and the not-so-good news to report. Anyhow, first the good news. Cosmo, Paty, and I want to thank everyone for working so hard to make your booths look good and for keeping your inventory truly old. A few of you have even remembered to remove the bar codes before you put the item in your booth," he sneered, staring directly at Bernice. "Seriously though, sales for September were the highest ever." Everyone cheered and whistled.

Walter held his hands up, signaling for everyone to quiet down. "Now for the not-so-good news: Jack is no longer with us."

"Oh, my God. Is he dead?" wailed Syd.

Before Walter could answer, Fred cupped his hands around his mouth and shouted from the back row, "Hey, who's getting Jack's space?" That question unleashed a verbal avalanche.

"I should get it. Walter promised I could move downstairs," claimed Donna, "because of my bad hip."

"You've got to be kidding!" Helen snipped. "Your bad hip? Try losing some weight and your hip will be just fine!"

"Helen, that was a cruel thing to say to Donna!" Annie exclaimed.

"Actually, I should be given a downstairs booth," Robert announced. "I'm the one who makes this place look classy, unlike some of you."

"Classy? You make the place look overpriced!" Joan snapped.

"Walter, didn't you say I could have a downstairs space?" Sadie piped up from the corner, raising her hand.

Robert was aghast. "You'll turn the downstairs into a dump!"

"How dare you, you pompous ass!" Sadie shot back.

Within a matter of seconds, the happy Antique Barn family was reduced to petty squabbling. Cosmo and Walter did not even bother to try to stop the landslide. They waited it out on the sidelines.

At last, everyone returned to their seats. Walter firmly admonished the backstabbing group facing him."Thank-you all for your show of compassion and concern about Jack's possible demise. You'll be relieved to know that he is alive. He, simply, decided that we weren't a good fit for him any longer. I will make a decision about Jack's space by next week."

Wendy could barely contain herself. "Walter, just tell everyone what really happened."

Without needing to be persuaded, Cosmo stepped forward and gave a colorful recap of the mêlée. A couple of dealers got up to inspect Cosmo's eye. Christopher was practically hyperventilating because the light bulb incident had occurred on his watch.

.

Before Walter could adjourn the meeting, the dealers began to whisper about Eddie Siricco's murder and the arson on Beekman Road. Cosmo was bursting to tell all. He was overjoyed to be the voice of scandal in Eddie's absence. He ceremoniously took the floor and had everyone's full attention.

"Okay," he sighed theatrically. "Here's the scoop. In case you haven't heard, the police think Joseph Van Dyke burned down his own house and made it look like a hate crime so he could collect the insurance! It's true. I swear!"

Wednesday, October 5

By morning, a rowdy, disenchanted crowd had gathered in front of the police station. 'Live with Lauren' was on the scene with the TV cameras rolling. Signs saying "*I'm crying for the Town Crier*" and "*We Love you, Eddie!*" were held high. Lauren addressed her TV audience. "*This is 'Live with Lauren' and I'm in front of the New Paltz Police Department. Only ten days ago New Paltz activists were rallying against a hate crime and now it is all about murder! New Paltz is where it's at, folks. Let's see what the demonstrators have to say.*" Lauren aimed the microphone at a group chanting, "*HEY, HEY, BOO HOO. EDDIE SIRICCO, WE MISS YOU!*"

Lauren's goal was to get one provocative sound bite. She spotted the perfect target: a skinny waif with a tie-dyed scarf around her head who was sobbing. Lauren shoved the microphone under her nose "*Please tell me why you are out here protesting today,*" she shouted to be heard over the crowd.

The young woman, dressed in fashionably tattered jeans and a skimpy crop-top sniffled, "*Eddie, our Town Crier, that's why! The police should have arrested someone by now,*" she wailed. "*We're pissed! Pissed!*"

Lauren asked the same question to a frail, osteoporotic woman old enough to be her grandmother. "*Please tell me why you wanted to be here this morning.*"

"*I want to know what the hell the police are doing about Eddie's murder!*" She faced the camera and angrily shook her finger at it. "*I'm representing everyone in my book group when I tell you that we're going to hunt down his killer and tar and feather the miserable bastard!"*

Lauren was elated. *"Well, folks, today is as much a love-fest for Eddie Sirocco as it is a demand for an arrest. The fans of Eddie Siricco, our Town Crier, are sobbing. They are angry."* She smiled, *"It appears that the residents of New Paltz have turned their grief into action."* She chirped, *"Enjoy a beautiful Wednesday and remember: you heard it first on 'Live with Lauren'! Now, back to you, Jonathan."*

Adam and Chief Liberti watched the protest from the second story conference room window. "Should I go out there and try to deescalate the situation?" Adam asked Liberti.

"You'd be out of your f--in' mind to get in front of a TV camera with that mob demanding an arrest! We have to keep doing our job and not worry about the optics."

"If you say so, Chief. Well then, I'm slipping out the back door. I have a couple of interviews scheduled before I meet with the Van Dykes later today. I plan to discover who Joseph's enemies are. I've decided that must be my strategy in this investigation. If someone wanted to destroy Joseph Van Dyke, they've sure found the way to do it. You know, Chief, I believe that everyone has an enemy-- even the nice guys like you and me," Adam said casually.

"Jacobson, I'm proud of you. That's the way a good detective has to think. Don't be swayed by what's going on out front. I like that you're beginning to think outside the box." Liberti nodded thoughtfully at Adam.

146

Dorothy was waiting in the courtyard for Detective Jacobson. She saw the young detective approach and flipped back her hair as if she were a twenty-year-old ingénue. "Detective! We meet again," Dorothy gushed.

"Yes, Ms. Dawson. The last time we met I almost had to put you in handcuffs, if I recall," Adam smirked.

"Detective, please call me Dorothy. And, I would never object being handcuffed to you," she said seductively."

Adam ignored her coquettish manner and began his interview. "Ms. Dawson, Dorothy, I appreciate your making time during a break in your rehearsal. I'm here because I'm aware that you spoke with Eddie Siricco a few days before he was murdered."

"Ah, yes, I did, very briefly, you understand."

"I'm meeting with anyone who had contact with Eddie, particularly the week of his murder. Please tell me what you and Eddie were talking about."

"It's hard to recall because it was small talk, really. He wished me well in my audition. That sort of thing."

"Now, Dorothy, I find that hard to believe. I happen to know that Eddie was your ex-husband. I would imagine that your conversation was much more volatile."

Dorothy gave Adam a sweet smile. "Eddie and I divorced twenty-five years ago. We've both moved on--or, at least, I have. Our meeting was quite cordial."

"Do you remember what day that was?"

"It was the day I auditioned for Desdemona. That's what made the day memorable for me. It was a Wednesday, but I don't remember the date."

Adam wrote down her comment and added, "That was Wednesday, September 21. Dorothy, did Eddie mention anyone else or mention going anywhere specific?"

Dorothy shook her head. "Sorry, Detective Jacobson. I'm not much help, I'm afraid."

"On the contrary. You've been very helpful," Adam stated with a smile.

Before Dorothy could respond, Leonard frantically scurried down the steps into the courtyard calling her. "Hey Dorothy, Dorothy! A reporter from the Daily Freeman wants to speak with you! I need you, stat!"

With a winsome look, Dorothy said, "My public awaits, Detective. I must depart." She fluttered away from the table and up the stairs to the theatre entrance.

Dorothy blew by Leonard and darted into her dressing room to refresh her make-up and fluff up her wiry, brass-colored hair. "Dorothy! Come out right now before that reporter takes off! You look fine. Actually, nobody even cares how you look!" Leonard yelled, knocking loudly at her door. "Harris and I have already had to stall her when you disappeared on us."

"Be right there, Leonard. Tell the reporter not to leave!" Dorothy emerged from her dressing room looking much the same as she did when she entered her dressing room. Nevertheless, she felt confident and ready to face the press.

"Hello, Ms. Dawson. I'm Mavis Redford, from the Daily Freeman."

"Pleased to meet you, Mavis. Please call me Dorothy," she replied, elongating the pronunciation of her name for emphasis.

Mavis Redford held up the microphone as the cameraman moved in to snap some photos. "So, Dorothy, is 'Desdemona' your comeback role?"

Dorothy gave a condescending smile. "I'd prefer to call it my charitable contribution. I must be perfectly honest and tell you that Leonard, the director, practically got down on his knees begging me to take this role. He insisted that it was meant for me. How could I disappoint him?" she asked with a wistful sigh.

Leonard was furious with Dorothy. He never even wanted her to audition for the part but she kept hounding him. She was a mediocre actress, at best. Besides, he did not want to contend with her tantrums and nastiness. What a bombastic liar! He tried to take several slow deep breaths, fanning his hands in front of his mouth, to keep himself from charging over to her and grabbing the mic out of her hand.

Dorothy was relishing this moment. "Besides, I am dedicated to supporting community theatres. I couldn't possibly refuse Leonard. That would have been cruel."

"Dorothy, is it true that you were arrested at the hate crime rally?" Mavis asked.

Holding up her left hand, Dorothy emoted, "Please, Maude, I really don't want to talk about it. It was too painful."

"Excuse me, but my name isn't Maude. It's Mavis," she whispered.

"Whatever. Anyhow, dear, about the arrest. It was a frightful experience and it hurts me to even mention it. But, I am here," she smiled, "and still committed to fighting hate crimes. In fact, the poor boys who were the target of this vile act have become, well, I call them my poor, little weekend refugees. See, I've invited them to spend their weekends in my flat from now on."

"That's very generous of you, Dorothy. They must be so grateful. In fact, the entire community is grateful to you for helping them out."

Dorothy continued her humble-brag. "It was nothing. I, simply, followed my heart." Dorothy posed for the camera as she finished her sentence, one hand on her hip, head tilted in an engaging manner. "Maude, or whatever your name is, when will this appear in the paper?" Dorothy inquired, careful not to disturb the inflated smile that was fixed on her face for the photo shoot.

"I'm Mavis," she said with a slight edge of impatience in her voice. "It should be in Sunday's entertainment supplement. I think you'll be pleased. And, thank-you, Dorothy Dawson." Mavis reached out to shake Dorothy's hand before bolting out of the theatre.

Myrna and Joseph Van Dyke arrived at the police station via the private back entrance to avoid any embarrassment. They were directly escorted to Adam's office. Knocking on the door, Sergeant O'Riley said, "The Van Dykes are with me."

Adam opened the door and invited them in. "Please sit down. I know this has been a difficult time for you, both."

"Difficult doesn't begin to describe the humiliation and degradation to which your department has subjected us!" Myrna spewed angrily.

Adam cleared his throat uncomfortably and said, "Right now things are not looking good for you. You can help me by telling me who would want to do this to you."

Myrna had not mentioned to Joseph that Phillip had visited her at home. Joseph had not mentioned to Myrna that Phillip had met him at Clemson Brewery. And, neither one of them was about to mention it to Detective Jacobson. Myrna and Joseph, each, had their reasons.

Joseph quietly said, "I don't know of anyone who would try to frame us. I don't even know of anyone in this town who would be anti-gay either."

"So, Detective, tell us where things stand right now," Myrna urged impatiently.

"Well, the anonymous note claims that Joseph was pouring, what the witness believed was, gasoline around the perimeter of your house on Beekman Road, as you already know. Without any help from you, I'm not likely to identify this person. And, Joseph, by your own admission, your alibi leaves enough time for you to have set the fire."

"But I didn't do it! Why should I have to prove my innocence?"

Adam shook his head, "Look, as soon as this allegation gets out, as it's bound to, your loyal followers will feel betrayed. So, you need to be realistic." Adam was through tiptoeing around Joseph's fear of Myrna. He wanted to be done with this. He had a murder to deal with. So, he dove in head first. "Besides, let's face it, Joseph, you've wiped out every bit of savings you and Myrna had. So, the motive is a strong one. You need that insurance money."

Myrna felt her face turn crimson as the heat quickly rose in her post menopausal body. "What is going on? Joseph? Tell me what you've done. I demand an explanation!"

Joseph was looking down, shamefully staring into his lap.

Adam spoke, "Joseph, would you like to tell Myrna or shall I?"

"Tell me what?" she shrieked. "Somebody say something."

Joseph did not look up, but gestured with his hand for Adam to speak.

"Myrna, between 2016 and 2018, your husband's online gambling depleted your entire savings. Your IRA, your investments. Everything." Adam looked directly at Myrna who looked directly back at him and said nothing at all.

Adam reached into his pocket and pulled out a piece of paper. "Joseph, I have a warrant to search your phone. Standard procedure." Adam handed Joseph the document to review. "Please hand it over. You can retrieve it after 4:00 this afternoon. It won't take our tech team long to check it out. You, two, need to return home. You've got a lot to discuss and I suggest you keep your windows closed when you do it. Good-day."

By late evening, Ellen and Charlie were relaxing on the porch, each, with a glass of sauvignon blanc when Ellen's phone 'can-canned', her default ringtone. "Catherine," she answered, "so good to hear from you! How are you and Ted doing?" Catherine was Charlie's sister-in-law. She and her husband Ted live in Cape Coral, Florida and are the reason that Ellen and Charlie spend the winter there.

"Ellen, put me on 'speaker'." Ellen did as she was told. "Hi there, Charlie! Tell us what you've been up to."

Charlie jumped right in. "Other than Ellen being arrested, nothing much is going on."

Ellen glared at Charlie. "It was nothing really. Just a rally about a hate crime that took place in New Paltz. I guess I was in the wrong place at the wrong time," she explained with indifference.

"No way! I know you better than that, Ellen! Remember, I've been to a rally with you before. But a hate crime in New Paltz? Hard to believe."

Ted cheerfully tried to diffuse the situation. "Well, at least this isn't a murder!"

Ellen and Charlie exchanged looks but neither one said anything.

Catherine surmised, "From the silence on your end, I am assuming the worst. There has been a murder. Right?"

"Yes, I suppose," Ellen squeaked. "But we're being very smart about this."

"Yeah, and I'm wearing nothing but a lace thong! We Bird-Watchers are not around to keep you, two, out of trouble, so behave yourselves!" Catherine scolded.

The Bird-Watchers are Catherine, Ted, and their closest friends, Karen and Bud. The four of them secretly protected Ellen and Charlie throughout each of their murder investigations. As Ellen and Charlie became increasingly reckless, the Bird-Watchers became increasingly vigilant. Their unconventional surveillance methods proved to be surprisingly effective.

"Well, we really called to say that we're heading up North for a visit. So, at least wait until we arrive before you start snooping around," Ted pleaded.

"What are you talking about?" Ellen asked.

"We're driving up with Karen and Bud in their RV," Ted explained. "I want to get some photos of birds at Minnewaska State Park and, it's leaf-peeping season. We leave tomorrow."

"Ted, that's really good news! We'll plan to get together for dinner when you get here. In the meantime, you have nothing to worry about," Charlie assured them.

"You're a terrible liar, Charlie Green," Catherine admonished. "When we arrive, you can tell us all about this murder that we have nothing to worry about."

As soon as they said their good-byes and ended the call, Catherine placed a call to Karen and Bud. "Attention Bird-Watchers. We just learned that geriatric Nancy Drew and her crusty sidekick are at it again," she sighed. "Pack your surveillance equipment and 2-way radios for our road trip. Looks like the Bird-Watchers are taking flight. This is Queenie. Over and out."

Yesterday, Myrna and Joseph, wisely, heeded Detective Jacobson's advice and sealed shut their townhouse before the implosion began between the two of them. After Myrna screeched and called Joseph every obscene name she could think of, she began smashing her Pyrex measuring cups, Stangl pottery, and Waterford crystal. Joseph sat stoically at the kitchen table, ducking as plates, bowls, and wine glasses flew by his nose. He knew he deserved her wrath. When the entire contents of the kitchen cabinets covered the floor in the form of shards of glass and smashed pottery, Myrna lashed out in a tirade that reached an ear-splitting decibel level. By the end of this interminable day, Joseph skulked off to the den to spend the night on the couch.

Today, Myrna and Joseph silently swept away the shattered pieces of their lives and Myrna made them some coffee.

Ellen drove to New Paltz to find Mrs. Brucker. She arrived at 681 Main Street and walked up the stairs to the second floor apartment to ring the bell. Ellen's arrival was announced with a chorus of yips coming from inside. "Yes?" asked a feeble voice peering through the peephole.

"Mrs. Brucker, I'm Ellen Green. May I speak with you?"

"Just a moment and I'll let you in." She unlocked the chain and spoke sternly, "Now, Fifi, go lie down!"

Ellen entered and was greeted by a twelve-pound, black poodle with a proprietary air. "Why, hello there! You're a little cutie!" Ellen bent down and held out her hand for Fifi to sniff. "Mrs. Brucker, Fifi is adorable! In fact, she reminds me of my little poodle, Truffle, who lived for seventeen years." After sniffing around at Ellen's feet, Fifi assumed her rightful place in the only comfortable chair in the room.

"Mrs. Brucker, I was a very close friend of Eddie Siricco," Ellen fibbed, "and wanted a chance to speak with you."

"That was a terrible night, Mrs. Green! Fifi and I will never be able to forget the sight of poor Mr. Siricco lying on the floor, not moving. Please have a seat." She motioned to a chair at the dining room table.

"Thank-you." Ellen sat across from Mrs. Brucker. "I can't imagine how you must have felt seeing him like that!"

Mrs. Brucker shuddered at the mere thought. "You say you were a close friend?"

Ellen nodded. "Yes, in fact, I saw him Sunday morning on the day he was murdered. We spoke briefly. Were you friendly with Eddie?"

"No, but he was always a kind neighbor. Even Fifi liked him and she doesn't like a lot of people. Would you care for some iced tea?"

"Thanks. I'd love some. Mrs. Brucker, did Eddie Siricco have any visitors on the day of his murder?"

Mrs. Brucker walked to the refrigerator and returned with two glasses of tea. "I already told the police that Mr. Siricco's visitors are none of my business, Mrs. Green. I'm not a nosy neighbor," she stated emphatically as she sat back down.

Ellen smiled and leaned towards Mrs. Brucker. "Of course you're not! But as neighbors, we all keep an eye out for one another. Right? It's the neighborly thing to do."

"Well, when you put it that way, I'd have to say that I do try to be a good neighbor," Mrs. Brucker nodded in agreement. "But, Mrs. Green, my hearing isn't the best and I'm afraid I never heard anyone in Mr. Siricco's apartment that day."

Ellen patted Mrs. Brucker's hand. "Please tell me what happened when you found our poor Eddie."

Mrs. Brucker pulled a handkerchief out from inside her blouse and blew her nose. "Like I said to the detective, Fifi had to pee and it was the middle of the night so I got up, put on my slippers and my coat and opened up my door. Fifi ran out the door and right into Mr. Siricco's apartment. It was almost as if she knew something terrible had happened!"

Ellen shook her head and smiled in the direction of the furball on the wing chair. "Fifi is, definitely, an old soul. I believe she probably did sense something. Please try to go on."

Nodding, Mrs. Brucker continued, "Well, there he was: flat on his back and not moving. I walked over to him to see if he was okay and he looked, well, he looked very strange. I picked Fifi up, called 911, and we waited in the hallway outside his apartment."

"Mrs. Brucker, did you see anyone else--someone leaving the building?"

"No. Nobody, Mrs. Green." She whispered, "But I have to tell you, I absolutely loved reading the Town Crier column every week. It was my favorite thing to do." Mrs. Brucker became animated as she explained, "See, I'd read the column and then spend the entire week trying to figure out who Mr. Siricco was talking about. He always liked to drop hints without naming names. It was like searching for buried treasure, trying to figure out his little secrets! My friends and I would get together and compare notes. How am I ever going to manage without the Town Crier?" she wailed.

"I'm not sure how any of us will manage without the Town Crier," Ellen commiserated.

"You know, sometimes I would see Mr. Siricco coming home and I would beg him to tell me about his next column. My friends were impressed that Mr. Siricco was my neighbor," she winked.

"Mrs. Brucker, did Eddie ever tell you anything about his next article? Any hints what it would be about?"

"No, he never would tell me. He always said that would spoil the fun."

"If I were you, I'd be bursting to know. I couldn't live next door to the Town Crier and not get a sneak preview!"

"Well, Mrs. Green, if you must know, I feel the same way," Mrs. Brucker said with a conspiratorial smile.

"I think you and I are very much alike, Mrs. Brucker. We're both curious, perceptive women."

"That we are." Mrs. Brucker began fidgeting with the buttons on her blouse. "Well, I must confess that, well, um, uh, this must stay between us, Mrs. Green. Promise?" Ellen quickly nodded, not wanting to interrupt whatever was to follow. "That night, I never thought about Mr. Siricco being dead, but all I could think about was the Town Crier column. Isn't that awful of me?"

"Not at all. The Town Crier column was your personal connection to him. Besides, at the time, you had no way of knowing Eddie was dead. Go on."

"Well, Mrs. Green, I did something I'm ashamed of. I saw his notepad on the coffee table next to the bottle of booze and," Mrs. Brucker put her head between her hands muttering, "I put it in my pocket."

Ellen's iced tea almost sprayed clear across the table. However, she swiftly composed herself. "You really must be one of his most loyal fans, Mrs. Brucker."

"See, I thought I would get a clue about next week's Town Crier piece and --oh, my God--what a selfish thing to do!"

Ellen reached across the table to reassure Mrs. Brucker. "You did that out of respect and admiration for Mr. Siricco." Mrs. Brucker did not lift her head, but nodded slightly. "Mrs. Brucker, did you show the notepad to the police?"

"No. I was afraid to say anything about it. Please don't tell anyone!" she pleaded.

"Of course not," Ellen lied. "May I take a look at it?"

Mrs. Brucker opened a drawer in the buffet behind her and handed Ellen Eddie Siricco's trusty notepad.

Meanwhile, Charlie was at Water Street Market where breaking news was erupting. The headline of an editorial in the Daily Freeman read: *'Van Dykes, Vamoose!'* The allegation about Joseph Van Dyke had gone viral and everyone from shop owners to customers to the college students was burbling to one another in shock-horror about it. Charlie saw Harris leaving the Antique Barn. "Harris, have a minute?"

"Barely." Harris was always on fast-forward and today was no exception. "But, okay. Let's sit down. I could use a little break."

"That's really something about Van Dyke."

"Yeah, Charlie. I feel kinda bad because I think I started it."

"What do you mean?"

"I heard it from Judith and told Cosmo. And, of course, once Cosmo heard it, everyone heard it."

"Cosmo announced it at our antique dealer meeting on Tuesday night. Actually, I'm surprised it didn't hit the paper until today," Charlie reasoned. "Do you think it's true, Harris?"

"Funny you should ask. Charlie, please keep this to yourself, but I'm not so sure. See, on Sunday I had breakfast with Phillip Edelstein and Ben Sheppard. You know about Ben's property?"

"Who doesn't already know about that?" Charlie asked.

"Well, the two of them want me to get the planning board to approve a hotel."

"That's not surprising, Harris. You're on the planning board."

"Right, but what is surprising is that when I warned them about the Van Dykes opposing the development, Phillip said something strange."

"Yes?"

"He laughed and said that he didn't think they would be a problem. Charlie, I remember. He said, 'Let me handle them'."

"What do you think he meant?"

"I couldn't say but, it is funny that he made that comment and now look at what's happened to the Van Dykes."

Ben Sheppard almost jumped right out of his Lazy Boy recliner as he read the headline: *'Van Dykes, Vamoose!'* He could not be happier with the way everything was unfolding. Eddie Siricco was off his back and now Myrna and Joseph were practically being run out of town. Phillip hadwiped out his property debts. Ben's plan, moving forward, was quite simple. After the closing, he would take the money and run. "Phillip will have to settle for whatever crumbs I throw his way and be grateful," Ben thought ruthlessly.

Phillip Edelstein was pouring a decaff latte from his Breville espresso machine into a glass tumbler as he caught the editorial in the Daily Freeman about the Van Dykes' alleged arson: *'Van Dykes, Vamoose!'* He stood in his kitchen and marveled at the power of a rumor. The more slanderous the rumor, the faster it spread and the more likely it was to be believed. Phillip wallowed in pleasure at how effortlessly Myrna and Joseph had been shaken from their pedestal.

Ellen was holding Eddie's personal notepad in her hand and was sorely tempted to sprint out the door with it and take off. She could, certainly, outrun poor Mrs. Brucker whose back was shaped like a question mark. However, Fifi was likely to be a problem. Therefore, Ellen resisted the temptation and, instead, asked for some more iced tea. Ellen's lucky break came when Mrs. Brucker called to her from the kitchen, "Mrs. Green, I'll be right back. Need to tinkle."

"Take your time!" Ellen called back. That was her cue. She quickly whipped out her phone and took photos of as many pages as time would allow.

Adam called a meeting with his team of officers and Chief Liberti. Adam began his briefing. "I am pleased to report that we have an update in the Eddie Siricco murder investigation. Listen to what our tech team discovered on Joseph's mobile phone. It's a voicemail that he had deleted and it's dated, Friday, September 23."

Adam played the voicemail for everyone to hear. *"Van Dyke. Eddie Siricco here. Funny, ain't it, that you need money and now your house burns down,"* Eddie cackled into the phone. *"Now, I'm not saying that you did this or you didn't, but if the police found out, boy, would it look bad for you! Last chance to change your mind before it's too late."*

Everyone strained to hear the message. One officer asked Adam to play the recording again. The officers were all buzzing with excitement.

Officer Larson asked, "Do you think Eddie Siricco could have typed the anonymous note?"

Officer Conrad shot back, "There's a problem with that possibility. Mail delivery isn't very reliable from six feet under, Larson!" A boisterous round of laughter followed.

"Good point," Adam grinned. "Remember, the anonymous note was received on Thursday, September 29--almost a week after Eddie's murder."

Another officer asked, "Jacobson, does Van Dyke have an alibi?"

"Not really. He and Myrna both swore they were home together but I don't believe a word they said."

The officer seated next to Adam concluded, "So, Van Dyke had a motive and, possibly, the opportunity to murder Eddie Siricco."

"That's right." Adam replied.

Chief Liberti cautioned, "We need to proceed carefully. The evidence from this voicemail only tells us that Eddie Siricco attempted to blackmail Van Dyke."

"But," Adam pointed out, "this message also tells us that Siricco had contact with Van Dyke prior to this voicemail."

"Correct, but remember, there's no evidence here that Van Dyke committed murder. We need to find out if Siricco was trying to blackmail anyone else. Basically, this investigation is still wide open."

"Okay, officers," Adam concurred, "our job, now, is to go wide and deep with this investigation, all at the same time. If we're going to consider Van Dyke a person of interest, we better have evidence to back it up or break Van Dyke down until we get a confession."

Friday, October 7

This morning, Ben had told Phillip to meet him for coffee in the courtyard at Water Street Market. Phillip breezed in eager to review the signed contracts. "So, Sheppard, let's see those signatures."

Ben put down his mug and stated, "Phillip, I'm pissed. I haven't received the contracts."

"So, what the hell is going on here, Ben? You better tell me!"

"I don't know. Maybe their attorneys don't think I'll get the approvals for the development."

"But the contract states that if the approvals are not granted, their deposit will be returned and the deal is null and void. They're protected. I'm not!" Phillip sipped his coffee in an attempt to calm himself down.

"Look, I'll call them this morning and see where we stand. In the meantime, you're sure you can get the planning board to okay this?" Ben asked skeptically.

"Cool it. I already told you that our biggest problem was the friggin' Van Dykes." With a malevolent grin he added, "And, now, they couldn't even get a swarm of hungry mosquitoes to follow them anywhere."

Ben stared long and hard at Phillip. Ben knew that Phillip had the brains in this partnership. He'd never be able to outsmart Phillip. But, he was scrappy and always ready to stab a partner in the back.

The truth is that Ben never had any intention of paying Phillip back that five hundred grand. And, if the deal fell through, there was no way in hell that he *could* pay it back.

Phillip continued, "I'm doing my part. Your job is to get the papers signed. Once that's done, we'll be golden." Pointing his finger at Ben, he growled, "And, sale or no sale, you'll pay me back that loan. Do I make myself clear?"

"You're my fixer and probably my only friend. I'm always going to need you, Edelstein. I'd never try to stiff you," Ben lied effortlessly.

"Bullshit. You'd love to, but you can't and you know it." Phillip warned, "Of course, if you want to spend the next ten years behind bars as a convicted felon, I could easily make that happen for you."

"You really are a son-of-a-bitch, Phillip." Ben's eyes darkened as he glared at Phillip. "I plan to find out what you don't want anyone to know about you." Ben stood up to leave. "And, I won't hesitate to use it against you, if I have to."

Phillip roared with laughter. "Sheppard, don't even try to outsmart me."

"Phillip Edelstein, you're every bit as corrupt as I am. In fact, that's what I like about you," Ben declared contemptuously as he walked away.

While Ben and Phillip were engaged in a heated discussion, Cosmo appeared to be busy placing dishes and knickknacks on the bargain table outside the Antique Barn. He pretended not to be listening, but he tried not to miss a single word of their conversation. "I think I'm channeling Eddie, may he rest in peace," Cosmo cackled to himself. His eavesdropping skills were still somewhat primitive. Therefore, Cosmo was unable to catch the details, but he heard enough to know that this was a savory morsel meant to be passed along to worthy individuals.

Chief Liberti and Detective Sergeant Adam Jacobson were meeting early this morning. The Chief had received an ultimatum from Mayor Bradley. "We've got a serious situation here, Adam. Apparently, parents of the college students in New Paltz are threatening to pull their kids out of school with a murderer on the loose. They plan to file a grievance against the police to the board of trustees, citing gross incompetence. So, Jacobson, we've got one lousy week to come up with a person of interest or the State Police will come strutting in here like a pride of peacocks!"

"Sir, I've gotta tell you, we're not even close to naming anyone, well, with the exception of Joseph Van Dyke."

Pounding his fist on his desk, Liberti concurred, "Then do whatever it takes to make that allegation stick. I'm counting on you, Jacobson."

Adam stood up and walked down the hall to his own office. The Greens had arrived and were waiting in the lobby. "Sergeant O'Riley, please ask the Greens to come to my office. No need to escort them. Thank-you."

168

Ellen and Charlie sat in their usual seats across the table from Adam. "So you two, any updates for me?" Adam asked.

"Adam, stop sulking," Ellen admonished.

In spite of himself, Adam grinned, "You're beginning to sound like my mother."

"Why, thank-you," Ellen smiled. "Now we do have information, so listen up. Charlie, why don't you start."

Charlie talked about his meeting with Harris who raised a concern about Phillip Edelstein. "And, Adam, Edelstein told Harris he would take care of the Van Dykes. If he wrote the anonymous note, I would say to him, mission accomplished."

"But why wouldn't Myrna or Joseph name him as a possible enemy?" Adam rubbed his imaginary beard.

"That's something the Van Dykes need to explain," Charlie concluded.

"Hmm, Phillip Edelstein is an intriguing possibility."

"Could I see the anonymous note?" Charlie asked. Adam removed it from a folder and handed it to Charlie. "Interesting. Look at this, Ellen. The note is typed on an old-fashioned typewriter."

"Adam, you're in luck. Charlie, what can you tell from this?"

"This was typed on a 1960's typewriter and, see, the style is cursive, which is fairly rare. There were several typewriters of that period that typed in cursive, but," Charlie examined the note with the magnifying glass that Ellen always carried in her purse. "I think it's an Olympia. That's my opinion. You find that typewriter and you'll find the person who wrote this."

Adam was duly impressed. "Charlie, good work. Well, here's what I have for you." Adam briefed Ellen and Charlie on the voicemail Eddie Siricco left on Joseph's phone. "Bottom line is that we know Eddie tried to blackmail Joseph. He must have known about Joseph's gambling losses and he had contact with Joseph prior to leaving that voicemail on Friday, September 23."

"What's your next step?" Charlie asked Adam.

"Bringing Joseph Van Dyke back in for questioning. So, are we done here for today?"

"Not quite," Ellen piped up. She reached in her purse and took out her cell phone. "Mrs. Brucker turned out to be most accommodating," Ellen announced, pleased with herself.

Leonard had to leave the theatre and get some fresh air. His acid reflux was keeping him awake at night. He popped another Tums into his mouth and bounded towards the courtyard to escape from Dorothy Dawson. She was driving him crazy. Every detail became a power struggle. Dorothy insisted that the playwright be fired. When Leonard tried to explain that without the playwright there would be no play, Dorothy began ripping up her script, tearing it to shreds. Leonard spotted Harris reading the New York Times and sipping a latte. He charged over to his table and sat down.

"Harris, I have to get rid of Dorothy. She's a friggin' beast!"

"Now, Leonard, she may be a bit of a diva, but she knows how to get publicity and she'll fill that theatre with patrons," Harris said, barely looking up from the newspaper. "Try to ignore her outbursts. Why don't you get one of Michelle's lattes and join me?"

"Harris, stop patronizing me. Everything I eat burns my throat. I can't sleep and when I finally do, I have nightmares. I'm taking Advil for headaches, my ears are ringing, my heart is racing and-- and, on top of all that, I'm constipated!" Leonard shrieked.

Harris glanced over at Leonard. "You should try meditation, Leonard. It would do you some good."

Leonard did not bother to reply. He stood up and headed back to the theatre to face his demon.

Adam and Charlie were stunned to see photos of Eddie Siricco's personal notes: page after page of notes. Adam cleared his throat as he tried to decipher the scribbles. "Can you make sense out of any of this?"

Ellen tried to clarify. "It appears that Eddie is focusing on several people. Look, here he talks about the Van Dykes." She read, "'*We can all hope that our resident geriatric hippies never decide to demonstrate by streaking through the Village. That would surely cause permanent blindness, folks!'* That was penned on Thursday, September 22. And much earlier, he refers to a *pair of bohippians.* I assume that's the Van Dykes, again. When he uses the term *'Birkenstock Bitch'*, I'm pretty sure we know who he's talking about."

Charlie and Adam were speechless as Ellen continued to scroll through numerous pages of Eddie Siricco's personal, hand-written notes.

"Now, here we have an excerpt of an article that never made it to his Town Crier column. It is dated, Wednesday, September 21. *'Hmm. A little birdie told me that a big tract of forested land is about to turn into--a Hilton, perhaps? I'll bet local businesses will welcome this economic boost to New Paltz or will they? Get ready to laugh when the Van Dykes mobilize their pathetic aging hippies to protest once again! I wonder how they can be stopped? Or do I? Star power has arrived to the Denizen--or has it? Dorothy Dawson will finally end her less than spectacular career. Watch her humiliation erupt. And I say good riddance.'* "

Ellen removed her glasses and looked up at Adam and Charlie. "Eddie seemed rather fixated on the Van Dykes and his ex-wife. Now, check out these pages and you'll see that since Monday, September 19, Eddie referred to someone as the *'friggin' fixer'* and there are many references to a *'lowlife land owner'* looking to *'snitch, sneak, and snatch'*. There's more for you to check out. I'll send these on to you, Adam." Ellen sat back in her chair, arms folded.

Adam stammered, "How the hell did you get hold of this?"

Ellen gave Adam a saucy smile. "Mrs. Brucker turned out to be very helpful. You just have to know how to ferret out the

172

information. As experienced sleuths, Charlie and I have learned that everyone--everyone--has something to hide. Even sweet little Mrs. Brucker. Our job is to keep at it until we find out what that is."

Saturday, October 8

Ellen showed up at the Antique Barn, ostensibly to bring in a couple of books and juicers. However, her real purpose was to pump Cosmo for information. "Hey Cosmo! How are you doing? You must really miss Eddie Siricco. Gossip has taken a big hit since he was murdered."

Cosmo's eyebrows danced up and down with mischief. "Well, I owe it to Eddie to do my best in that department, Ellen. In fact, wait till you hear this one. Everybody knows about Ben Sheppard's property." Cosmo moved closer to Ellen so he could speak softly. "But nobody knows about Ben and his business partner going at it like a couple of rabid hippos!"

"Rabid hippos?" Ellen stifled a giggle. "Do tell!"

"Oh, yes. It was yesterday and while my hands were busy putting stuff out on the bargain table, my ears were busy listening to them threaten each other. They were sitting just below at a table in the courtyard."

"What were they saying?"

Cosmo scrunched his face up, shook his finger, and mimicked, "You better pay me back or I'll see that you're behind bars for the next ten years!"

"Oh my God!"

"But Ben swore he'd find out something big to hold over his partner. Let me put it this way, Ellen. I wouldn't put it past either of them to steal something right off the dollar table outside!"

Ellen laughed, eager for more. Cosmo did not need much encouragement. Her reaction was enough inspiration for him. "Oh, and one more nasty little detail."

"Yes?"

"You know about Joseph Van Dyke burning down his house?"

"Yes, Cosmo. If you recall, you made a big announcement about it at our dealer meeting last week. Everybody knows about that. Go on."

"Well, Ben and his little co-conspirator seemed to be very happy about what happened to Joseph Van Dyke. Very! Ben's partner kept saying that the Van Dykes were their biggest problem and now everybody hates them so they're no longer an issue."

"You think the planning board will approve this development now?"

Cosmo replied impatiently. "Ellen, think about it. Without the Van Dykes to protest, the planning board will cave. I'm sure they will. Look, Harris is on the board. You think he'll block it?" Cosmo scoffed.

"No. Harris would probably welcome the extra business it would bring in. Very interesting, Cosmo. Eddie would be proud of you!"

"Well, thanks, honey!"

"I'm going to straighten up my booth. Be downstairs in a little while." Ellen waved as she practically skipped up the stairs to her booth.

This morning, Matthew and Pablo drove directly from Manhattan to Water Street Market. Cosmo rushed over to give them, each, a hug. "Hello, boys. How are you doing?"

"We're great, Cosmo. And you and Walter?"

"We're marvelous!" he replied.

While Pablo stayed to talk with Cosmo, Matthew darted up the stairs to check out Ellen and Charlie's typewriters. Not wanting to interrupt her, he stopped and watched from another booth as Ellen walked over to speak with a couple of young men who were examining one of her typewriters.

Ellen could not resist inserting herself into their conversation. "Hi. If you have any questions about the typewriter, I'm happy to try to answer them."

"I think we're okay. Looks interesting," one of the men answered politely.

"I realize that your generation has no idea how these amazing machines work. There isn't even an on/off switch. No passcodes," she announced flippantly. "You put the paper in here, turn, and hit the keys fairly hard. Worst part is--you can't get rid of typos."

"Hey, look at this!" Ignoring her, the other young man examined the ribbon tape.

Ellen had seen too many people under the age of thirty who mangled the keys and played with the ribbons. "You do need to be careful. The ink will be all over your fingers," she warned, gritting her teeth. "And just what are you doing to the keys?" Ellen watched with annoyance as they examined individual letters. "They are very delicate! You break it and it's yours!" She wanted to grab it out of their hands.

The first man smiled at her while the other man stepped aside to use his phone. "If you're looking this up on Ebay, you'll find this model is very pricey. It's a rare machine." Ellen insisted. "And, it was working just fine before you, two, came along!" she barked.

"Thank-you. I think we'll take it," the other man said, placing it in the case. They walked downstairs to the counter to pay.

Matthew walked over to Ellen. "Well, Ellen, seeing you in action, it's obvious that you sure know how to win over your customers," he laughed.

"Did you see the way they handled that delicate machine, Matthew?" Ellen was outraged. "They were ravaging it!"

"Look, they bought it," he shrugged with amusement. "Anyhow, it's good to see you. How's Charlie?"

"We're fine. Good to see you, too," Ellen smiled as they hugged. "Hey, you guys heard about the Van Dykes, I assume."

"What do you mean?"

Ellen shook her head. "We need to go downstairs. Cosmo can tell you and Pablo what's been going on."

Matthew headed right for Cosmo. "What's been going on? Are the Van Dykes okay?"

Cosmo put his arms around Matthew and Pablo's shoulders and walked them behind the counter to whisper. "Word on the street is that Joseph staged the fire and burned the house down to get the insurance money."

"No way!" Pablo exclaimed. "Joseph would never do that!"

"Well, it seems that Joseph did just that!"

Matthew and Pablo were attempting to absorb this astounding information. "Is that a fact or a rumor?" Matthew asked.

"It's what I call a 'frumor'," Cosmo quipped. "Just made that word up. A rumor that is very, very close to being a fact."

"Cosmo," Matthew cautioned, "Myrna and Joseph could be perfectly innocent and you've pegged them as guilty."

"Matthew, what fun would it be if every juicy rumor had to be fact-checked? Huh?" Cosmo shot back. "Nobody would bother to gossip anymore."

Matthew shook his head. "Well, I plan to give them a call and see how they're holding up."

This morning, Myrna was troubled that Detective Jacobson insisted on meeting privately with Joseph. Therefore, she tried to distract herself by searching again for the missing earring she lost the night of the rally: the only gift Joseph ever gave her that she actually liked. She did not want Joseph to know that she lost it.

However, Myrna could not shake her anxiety about Joseph being questioned. She really wanted to be there with him to mitigate any damage that might result. A careless disclosure could be devastating. One fact remained clear to Myrna. She would do whatever needed to be done in order to learn who sent that anonymous note to the police.

Joseph was sweating in the air-conditioned police station as he waited to be called to Detective Jacobson's office. Within a couple of minutes, Detective Jacobson, himself, walked over to escort Joseph to his office. Adam closed the office door, sat down, and cleared his throat. "Joseph, have a seat. Our tech team searched through your mobile phone and found this voicemail dated Friday, September 23. I'll play it for you."

Adam studied Joseph carefully as Joseph listened to the message. *"Van Dyke. Eddie Siricco here. Funny, ain't it, that you need money and now your house burns down,"* Eddie cackled into the

179

phone. *"Now, I'm not saying that you did this or you didn't, but if the police found out, boy, would it look bad for you! Last chance to change your mind before it's too late."*

Adam waited silently as Joseph crossed and uncrossed his legs, rubbed his hands together, and stared down at his lap. At last, Adam merely asked, "Well?"

Joseph rested his elbows on the table and his head in his hands. "But I don't get it. I deleted that right away," Joseph declared dumbfounded.

Adam shrugged, "That's technology for you, Joseph. So now, start filling in the blanks. From his message, we know that Eddie tried to blackmail you. You need to tell me when he contacted you. You better give it to me straight." Adam folded his arms across his chest and leaned back in his chair.

"Eddie had found out about my gambling losses. No idea how he knew about them, but he did. He wanted money from me. He came to see me at home and I told him to get the hell out. That's about it."

"When did he do this?"

"It was Thursday. The same night as the fire."

"When you refused to pay him for his silence, what did Eddie say?"

"He told me I'd regret it."

"What did Eddie mean about your regretting it?"

180

"He threatened to tell Myrna and expose me to the entire Village. I'm on the board of the bank, you see."

"What stopped you from paying Eddie off?"

Joseph looked up at Adam and stated candidly, "I had no money. I had lost everything. How could I pay him off?"

Adam stood up and began pacing in front of Joseph. "So, you had no money and that same night your investment property happens to burn down. This is not looking good."

Joseph squirmed uncomfortably and nodded.

"Now, it's Friday and you get that voicemail from Eddie. It certainly looks to me as if the stakes have gotten much higher overnight. If Eddie manages to spread a rumor around that you burned your own house down, you're in deep shit." Adam stopped pacing and stood in front of Joseph. He raised his voice in exasperation. "You're on the board of the bank and probably could have managed to secure a loan. I don't understand why you didn't do whatever it took to pay Eddie off. Can you explain that to me, Joseph? I need to understand this. Tell me!" Adam leaned the palms of his hands on the table and glared at Joseph.

After an agonizing silence, Adam continued, "Now tell me the truth. Where were you on Sunday, September 25 between 9:00 and 11:00 in the evening?"

Joseph closed his eyes and muttered, "I was at home with Myrna all evening." Joseph did not have to look at Adam to know that Adam did not believe him. Shaking his head Joseph mumbled angrily,

"You didn't know Eddie Siricco! He would never have kept his damn mouth shut anyway."

"I guess there was only one sure way to shut Eddie Siricco up for good. That sounds like what you're telling me, Joseph Van Dyke." Adam sighed and sat down across from Joseph.

"No, that's not what I'm saying!" Joseph's lips tightened. "Damnit, I'm saying that Eddie Siricco wasn't capable of shutting his mouth! It wouldn't matter how much I paid him, Eddie would still..." he abruptly stopped talking. Joseph realized, too late, that his mouth had gotten way ahead of his brain. He had fallen, headfirst, right into Adam's trap.

Ellen's first opportunity to tell Charlie about her day occurred when she and Charlie were preparing dinner. Charlie was making a lemon spaghetti dish when his phone rang. He left the kitchen to take the call while Ellen made the salad. When Charlie returned, Ellen told him all about her conversation with Cosmo. "So, bottom line is that Phillip Edelstein and Ben Sheppard are in cahoots, Charlie. They are both out to destroy the Van Dykes "

"Okay, Ellen. This confirms what we already knew."

"And Cosmo heard them both threatening to destroy each other."

Charlie laughed, "Cosmo has no idea how helpful he has been!"

"I know. And, Charlie, I sold an expensive typewriter today. These two Millennials didn't know a thing about typewriters. I was so smooth, Charlie, you'd have been proud of me. I must humbly admit that they never would have bought it if I hadn't explained the fine points," Ellen boasted.

Charlie swallowed hard before speaking. "Ellen, please sit down." Charlie waited for Ellen to move to the table. "I just got a call from Adam. The two Millennials you're referring to were from his tech team. The Olympia typewriter you just sold types in cursive. They checked the imprints on the ribbon tape and found the exact words that were typed in the anonymous note."

Ellen was stunned and befuddled. "What are you saying, Charlie?"

"I'm saying that someone walked into our booth and typed the anonymous note for the police on our 1960's Olympia typewriter, Ellen."

Sunday, October 9

The rain today had very little impact on Water Street Market traffic on this holiday weekend. From the Mudd Puddle Cafe all the way to the Fry Shack, walkers left the rail trail to escape the rain. Customers were lining up at the Grazery for cheeses. They were enjoying brunch at The Parish. Cosmo was entertaining everyone with his witty repartee at the Antique Barn.

Dorothy opened up the Sunday supplement of the Daily Freeman and there was a centerfold with a photo of her in the middle. She greedily read aloud part of the article that followed. "*Dorothy Dawson has made a generous and charitable contribution to New Paltz. She has opened up her home and her heart to the gay couple who was left homeless after their house was burned to the ground on Beekman Road. Ms. Dawson wistfully referred to them as her 'poor, little, weekend refugees'.*" She walked to the mirror in the bathroom and crooned, "Academy-award winning performance! Bravo, Ms. Dawson."

Matthew made numerous attempts to contact Myrna and Joseph, but they never answered their phones. They were definitely avoiding him. Matthew began to wonder whether Cosmo's preposterous rumor could be true.

Joseph returned home from the police station yesterday having aged an entire decade in a single hour. He refused to speak with Myrna about it. She realized that her worst fear had, likely, materialized: Joseph had not kept his mouth shut when he needed to.

Phillip Edelstein relaxed at home with an espresso, strains of Vivaldi, and the New York Times this morning. He was supremely confident that he could easily manipulate the planning board into granting the necessary approvals in order for the land sale to go through. The greatest obstacle was conveniently out of the way: the Van Dykes.

Ben Sheppard was on his third mug of coffee this morning but that was not why he was jittery. He had expected to receive a signed contract several days ago from the development group looking to buy his property. If the buyers were getting cold feet about this deal, Ben was screwed. Or, better yet, he needed to make damn sure that it was Phillip who was screwed.

The Bird-Watchers, Catherine, Ted, Karen and Bud, were very excited to be arriving in Gardiner, just outside of New Paltz. The trip from Cape Coral, Florida to Gardiner, NY had been an epic journey. Bud was at the wheel of the RV with the women in the back belting out every Beatles song they could remember at the top of their lungs. Ted was the navigator and had spread out huge maps in front of him. He never trusted a G.P.S. There was no way he would allow a disembodied voice to tell him where and when to turn.

When they arrived at the entrance to Yogi Bear's Jellystone Park, they all began cheering wildly. For each of them, this trip had been both a joy and a challenge. For Catherine, her biggest challenge was relinquishing command of the expedition. For Ted, the challenge was to navigate and ignore everyone shouting directions at him. Driving had a hypnotic effect on Bud. His challenge was to stay awake while driving. Karen's challenge was to put on her make-up with substandard lighting. They checked in, received a tour of the resort and the facilities, and crashed for the rest of the afternoon.

Ellen and Charlie were surprised that Adam called them today. He invited them to the police station to observe his questioning of Phillip Edelstein scheduled for noon on Monday.

Adam Jacobson was looking forward to a completely non-productive day. This was his first full day and evening off in weeks. Aside from his one call to the Greens, Adam planned to chill and do absolutely nothing As soon as he sat down to check out the sports section of the Sunday paper, his phone beeped. Adam immediately regretted taking the call. "Hi, Mom." Adam paused as his mother spoke. "Really, Mom? Do I have to?" he pleaded. A few seconds later he moaned, "A lawyer? You know I don't like lawyers and I don't care if your friend Trudy thinks we'd be perfect for each other!" Adam listened impatiently. "Tonight? Yes, I'll be there. Of course. I promise not to be late," he grudgingly agreed and ended the call.

Monday, October 10

This morning, as Myrna poured them each a second cup of coffee, she demanded, "Joseph, you have to tell me what happened with Jacobson on Saturday. What did you tell him?"

Joseph shook his head. "Too much." Joseph told Myrna about the voicemail from Eddie.

Myrna tried to modulate her voice, but she could not contain her mounting anxiety. "You should have told me about a voicemail, Joseph!"

"I thought if I deleted it, it would disappear. Apparently, I was wrong."

"No kidding! What else happened?"

"Jacobson didn't believe my alibi. From the voicemail, he knows that Siricco tried to blackmail me. So Jacobson is convinced that I burned down the house and, then, murdered Eddie to keep him quiet. Other than that, nothing much," Joseph snapped.

"But, remember, we stick to the alibis no matter what. Agreed?"

"Yes, but Eddie's voicemail gives Jacobson's theory more weight and besides, I said something I probably shouldn't have."

Myrna barked back, "You might as well tell me what you said. I'll find out soon enough."

"I told him that I knew Eddie could never keep his mouth shut no matter how much I paid him."

"Shit, Joseph! I knew I shouldn't have left you alone with Jacobson. That was a stupid comment to make! Stupid!" Myrna added for emphasis. "I've heard enough. I'm heading into town."

Myrna stormed out of the townhouse and drove to Phillip Edelstein's office on Main Street. An officious-looking receptionist peered up and over her glasses at Myrna. "Yes? Do you have an appointment?"

"I am Myrna Van Dyke and I need to see Mr. Edelstein immediately. It is an urgent matter," Myrna retorted.

"Let me see if he's available," the receptionist replied, pressing a button. "Hey, wait! You can't go in there!"

Before the receptionist could stop her, Myrna marched to Phillip's office door and barged right in. Phillip was talking on his hands-free phone, legs propped up on the desk, a mug of coffee in his hand. Startled by the intrusion, he spilled his coffee and abruptly ended his call. "What the hell is going on, Myrna?" He grabbed a pile of napkins and began cleaning up the spill, furious that the coffee dripped onto his linen slacks.

"That's what I intend to find out, Phillip. It's more than a coincidence that after you threaten me if I don't support turning Ben Sheppard's property into a mega convention center, an anonymous note is sent to the police accusing Joseph of setting fire to his own house!"

"Sometimes, Myrna, coincidences do happen." Phillip gave a cocky grin. "Feel free to leave now."

"You sent a note to the police, didn't you?" Myrna accused.

"If you're so sure I sent it, why didn't you tell that to the police? Huh?" Phillip clasped his hands behind his head and leaned way back in his ergonomic desk chair. "I think you've got a couple of secrets of your own, Myrna."

Myrna chose to ignore that comment and, instead, took the offensive. "If you think you can destroy us, you're wrong. You're an arrogant bastard!"

"Why, so I've been told. Thank-you, Myrna. That reputation is purely the result of hard work," he said derisively.

At that moment, the receptionist buzzed in to Phillip's office. "Mr. Edelstein, your 10:00 appointment is here. Shall I send him in?"

"Mrs. Van Dyke is leaving now. Yes, please. Thanks, Sandra."

Before Myrna left Phillip's office, the 10:00 appointment entered. Phillip relished his turn to surprise Myrna. He graciously said, "Myrna Van Dyke, I don't know if you've met my client, Ben Sheppard. He's selling his property on Milo Road."

"I certainly know of you, Mr. Sheppard," Myrna responded sweetly, reaching out to shake his hand. "If I were you, I'd hire an attorney who can do more than cower behind anonymous notes. You're going to need one with some balls." She continued moving towards the door without even glancing back at the two buffoons left in her wake.

As soon as Myrna walked out the door, Ben roared with laughter. "Well, well, well, Phillip. Myrna Van Dyke has got your number. So, you snitched on Joseph, you sneaky rat!" Ben decided that he needed more dirt on Phillip and now he knew exactly where to get it.

Dismissing Ben's comment, Phillip got right down to the business at hand. "Look, Sheppard, we're meeting here to call and find out why the buyers are screwing around with this contract. I'll put the call on 'speaker'. Go ahead."

By the time Ben was able to get past the various assistant administrators and office staff, he was connected with Kevin, an up-and-coming real estate magnate. In a cheery voice, Kevin said, "Hi there, Ben. It's Kevin. What's up?"

"Kevin, that's what I'd like to know. The contract has not been returned and I've got some eager buyers waiting in the wings, hoping that you back out of this."

Kevin gave a hearty chuckle. "That's an old trick, Ben, and nobody's fallen for it in the last fifty years. Here's what's happening at our end. I'm going to send you an amended contract stating that prior to a formal commitment to buy, the buyer needs proof that all the necessary land use approvals have been okayed. Not a big change, but that's the only way they'll be willing to proceed."

Ben sighed, "We'll need another week to secure the planning board's approval."

"Not a problem. I'll have my people draw up an amendment to the contract and we'll get it out to you."

"When should I expect to receive it?"

"Ben, hah! You really are a dinosaur," Kevin chided. "I'll send it to you today, virtually. You can sign it, virtually, and email it back to us. Good talking to you, Ben. Gotta go."

Phillip Edelstein's reputation as a barracuda was well-earned and something in which he took great pride. As Ben Sheppard's lawyer and fixer, Phillip had access to Ben's confidential files. Within those incriminating files was all the documentation Phillip needed to be sure that Ben lived up to his end of the agreement no matter what happened with the land deal.

Sergeant O'Riley escorted Ellen and Charlie to the observation room where a one-sided window looked out into the small room where Adam was going to question Phillip Edelstein. From Adam's side, the window appeared to be, merely, a mirror. Ellen and Charlie each received headphones to wear to access the audio. After testing the microphone, Adam was ready to begin his interview. He asked Sergeant O'Riley to escort Phillip to the interrogation room, affectionately known as 'The Closet'.

Phillip had no idea why he had been summoned, but strode in with his usual air of arrogance. After introductions and a couple of formalities, Phillip casually pointed out, "I'm used to being the one asking the questions rather than the one answering them, Detective."

"Just tell the truth and you'll do fine," Adam reassured him. "Please confirm that you have chosen to be questioned without the presence of an attorney."

Phillip smiled, "I'm the best attorney I know, so yes, I am willing to be questioned without another attorney present. But, please tell me why I am here."

"You're here because you've been summoned here. Now, have you ever been to the Antique Barn at Water Street Market?"

Phillip shrugged, "Probably. Hasn't everybody?"

"Mr. Edelstein, let me remind you. I ask the questions and you answer them. When were you last at the Antique Barn?"

"I might have wandered around there to waste some time--oh, perhaps, a few weeks ago."

Adam opened up a cabinet and placed Ellen and Charlie's 1960's Olympia on the table. "Ever see this before?"

"Well, Detective, I used one of these back in college. But haven't used a typewriter in almost fifty years."

"Someone used this very typewriter to send an anonymous note to the police alleging that Joseph Van Dyke appeared to be setting his own place on fire." Adam placed a copy of the note on the table in front of Phillip. "Did you send this note?"

"Absolutely not. Why would I do something like that?"

"Again, Mr. Edelstein, I ask the questions," Adam said flatly. "Well, perhaps you can tell me where you were on Thursday, September 22 throughout the evening."

"Let me see. I worked late that night and went to the Clemson Brewery for a quick burger and a beer. That's about it. I had some briefs to review at home before going to bed."

Adam scratched his head looking bemused."You know, Edelstein, if someone asked me the same question, I'd be hard-pressed to remember. The week nights all tend to blend together. How did you instantly recall where you were weeks ago?"

"My extraordinary memory, Sir. My work as an attorney is dependent on my remembering the smallest detail. That's one of my strengths. I'd probably make a great detective," Phillip said glibly.

Adam continued. "Can anyone verify your whereabouts that evening between 9:00 and 10:00?"

"No way. You've got to take my word for it," Phillip smiled amiably.

Abruptly changing the subject Adam stated, "How do you get along with the Van Dykes?"

"I know who they are but I don't have anything to do with them personally." He shrugged dismissively, "I don't have any problems with them."

"Now, Edelstein, I'm surprised to hear that." Adam opened up his laptop. "I'm looking at minutes from several very tense planning board meetings over the last couple of years. In each case, you were looking to turn farmland into a commercial development and in each case, the board would not grant you the land use approvals."

Phillip nodded, "That's right. I see you've done your homework, Detective. What of it?"

"At every one of these contentious meetings, the Van Dykes had mobilized their troops in protest. Without their demonstrations, you might have received permission to develop those properties."

"You win some and you lose some," Phillip shrugged indifferently.

"Mr. Edelstein, quite frankly, you lost every single time," Adam pointed out. "By the way, how much did you lend Ben to clear up his debts on the Milo Road land?"

"Sir, that's strictly between me and Ben."

"And what percentage of the sale price do you get, Edelstein, when the deal goes through? Twenty? Thirty? More? Come on. What's in it for you?"

Phillip tried to steady his left leg by crossing it over his right one. He remained stonily silent.

Adam continued, "What a lucky break for you that Joseph Van Dyke is accused of burning down his own house. At long last, you should be able to get the necessary land use approvals from the planning board with no problem." Adam began pacing in front of Phillip. He stopped pacing to lean the palms of his hands on the table. "Ben Sheppard's property on Milo Road would sure be worth a lot of money if a hotel could be built on it."

Ellen noticed that whenever Phillip was uncomfortable with a question, he rubbed his upper right arm.

"Like I said, Detective, you win some and you lose some," Phillip replied with an insolent grin. "Looks like I won this time. Lucky coincidence."

"I don't believe in coincidences and neither do you," Adam shot back. He stood up and began pacing once again. "In fact, Edelstein, I think you made absolutely certain that the Van Dykes couldn't stand in your way this time."

"What the hell are you saying?" Phillip asked, vigorously rubbing his upper arm.

Adam sat back down across the table from Phillip and in a measured tone stated, "It wouldn't surprise me if you started that fire in order to frame Joseph Van Dyke. Maybe you did and maybe you didn't. But I sure as hell think you saw the fire as an opportunity to nail Joseph Van Dyke." Pointing his finger accusingly at Phillip Adam declared, "You wrote that anonymous note."

Phillip leaned back in his chair and snickered, "I've got to hand it to you, Detective. You've got a great imagination! Why would I do that when I'll have no problem getting the planning board to approve the development with or without the Van Dykes? This development is a win-win for the community. Simple as that."

"I'm asking you again, Edelstein. Did you send that anonymous note to the police?"

Phillip folded his arms across his chest and announced, "I already answered that question. Are we finished here?"

"No. You're staying right here. I'm not through with you. But, we'll take a five minute break. Help yourself to water. I'll be right back."

Adam stepped into the observation room to join the Greens. "So, what are your impressions?"

Ellen said, "Watch whenever Phillip rubs his right upper arm. You've obviously made him uncomfortable and whatever follows is probably a lie."

"Why, thanks, Ellen. Never noticed that," Adam admitted.

"And that's why I think Phillip was the one who sent the note," Charlie added. "But why wouldn't he just admit that he sent it and be done?"

"Because he's an attorney and he knows that if you admit to anything at all, a lot of questions are apt to follow."

"So, where is the next round leading?" Charlie asked.

Adam winked, "Stay tuned." He left and walked back into 'The Closet' to finish questioning Phillip.

"Let's start a new topic: Eddie Siricco," Adam began. "When did you last see him?"

"Eddie was painting the trim at Water Street Market at Antiques on Main. It was a Monday morning."

"That would be Monday, September 19," Adam clarified as he looked at his notes. "Did you talk to him?"

"No, well, we greeted each other," Phillip said, rubbing his arm.

"Were you there alone?"

"No, I was with Ben Sheppard. We were having coffee that morning."

"Where were you sitting?"

"In the courtyard at a table."

"Where was the table? Near the Mudd Puddle?"

"No. It was at the opposite end. Eddie was working right above us that morning." Phillip began rubbing his upper arm again.

"So, that's when Ben told you about his Milo Road offer," Adam added. "Could Eddie have overheard your conversation?"

"I suppose, but not likely. He didn't seem to be paying attention."

"Was he close enough to hear you?"

"I suppose. Yes."

"Well, suppose, for a minute, that Eddie did hear your conversation. That could present a serious problem, Edelstein."

"Absolutely not. We weren't plotting anything illegal. Ben talked about having a possible buyer for his property. That's it." Phillip continued rubbing his upper arm.

Adam stood looming above Phillip. "You're lying. Eddie knew that you were going to, and I quote, take care of the Van Dykes. What did you mean by that?"

"Is this what you call an investigation? You're pathetic, Jacobson."

"Just answer my question."

"I planned to speak with the Van Dykes and enlist their cooperation."

"When did you do that?"

"I, uh, I met up with Joseph later that same day--at Clemson Brewery."

"Go on."

"He told me he'd think about it," Phillip said as he vigorously massaged his upper right arm.

"I'll have to see if Joseph's version is the same. You know, Eddie called you a 'friggin' fixer'." Adam folded his arms across his chest. "Eddie Siricco must have known exactly what you were up to."

From the observation window, Ellen nudged Charlie. "Look at that. Phillip's going to rub a hole right through his designer shirt sleeve if he keeps at it!"

Phillip glared at Adam and said, "Siricco knew how to stir up trouble where there wasn't any. Everybody knew that. That was his job. And nothing I did was illegal."

Adam was beginning to connect the dots and decided he had learned what he needed to learn from this arrogant, egotistical bullshitter. "Where were you on Sunday, September 25 between 9:30 and 10:30 at night?"

"I can tell you exactly where I was. I was meeting with a client in my office late that evening."

"I'd like to verify that information."

"I'll bet you would, but you and I both know that's privileged information. I'll never give up my client's name to you. Now, are we finished?"

"Stay close to home. We're not nearly finished, Edelstein."

Tuesday, October 11

Adam decided to pay a visit to the Van Dykes this morning. He rang the bell.

Myrna scowled, ""Oh, it's you. Come on in. What good news have you got for us today?"

"Hi, Myrna. I'd like to speak with Joseph if he is available."

Myrna turned towards the den and shouted, "Joseph, are you available? It's Inspector Clouseau."

Joseph shuffled to the living room to greet Adam. "You came to our place. This must be important."

"May I sit down?"

"Of course."

Myrna said, "I'd offer you some coffee, Detective, but I'm hoping you won't be here long enough to drink it. How about a quick shot of whiskey, instead?"

Adam tried to hide the smile that wanted to emerge. "No thanks, Myrna. Since we last met, Joseph, I've learned that Phillip Edelstein met with you at the Clemson Brewery on Monday, September 19. What did he want to see you about?"

Myrna answered for Joseph. "He never met with Joseph! Right?"

"Myrna, I asked Joseph the question, not you. Joseph, please answer the question."

"I don't really remember it very well."

"Well, let me refresh your memory. It seems that Edelstein wanted to make sure you didn't stand in the way of the planning board approvals for the Milo Road property."

"Oh, yes," Joseph mumbled hesitantly. "We met for a beer and he talked about the hotel/conference center proposal."

"Did you agree to back off and let the board approve this use of the land?"

Myrna began fiddling with her peace sign pendant as she waited for Joseph's response.

"Joseph, I've asked you a question. Did you agree to back off or not? Yes or no."

"No. I refused." Joseph spoke in a barely audible whisper.

"And how did Phillip respond?"

"He was not happy."

"Look, Joseph, tell me what he said to you. This is very important."

"He got angry and said that he would destroy me. He was talking about exposing my gambling debts. He said, and I do remember his exact words, 'don't say I didn't warn you'."

Myrna stiffened as Joseph revealed meeting with Phillip. She had no idea that Joseph had met with him. "Why the hell didn't you tell me you met with that big shot wannabe?" she fumed.

Adam asked impatiently, "I'm wondering the same thing. Why didn't you mention meeting with Phillip Edelstein before today? I don't get it."

Joseph merely shrugged.

"Joseph, if you knew that Edelstein was out to destroy you, why the hell wouldn't you want me to know?" Adam was becoming very frustrated. "You're hiding something," Adam stated. "Whatever it is, I'll find out," he warned.

Joseph did not budge. Instead, he tried to shift the focus. "So, you think Edelstein sent the anonymous note?"

"What do you think?" Adam asked.

"It's becoming more and more likely."

"Now I know that Edelstein was threatening you and Eddie Siricco was attempting to blackmail you. I have to wonder if you had reached your breaking point," Adam surmised, staring into Joseph's face. "So, once again, Joseph, where were you on Sunday, September 25 between 9:00 and 11:00 PM?"

Myrna stood up and yelled, "Joseph was with me! We were sitting right here in our condo. Now, you can get the hell out of here, Detective!"

Adam ignored Myrna's outburst and turned to Joseph again. "You need to tell me where you were on Sunday, September 25 between 9:00 and 11:00 PM."

Joseph stammered, "Myrna's right. We were both here in our condo."

Dorothy fluttered out the entrance of the Denizen Theatre with Leonard close at her heels. She cried out, "Leonard, Desdemona is a tortured soul. She is a veritable kaleidoscope of conflicting emotions. She cannot be contained!" Dorothy spotted Ellen at a courtyard table and swooped down, landing in the chair across from her. "Ellen, I swear, Leonard thinks he can control Desdemona! What madness!"

Ellen was in the middle of reviewing her list of sales at the Antique Barn for the month of September. She was startled by this rush of indignation that suddenly arrived. She looked up, removed her glasses, and said, "When men try to control women, they play right into our hands, Dorothy. As soon as they underestimate us, the fun begins."

"How true, Ellen. I must remember that."

"Dorothy, tell me about your career. Were you always a stage actor?" Ellen leaned her elbow on the table and rested her head in the palm of her hand.

Dorothy entertained Ellen with a highly fictionalized account of her starring roles, beginning with the Westport Playhouse in Connecticut. "And, did you know that Paul, Paul Newman that is, was very limited as a stage actor?"

"Do tell, Dorothy!" Ellen urged. "Paul Newman? You acted with Paul Newman?"

"Well," she whispered, "we played opposite each other in 'Streetcar Named Desire' and, let me put it this way. My 'Stella' was considerably more powerful than his 'Stanley'."

Ellen was loving this insider info. "But, Dorothy, how did you get your big break?"

"Ellen, it's a bittersweet story. One summer, when I was barely out of high school, I was part of the costume crew for 'The Miracle Worker'. That's the story of Helen Keller. But, I studied every line of Annie Sullivan and could play the part better than the little birdbrain who was cast in the role. Anyhow, two days before we opened, she had an unfortunate accident during the dress rehearsal."

"What happened?" Ellen asked.

Dorothy began to giggle as she recalled the incident. "She was changing her costume for the second scene and, by mistake, a razor blade had been left in the side seam above the waist."

"Ooh!" Ellen cringed on hearing this.

"Poor thing lost so much blood, she had to go to the hospital and the director needed someone to fill in for her. I volunteered, received rave reviews, and the rest is history," she smiled.

"Oh, my God! Just like 'Sunset Boulevard' and Norma Desmond," Ellen declared.

"Alas!" Dorothy lamented.

Ellen and Charlie were looking forward to seeing Catherine and Ted, Karen and Bud tonight. They were all meeting at Ward's Bridge Inn for dinner. By the time Ellen and Charlie arrived at Ward's Bridge Inn, the bar was overflowing with happy hour customers. Marc was bartending tonight and he was moving at an impressive pace to fill drink orders and shmooze with everyone.

Charlie had called ahead so they could reserve the big round table in the front dining room. He and Ellen were seated and waiting when the four traveling vagabonds arrived. They greeted each other with a rowdy round of hugs and back-slaps.

Catherine spoke up first. "It's great to see you both, but it's even better to be waited on and eat whatever I want." She gave Ted an imperious look.

Karen chimed in, "Bud and Ted wanted us to fully experience camping by grilling our dinners every single night. I never want to eat another hot dog again! Tonight, I want to start with a whisky sour and a shrimp cocktail." Karen purred.

Tara came over to take their drink and dinner orders. Charlie introduced her to everyone. "Tara, these friends have saved our butts when Ellen and I were investigating murders."

"Well, then, I'm pleased to meet you. Now, what would you like to order?" Tara asked with a smile.

After everyone placed their dinner orders, the four of them regaled Ellen and Charlie with their adventures on the road. They heard about getting lost in the Smoky Mountains and running out of gas near Savannah. And, there was the bear that joined Karen and Catherine on their walk one day. Throughout dinner, the laughter proved that what had been viewed as catastrophic at the moment, had already become a priceless memory.

By the time they were finishing up their dinners, Ellen and Charlie's friends, Hugh and Ginger, headed over to greet them. Hugh said, "We just arrived for dinner and saw you sitting in the corner."

"Hey, there! Let me introduce you. These are our good friends, Hugh and Ginger. Meet our Cape Coral adopted family: Catherine, Ted, Karen and Bud," Charlie announced. "They've all driven up North together in an RV."

"And you're still speaking to each other?" Ginger asked in amazement. "Wait a minute. Aren't you the Bird-Watchers Ellen has told me about?"

Catherine nodded with pride. "Yes, we are!"

"I'm so glad to meet you at long last. I've heard all about how Ellen and Charlie have had to protect you. It sounds like they've been your--well, your guardian angels!"

All eyes shifted to Ellen who slid so far down in her chair, her head was barely visible. Catherine's raised eyebrow and unrelenting glare said it all. She declared, "Well, Ginger, perspective is everything. Right, Ellen?"

Charlie came to Ellen's rescue. "Ginger, I think there may have been a miscommunication. Ellen meant exactly the opposite. Actually, the Bird-Watchers have saved our butts. Not the other way around." He put his arm around Ellen's shoulder. "Isn't that right, my dear?" Ellen nodded docilely.

"Glad we cleared up that little slip of the tongue," Bud grinned. "Nice to meet you both."

"You, too!" Hugh agreed. "Have a wonderful visit up North."

"Thanks. We're enjoying it already. Hope you enjoy your dinner," Catherine added.

"Great to meet all of you! See you soon, Ellen," Ginger said with a wink.

Karen spoke softly, "Ellen and Charlie, now tell us about the murder that you're investigating."

"What murder?" they both lied in unison.

Catherine finished chewing a bite of her strip steak and shot them a haughty look. "You, two, are terrible liars. We came prepared for action, so you might as well make it easier for yourselves and tell us what the hell you've stuck your noses into this time. Isn't that right, Bird-Watchers?"

Ben Sheppard wanted the power to destroy Phillip before Phillip destroyed him. Ben may not be the quickest guy in the race but, he had learned enough to crush Phillip. Still, Ben decided he needed more ammunition. It was about shifting the balance of power clearly in his direction. Ben wanted to arrange a meeting with an unlikely ally: Myrna Van Dyke. Ben knew that he and Myrna were both determined to have the power to screw over Phillip Edelstein.

Chief Liberti called a meeting with the team of detectives investigating the Eddie Siricco murder. "Detective Jacobson will brief you on the progress." He gestured to Adam at the opposite end of the table.

Adam began, "Here's where things stand. We have discovered Eddie Siricco's personal notepad. He liked to write down ideas, phrases, tidbits to use in his Town Crier column. If you look on the screen behind me you will see photos of his most recent pages in his own handwriting." Adam used the cursor to point to various scribbles. "Eddie seemed to have an adversarial relationship with our most likely suspect: Joseph Van Dyke." Adam turned around and pointed out the various slurs Eddie used to refer to the Van Dykes.

Adam continued, "Here you can see that Siricco began a draft of a Town Crier piece that never made it to the newspaper. It was dated Wednesday, September 21. On that date he wrote this line that refers to the Van Dykes protesting the Milo Road development. The word 'they' refers to the Van Dykes. *I wonder how they can be stopped? Or do I?*"

"Jacobson, you're saying that Eddie Siricco knew that Edelstein was going to stop them."

"It sounds that way to me."

"Why not Sheppard? It was his property." Detective Larson asked.

"Some good, old-fashioned digging uncovered the history that Edelstein had with them. The Van Dykes had been his nemesis, successfully opposing every development that Edelstein invested in. We're almost certain that Edelstein wrote the anonymous note."

"Do you think he framed Van Dyke and started the fire himself?" asked the detective seated on his right.

"It's a possibility, but Edelstein is smart and not likely to do something that could result in criminal charges. Besides, he didn't have to. The accusation, alone, was enough to destroy the Van Dykes. But, Eddie Siricco was a scoundrel and saw how to leverage this information. We know Siricco definitely blackmailed and threatened Van Dyke and possibly did the same to Edelstein."

"So both of these guys would want to get rid of Siricco for good," Larson surmised.

"That's right, Larson." Adam continued, "Siricco's notes are filled with references to Ben Sheppard, as well." Adam pointed out, "*'lowlife land owner'* and *'snitch, sneak, and snatch'.* Siricco had nothing good to say about Ben Sheppard. Not sure what Siricco had on him."

"But what about the comments about Dorothy Dawson? That makes no sense. Why tear her apart?"

"She was his ex-wife. Any of you have an ex?" A rumble of groans traveled around the table. Adam grinned. "Need I say more?"

Liberti jumped in. "All of this is good intel but, damnit, we've got just a few more days before the Mayor kicks our butts out of this building for good! I won't stand for it. I know you are better than this. Now act like you are!" Shaking his finger at each one seated around the table, Liberti warned, "You need to name a person of interest for his honor the Mayor and it better be done by Friday! No excuses!"

Liberti stood up and lumbered out of the conference room. The remaining officers sat with their mouths gaping open, unable to speak. Adam somberly adjourned the meeting. He dragged himself back to his office and poured over Eddie Siricco's scribbles. Adam was certain that he was overlooking something important.

This morning, Ben Sheppard waited to speak with Michelle at the Mudd Puddle. He ordered a cappuccino and explained his predicament. "Hi, Michelle, I left my sweatshirt in the courtyard when I was here for the rally, a couple of weeks ago. Could you give me Myrna Van Dyke's phone number so I can see if she found it?"

"You were at the rally?" Michelle asked skeptically, but was too busy to question him further. Besides, she was too disillusioned with the Van Dykes to care. "Here you go." She quickly showed him Myrna's contact information.

"Thanks, Michelle," Ben said, stepping aside to make his call. He left Myrna a voicemail inviting her to meet him at Water Street

Market to discuss their mutual contact. Within a few minutes he received a text reply: "OK".

Ellen arrived at the Antique Barn this morning, waving hello to Barbara and Paul, two other dealers in the shop. They waved back as they privately huddled together with Cosmo and Walter.

"Oh, my God! I can't believe it." Cosmo caught Ellen halfway up the stairs. "Hey, Ellen, honey, you've gotta hear this!"

Not wanting to miss a single word, Ellen rushed back down and joined them. "What's going on?" she asked eagerly.

Barbara explained, "Well, you know how our space is tucked away in the corner. A few items have been stolen from our booth so we installed a fake camera last week."

Ellen nodded, "That's a smart move on your part."

Paul was totally baffled. "That's what we thought until this morning."

"What do you mean?"

"Someone stole the damn camera! They had to climb up on a ladder and unscrew the entire piece to get it down. I can't believe it!" Barbara exclaimed.

"Nine bucks thrown away. Just like that!" Paul replied snapping his fingers.

"Your fake camera? You've gotta be kidding!" Ellen shook her head. Cosmo burst out laughing.

Raising one eyebrow, Walter matter-of-factly stated, "You may want to check out Robert's space. Wouldn't surprise me if it happened to end up there." Walter walked away to unpack a box of glasses.

Ellen looked out the door at the courtyard. She squinted to get a better look at a sturdy woman wearing a wide-brimmed, floppy hat and sunglasses. The woman's identity would have been completely camouflaged were it not for her signature Birkenstocks. "Myrna Van Dyke," she muttered to herself. Turning to Cosmo she asked, "Cosmo, see the woman with the big hat?"

"Quite the looker," he quipped sarcastically.

"Stop that, Cosmo!" Ellen scolded. "Who is that man with her? Do you know?"

"Oh, yeah. That's Ben Sheppard, the owner of the property..."

As soon as Ellen heard the name, she stepped outside to get a closer view.

"We both know why we're here," Myrna snarled.

"You don't know as much as you think you do," Ben retorted.

"Let's skip the pleasantries. We both want to screw Phillip Edelstein. So, tell me what you've got on him," Myrna demanded.

"Now, Myrna, not so fast."

"Look, just tell me what you can hold over the conniving weasel."

"Let's start with what we both have figured out: Edelstein wrote the note to the police."

"Look, Sheppard, I'm not comfortable talking to you here. Someone is going to recognize me. Come to my place. Joseph isn't around today. Here's the address." Myrna wrote her address on a napkin and handed it to Ben.

He nodded. "Okay. I'll meet you there."

Ellen saw them both get up to leave. She darted to the back door to watch Myrna get into her white Prius. As soon as the coast was clear, Ellen bolted to her own car, put on her sunglasses, pulled down her baseball cap, and tailed Myrna. She arrived at Myrna's townhouse and parked further down the street to avoid detection. A second car pulled into Myrna's driveway. Ben Sheppard got out and went to the front door.

"Come on in. We can sit on the porch out back where it's more private," Myrna suggested leading the way. "I'll make us some coffee." Myrna reheated the leftover coffee in the microwave. "You want milk? Sugar?"

"Just some milk. Thanks," Ben replied.

Myrna joined him on the screened-in porch. "Okay, so we figure Edelstein wrote the note. Big deal. Tell me, Sheppard. What is it that you want out of this?"

"No way. You tell me what you're after."

Ellen was frustrated. She needed to get closer to hear what this covert rendezvous was all about. She got out of her car and sneaked around to the side of Myrna's townhouse. Ellen crouched down on the strip of lawn separating Myrna's townhouse from her neighbor's. She pulled out of her purse the glass she always carried with her for eavesdropping. By placing one end on her ear and the other end on the outside wall of the porch, Ellen was able to hear their conversation.

"You already know. I want the insurance settlement from the fire."

Ben gave Myrna a lop-sided grin. "Good, now we're getting somewhere. And I want the approvals to go through so I can finally sell off my Milo Road property."

"But without Phillip, you haven't got a chance. You'd have to shower that week before the planning board would even let you in the door." Myrna eyed Ben critically.

"Now, Myrna, I'm going to ignore that nasty comment. See, that's what makes my situation particularly sensitive. You're right. I need Phillip and I wish I didn't. I need him to use his connections but then I want to have the power to make him go away."

"And why, might I ask?"

Ben cackled, "You don't need to know why. Just know I want to get him as bad as you do. So now what?"

"Look, Sheppard, this meeting was your idea. You tell me!"

"Okay, here's what we can do. We've got to blame the fire on someone else or you're going down. Plain and simple. Let's say Phillip set the fire."

"You really are a nincompoop. How do we prove that?" Myrna was certain that although Ben was a con artist, he had the IQ of a gnat.

"Myrna, Phillip alleged that Joseph burned down the house. If he had proof, he would have shown it by now. So he doesn't have any more evidence than we do, but he has a motive. He wanted to destroy you and Joseph to get the approvals. Isn't that a worthy motive?" Ben raised his hands, palms up.

"So, why didn't you accuse him of arson before now?" Myrna asked.

"I need him to sway the planning board. Why haven't you said anything to the police about your suspicion that Phillip wrote the note?"

"I have my reasons," was all Myrna was willing to admit.

"But, if we frame Phillip..." Ben ruminated.

"Sheppard, *we* cannot frame Phillip. It has to be *you.* Nobody would believe a thing I said." She took a long sip of her coffee. She knew they would have to create an elaborate series of lies to convince the police. Could Ben really pull it off, she wondered?

Ben seemed to mull this thought over in his head. "Okay, but it has to wait until after the planning board meets. Until then, I need the bastard."

"When do they meet?"

Ben grinned, "Thursday, tomorrow, at three."

Myrna lifted her coffee cup to toast their hostile alliance. A loud commotion outside caused Myrna to spill her coffee. She popped out of her chair and flew out the porch door to see what was going on. Ellen had attempted to edge her way closer to the door when she tripped over the handle of a shovel that was on the ground. Her glass dropped and shattered loudly against the shovel. "What the hell are you doing snooping around?" Myrna shouted as she grabbed Ellen by the arm. "Go on inside and tell me what you're up to."

Ellen was mortified by her own clumsiness but secretly delighted with what she was learning. Scanning the room, she saw no sign of Ben Sheppard. "I've been worried about you and Joseph and wanted to see how you're holding up."

Myrna put her hands on her hips and glared, "You're full of it! You were spying on me. Who do you think you are, anyway? Wonder Woman?"

Ellen knew she had to take the offensive. "Aren't you even going to offer me some coffee?" she shot back, returning Myrna's glare.

"Sit down and don't you dare move! I'll get it."

"Black, please," Ellen said sweetly.

Dorothy was beyond exhausted. This one-woman play had her frazzled. Leonard was insistent that she remember every line, exactly as that little twit wrote it. Dorothy truly believed that she, Dorothy, was the embodiment of Desdemona and, therefore, perfectly equipped to utter extemporaneous monologues. This free-styling covered up the truth; memorizing all those lines was impossible for her. With barely one week before her opening, Dorothy was on that fragile cusp teetering between glory and catastrophe.

Therefore, when Detective Adam Jacobson summoned her back in for questioning, she had little appetite for this unwanted intrusion into her already tumultuous life. Dorothy presented herself at Sergeant O'Riley's desk wearing oversized sunglasses to cover up the ravages of age. Puffy eyelids and bags underneath her eyes needed a full two hours of vigorous cucumber treatments before the fluids finally chose to redistribute themselves.

"I'm Dorothy Dawson here to meet with Detective Jacobson."

"Certainly, Ms. Dawson. This way."

Adam's door was open. "Ms. Dawson, please come in and have a seat."

"Detective, what was so urgent that you needed to see me again?" Dorothy reprimanded him.

"My apologies, Ms. Dawson. Would you like some coffee?"

"Yes. Black, no sugar. French press would be nice," she added.

Adam gave her an amused shake of his head as he walked to his Mr. Coffee machine. "Here you are."

"Thank-you. Now, what is it that you want to ask me about? I have to be at rehearsal by one."

"Dorothy, tell me more about Eddie and why you divorced."

"Not much more to tell. He was a scoundrel. Always looking to get the goods on someone and use it against them. He liked to run his mouth about people. A small-time crook. His drinking was what did us in."

"Were you in touch with him over the years?"

"No. I saw him for the first time at Water Street Market when I arrived back in town."

"And tell me, again, what you talked with him about."

"He made some disparaging remarks about my acting ability. I think he was terribly jealous that I have been a successful actress and am about to reach the pinnacle of my career."

Ignoring Dorothy's grossly inflated self-assessment Adam stated, "Eddie had written parts of a Town Crier piece that was never completed. In it, he talked about you. And I quote, '*Star power has arrived to the Denizen--or has it? Dorothy Dawson will finally end her less than spectacular career. Watch her humiliation erupt. And I say good riddance.*' After all those years, Eddie sounded very bitter."

"Like I said, he was very jealous of my success."

"What did he mean by '*Watch her humiliation erupt*'?"

"Haven't the faintest, Detective. He was a bitter, vindictive man," she said nonchalantly, peering over the top of her glasses.

"You both shared a history."

"An ancient history, Detective, from the bowels of the pyramids."

"Regardless, Eddie knew a lot about you. He was killed because he knew a lot about someone and didn't keep his mouth shut. What did he know about you that you wouldn't want anyone to know?"

"Tsk, tsk. That's a very impertinent question, Detective Jacobson," Dorothy replied shaking her finger at him. "Well, I suppose Eddie knew that I had several indiscretions with my leading men. And, I suppose that may have contributed to our marital problems, but," Dorothy whispered, "Eddie's drinking left him, well, shall I say, lacking in that department. I have a very passionate nature,

Detective, and needed to find a suitable outlet. It was a matter of survival."

Adam found Dorothy entertaining, but frustrating. He took a deep breath and continued. "Dorothy, where were you on Sunday, September 25 between 9:00 and 11:00 in the evening?"

Dorothy's jaw dropped with that question. "Sir, are you implying...?"

"Please answer the question, Dorothy."

"I was home starting to rehearse my lines." Dorothy thrust back her shoulders. "You see, I had recently received word from Leonard, the director, that I was to play Desdemona. And I am a seasoned professional. It is a complex process when one begins a new role. I went to my flat and spent uninterrupted hours dissecting the script. Anything else, Detective?"

"Did you leave your flat at any time that evening?"

"Detective, listen to my words. I was totally immersed in, not just playing but, becoming Desdemona. Now, if you'll excuse me, Desdemona calls. Tada!" With her parting line, Dorothy floated out of Adam's office.

While Myrna was in the kitchen heating up coffee, Ellen was dying to find out what happened to Ben Sheppard. She tiptoed inside and peered around the living room. As she quietly turned to where the bedrooms were, a hairy arm reached out and grabbed her arm, twisting it behind her back. A hand covered her mouth, silencing her as Ellen was dragged back into the living room.

"Who is she and what the hell is she doing here?" Ben Sheppard growled.

Myrna put down the mug of coffee and spewed. "I told you not to move!" Turning to Ben she explained, "She's Ellen Green, general pain-in-the-ass busybody. Doesn't know when to butt out!"

Ellen's phone 'can-canned'. She tried to reach for it, but Ben warned her, "No way, lady. Now sit down." He plunked Ellen down on the dining room chair and warned, "I'll remove my hand, but one loud squawk out of you and that mouth'll be duct-taped. I want to know what you heard!" he demanded.

Ellen was determined not to panic as she assessed this dire situation. Myrna was sluggish and Ellen could outrun her, but Ben Sheppard could be trouble. She feigned a sneezing fit. She could barely catch her breath before the next round of sneezes began. "A tissue, please," Ellen muttered. "I know I brought some. Allergies," she gasped, rummaging around in her purse.

Myrna went to get some tissues. She returned with a wad of toilet paper which she handed to Ellen. Ellen knew that she had a slim chance of escaping and she had to go for it in the next second. In one swift motion, Ellen whipped out the pepper spray she always carried with her, squirted Myrna smack in the eyes, and aimed the spray right at Ben Sheppard's craggy face as she darted out the front door.

Ellen sprinted to her car and drove off. When she reached the Albany Post Road, she finally pulled over and waited until she stopped shaking. She reached in her purse and cradled the can of pepper spray that Detective Sergeant Raul Swann, back in Cape Coral, had insisted she carry with her at all times.

Later that evening Ellen wanted to share what she learned about Myrna and Ben Sheppard today. She was willing to endure the safety lecture from Charlie that was sure to follow. Ellen waited until Charlie was on his second glass of sauvignon blanc before embarking on this delicate mission. "So Charlie, I finally met the elusive Ben Sheppard today."

"Really? Tell me about it."

"He and Myrna met at Water Street Market and Myrna was barely recognizable. She was trying to be incognito but her Birkenstocks gave her away," Ellen laughed attempting to keep this rendition light and fluffy. "Anyhow, I followed them to Myrna's condo and got quite an earful," Ellen added with a distinct touch of smugness.

"You followed them? That was crazy, Ellen!"

"Perhaps, but, Charlie, wait till you hear what they're up to! They both are out to get Phillip Edelstein and have decided that Ben is going to claim that Phillip started the fire in order to frame Joseph."

Charlie made the mistake of taking a sip of his wine at that moment. He gagged and began to turn red as Ellen rushed to get him a glass of water. When Charlie was able to speak he asked dubiously, "You're sure you heard this correctly, Ellen? That's a bold accusation to make."

Ellen nodded. "I used my trusty glass-between-the-ear-and-the-wall technique."

Charlie took another drink of his wine as he attempted to process this information. "Ellen, wait a minute. Anything else happen that you're not telling me?"

Ellen rolled her eyes, unable to look in Charlie's direction as she mumbled, "Nothing I can think of."

"Damnit, Ellen. I know that look! You better tell me what happened. Everything. Stealth is not your strongpoint. They caught you, didn't they?" Charlie looked intently at Ellen, trying to gage her reaction. "Aha! I was right. I knew it! You had that look on your face!"

"I did not. What look?" She was indignant that she got caught.

Charlie mimicked Ellen's eye-roll and the way she tightened her lips. Pouring each of them another glass of wine, he sat back in his chair and raised his eyebrows. "Now, start talking."

Later while Ellen was brushing her teeth, Charlie secretly placed a call to Catherine who, in turn, announced to Ted, Karen and Bud, "Bird-Watchers, I just got an S.O.S. from Big Package. Little Package has gone rogue once again. Need to mobilize. Meet at eight hundred hours. Over and out."

Thursday, October 13

Early this morning, Catherine was pacing back and forth trying to warm herself up. "Jesus, it's freezing here! Bud, turn up the heat. Karen, I need to use the bathroom. Hurry up!"

"Catherine, our heaters are on high," Bud calmly explained. "You know, this isn't Cape Coral. Just put on a heavy sweater and you'll be fine. Where's Ted?"

"He's been out for hours with his binoculars," Catherine muttered. "See if you can find him. Coffee's ready."

Catherine began her meeting as soon as Bud returned with Ted. "Bird-Watchers, we need to strategize. Charlie will serve as our informer. As soon as we hear from him, we get ourselves armed and ready for action."

Karen gave Catherine a look of annoyance. "Armed? Really, Catherine, don't you think you're taking this too far?"

Bud responded, "Karen, we're not packing AK-47's! Catherine is talking about our super-soakers."

"And, I've got my hidden spy camera," Ted declared proudly."See, I'll bet you thought it was a water bottle."

Karen exclaimed, "Ooh! I want one of those!"

"Back to business. Let's review our code names." Catherine announced, "This is Queenie. Over."

Karen piped up, "Dragon Lady, here. Over."

"Eagle One reporting for duty," Ted stated. "Over."

"Firefly, signing off. Over and out."

Ellen and Charlie drove to the New Paltz Police Department to update Adam. They waved to Sergeant O'Riley who, in turn, waved them right in. Adam was seated at his desk looking glum.

"Another hot date with the daughter of one of your mother's bridge ladies?" Ellen jeered.

Adam scowled back at Ellen. "Hope you have some good intel for me. I sure could use it."

"Myrna Van Dyke and Ben Sheppard are in cahoots against Phillip Edelstein." Ellen stated flatly.

"What are you talking about?" Adam asked skeptically.

Ellen proceeded to tell Adam about her adventure tailing Myrna.

"So, you're telling me that Ben is about to walk in here and claim that Phillip set the fire?"

"Exactly," Ellen confirmed. "But not until after the planning board meets."

"Well, that should be happening at 3:00 today," Adam smiled. "I almost hope it's true. I'd love to nail Phillip Edelstein for something."

"So how do you handle, what appears to be, a bogus accusation?" Charlie asked.

"Charlie, the same way I handle all the bogus accusations I receive: as if they're legit. Believe me, I know what I'm doing." Adam sighed, "But, I just want to give you guys a heads-up. Joseph Van Dyke is likely to be named a person of interest in the Siricco murder. Chief Liberti's directive came yesterday."

"I don't buy that, Adam," Charlie stated emphatically.

"I've examined Eddie's scribbled notes so much I'm dreaming about them at night. I'm sure he's left us a clue, but I'll be damned if I can figure it out," Adam claimed in frustration. "Anyhow, Ellen, you've got to back off. That was a reckless thing to do. Ben Sheppard is, to quote Eddie Siricco, 'a lowlife landowner'. I don't know what he's capable of and you don't want to find out."

Ellen gave Adam a condescending stare. "Perhaps, even murder?" She walked out the door.

Charlie held back. "Be right there, Ellen!" Turning to Adam he whispered, "Adam, you need to give me Sheppard's contact info."

"Charlie, now I've got to tell you the same thing I told Ellen--back off! Raul warned me about you, two, and I see he was right."

"I'm not reckless. I leave 'reckless' to Ellen," he smiled. "But I need to have a talk with this guy and make sure he doesn't come after my wife!" Charlie's voice was getting louder with every word.

Reluctantly, Adam placed a piece of paper on the table for Charlie to view. It contained Ben Sheppard's home address and phone number. "Just look. Don't touch. Remember, I never gave this to you, Charlie," he warned.

Charlie nodded and left the office.

Phillip and Ben had planned to meet at Water Street Market at noon today. They were both amped up. They ordered sandwiches and coffee from the Mudd Puddle and sat down to review their plans. "So, Phillip, you're sure the planning board will vote to approve this?"

Phillip leaned back in his chair and with a cocky grin said, "Sheppard, we're cool. In fact, look over there. It's Harris." Phillip waved to Harris. "Hey, come on over, Landau!"

Harris strolled over and sat down to join them. "I just have a minute. Hello there, Ben."

Ben nodded without saying a word.

"Harris, Ben is asking me if the planning board is going to approve his land use request. He's getting the jitters. Tell him."

"Ben, I'm not a fan of yours, by any means," Harris began, "but I believe this development would benefit the community. I'm planning to approve it and the other members are on board, as well. Nothing to worry about." Harris slapped his hand on the table and got up to leave. "Now I get to mediate another fight at the Denizen between Leonard and Dorothy. If you'll excuse me..." Harris took off.

Phillip turned to Ben, "Okay?"

"Yeah, Edelstein. We're good."

Charlie informed Catherine that he had an appointment this afternoon that could not be changed but he was worried about Ellen. She had planned to spend the afternoon walking the Wallkill Valley Rail Trail in New Paltz with her friend, Pat. She needed protection. He texted Catherine the details.

She texted back, "*And what trouble are you planning to get into?*"

When Charlie texted, "*LOL!*" Catherine knew she had to revise the Bird-Watchers' plan.

"It's obvious that Charlie is up to something, too. He's being evasive and trying to blow me off. We need to split up and tail them both, I'm afraid."

"How? We only have the one car." Karen reasoned.

Bud took command of the operation. "Here's what we'll do. Ted and I will drop you and Catherine off at Water Street Market. You can tail Ellen. The rail trail goes right next to Water Street."

Catherine and Karen nodded in agreement.

"Ted and I will drive to Montgomery and follow Charlie wherever he's going. We can keep in radio contact. Okay, Bird-Watchers?" They placed their right hands in a pile and let out a hardy "Woohoo!"

Charlie was free to track down Ben Sheppard, knowing Ellen would be safe. He turned down Putt Corners Road and made the left onto Ben's road. He parked in the driveway and strode to the front door to ring the bell.

Ben was surprised to have a visitor. "Yes, can I help you?"

Charlie gave him a cordial smile. "You're Ben Sheppard?" he asked. Ben nodded. "May I come in?"

Ben stepped aside to let Charlie enter. "What is this about?"

Charlie's smile immediately transformed into a sneer. "I'm Charlie Green and you assaulted my wife yesterday."

Bud and Ted discreetly parked just past Ben's house. They put on their gear: canvas birding hats, oversized sunglasses, binoculars, and 2-way radios. They surveyed the territory and saw there were numerous overgrown shrubs to hide behind. The plan was to surround the exterior of the small house. Ted hid on the left side of the house and Bud went to the right. Side windows gave them each a line of sight into the house.

"Eagle One to Firefly. Big Package and unknown are talking. Over."

"Firefly to Eagle One. Unknown looks like a punk but I can take him down. No problem. Over."

"Eagle One to Firefly. Not yet. They're just talking. Hey, got any snacks? Over." Ted was willing to risk his life for Charlie but had no intention of going hungry.

"Firefly to Eagle One. Pringles. Meet you around the back. Over and out." They each got on all fours and crept around to the back of the house to make the exchange and return to their posts.

"Charlie Green. Hah! Your wife was trespassing and snooping around where she didn't belong!"

"My wife had stopped by to try to offer support to Myrna Van Dyke. That was all!" Charlie yelled back.

"I don't think Myrna Van Dyke would agree with that. She was pissed!"

"Whatever you and Myrna were talking about is your ugly business. That's between the two of you. I don't give a damn what's going on and neither does my wife," Charlie hissed.

"Anything that old broad heard is nothing more than hearsay," Ben growled.

Ted groaned as he slowly tried to stand up to peek in the window, chips in one hand, binoculars in the other. After years with the NYFD, Bud's knees were in no better condition than Ted's. He winced in pain as he rose to look inside the house. They witnessed an enraged Charlie whose shouting could be heard throughout the neighborhood.

"Firefly to Eagle One. Code red. I repeat: code red. Over." Bud was ready to spring into action.

"Eagle One to Firefly. Stand by. I repeat: stand by. Over." Ted was praying they would not have to rescue Charlie.

"Firefly to Eagle One. Roger that." They each held their breath as they watched the scene unfold.

Charlie grabbed Ben by the front of his tee shirt and glared down at him. "First of all, you shut up about my wife. The only thing she heard was that you threatened her. And now I'm going to return the favor," Charlie roared as he shoved Ben so hard he landed on his own threadbare couch. Ben attempted to stand up and Charlie shoved him back down with the palm of his hand. Shaking his finger at Ben, Charlie gritted his teeth and bellowed, "Anyone threatens or harms my wife and I'm holding you responsible, you miserable, lowlife. And now I know where you live!" Charlie turned and walked out the door.

"Firefly to Eagle One. Big Package heading to car. Over."

"Eagle One to Firefly. Thank God! Over and out." Ted closed his eyes in relief, put away his camera, and waited behind the overgrown forsythia until his breathing returned to normal.

Even in the midst of his fury, Charlie stopped and bent down to pick up a piece of litter he found in the driveway. "Ben Sheppard really is a pig," he muttered to himself stuffing the paper into his pocket.

Ben did not dare move from the couch until he heard Charlie's car drive off.

Karen and Catherine set out to find Ellen. They wore over-sized sunglasses to hide their faces. Karen wore a scarf, Grace Kelly style, and a large straw hat over it. When they arrived at Water Street Market, they spotted Ellen's car parked just where Charlie had said it would be. Catherine and Karen split up. Catherine remained at Water Street Market. Karen hit the rail trail. They were each equipped with a 2-way radio for emergency communications.

Ellen dropped off a few small items at the Antique Barn before meeting up with her friend, Pat, to walk the rail trail. They started their trek at Water Street Market and headed out at a brisk pace. Their route took them through the village along historic Huguenot Street, a designated National Historic Landmark District.

Their walk conveniently ended at Jar'd, a lively wine bar at Water Street Market. They ordered a bottle of local wine from Whitecliff Winery. Pat asked, "So, any more gossip about Eddie Siricco's murder?"

Ellen answered evasively, "Not really. I guess the police are on top of things."

Their server brought them their wine, poured it, and placed it in the iced cooler at the end of the table.

"Well, I heard that residents are going to storm the Mayor's office if a suspect isn't named," Pat whispered. "Hey, Ellen, did you see that?" she pointed to Maglyn's Dream, a shop several doors down.

Catherine whispered into her shoulder having cleverly hidden her 2-way radio in her shirt pocket. "Queenie to Dragon Lady. Little Package is turning into a wino! It's mid-afternoon and she's downed one full glass already! Over and out."

"What are you talking about?" Ellen asked.

"I swear I saw someone staring at us. She's sitting alone at a table. She's wearing a ridiculous floppy hat and keeps turning around. I'm going to give her my 'don't mess with me' look," Pat stated defiantly. "See? There she goes again."

Ellen turned to look but was too late. "Pat, I don't see anyone staring at us. Have some more wine. I think you need it."

"Dragon Lady to Queenie. I'm exhausted! Order me a glass of wine, too. I could use it. Over."

"Queenie to Dragon Lady. If you insist. But do not come to my table. I repeat: do not come to my table. Take cover. Over and out."

Ellen refilled Pat's glass.

"Ellen, turn around right now!" Pat ordered without moving her lips.

Ellen whirled around and shook her head. "Pat, there is nobody staring at us! Just relax. You're beginning to sound like me."

"Puhleeze! Spare me!" They both laughed and chattered away as they sipped their wine. "And you should have seen Bill's face when

235

I served him sushi for dinner the other night. I swear, you'd think I had served him fish bait!" They both guffawed. "Ellen," Pat muttered, slinking down in her chair. "Now I'm seeing another floppy hat peeking up from behind the tall shrubs."

Karen mumbled into her 2-way radio, "Dragon Lady to Queenie. I have a clear visual on our target, but her damn friend keeps looking at me every time I pop up. Over."

"Queenie to Dragon Lady. Then don't pop up! Over and out."

Ellen turned to look. "Pat, you're becoming paranoid. I don't see anyone staring at us."

"I swear, you'd think someone just spotted a Cuban Peewee," Pat fumed, gulping down her wine, not taking her eyes off the shrub.

Ellen teased, "Maybe someone thinks you are a rare specimen."

"Yeah, well, cheers to that," Pat grumbled as they clinked glasses.

By late afternoon, Adam walked outside for some air. He needed to clear his head before digging into Eddie Siricco's personal notes all over again. "Detective," Sergeant O'Riley called. "I've been trying to reach you."

"Sorry. I came out here to think. What is it?"

"Ben Sheppard is here and wants to see you. He says it's urgent."

"Okay, Sergeant. Give me five minutes then you can send him to my office."

"Well, Ben, this is, indeed, a surprise. What is it?" Adam asked.

"It's about Phillip Edelstein."

"What about him?"

"Detective, Joseph Van Dyke did not set fire to his own house. Phillip Edelstein did it."

Adam's acting ability had improved since he was in the chorus of *Fiddler on the Roof* back in high school. He took a couple of deep breaths and calmly asked, "What makes you so sure that Edelstein set the fire?"

"Because he told me he did it," Ben said. Adam gave Ben a skeptical look. "Look, you already know I'm trying to sell my property. Edelstein loaned me the money to clear up the liens on my property in exchange for a piece of the action. His job was to get the planning board's approval."

"Why didn't you tell me any of this the last time we met?"

"Because I didn't know for sure until yesterday. That's when he told me."

"He confessed? That doesn't make sense to me."

"Detective, he didn't confess. He bragged about it. Tried to show me how cleverly he destroyed the Van Dykes. I've got to get out of here. If Edelstein discovers that I ratted him out, he'll kill me!"

"You think he would go that far?"

Ben shrugged in response. He wanted to screw Phillip but not necessarily accuse him of murder. Phillip still could be useful.

Adam stood up, put his hands in his pockets, and announced, "Sheppard, don't leave town. We're not finished here. Not at all."

Ben gave an exaggerated salute to Adam, left the police station, and sent a text to Myrna.

Pat was becoming agitated. "Ellen, look right now!"

Ellen abruptly turned her head and saw the brim of a floppy hat lower itself behind a manicured shrub. She walked over to talk to the hat. "Have you lost something besides your mind?"

The hat rose up. "Why, Ellen. What a surprise to see you here!" Karen exclaimed.

"Where are the rest of you?" Ellen asked impatiently.

Karen gestured with her head to the table near Maglyn's. "Over there."

"I know Charlie put you up to this," Ellen accused as she walked over to Catherine's table.

Catherine, ever unflappable, shot Ellen an uppity look as she reprimanded her. "I can see why we have to keep an eye on you, Ellen. One more sip of wine and I take away your car keys!" She stood up and winked, "Now, introduce us to your friend. I'd like to meet her."

Much later, Ellen and Charlie sat on their porch and it was Charlie's turn to come clean about his activity for the day. "Eddie was right when he called Sheppard a 'lowlife'. But," Charlie grinned, "I must admit, it felt great to know that I'm still the toughest guy in the room."

"Right. And I'm Lady Gaga," Ellen retorted. "Ben could have met you at the door with a shot gun, for all you knew. That was a foolish thing to do."

"Look, I guarantee that he's not going to mess with you or me ever again." Charlie was quite pleased with himself. He took a generous swallow of his wine.

"What's that sticking out of your pocket? More receipts from the last decade?" Ellen teased. Charlie had the annoying habit of never throwing away a single scrap of paper, receipt, grocery list, or expired coupon. To locate an item in the top drawer of his dresser required an archeological dig.

"Oh, that! I forgot. I picked it up in Sheppard's driveway. Couldn't leave litter sitting there--even at his place." Charlie removed the paper and got up to throw it away. He glanced at it and walked back onto the porch. "Ellen, look at this. It looks like Eddie's handwriting." He read, "*Peek-a-boo. Shame on you! For my silence, 5 grand should do.*"

Phillip tried to contact Ben. Ben never bothered to answer his calls. Phillip never bothered to leave a message. He wanted to let Ben know that the planning board met to vote on the land use approvals at 3:00. However, two of the board members were unable to attend. They did not have a quorum. The planning board will reconvene in two weeks.

Friday, October 14

Today, Adam and his team of detectives were expected to name a person of interest in the Eddie Siricco murder. Adam began his remarks. "Good morning, officers. We have a challenging task ahead of us. Once we name a person of interest, that person will be guilty in the court of public opinion." The other officers nodded in solemn agreement. "We are fortunate to have obtained Eddie Siricco's personal notes. They have shed a lot of light on Eddie and his relationships with various members of the community."

Adam projected a visual onto the screen behind him. "If you look at the screen you will see Eddie Siricco in the bull's eye. In the upper left is a photo of Joseph Van Dyke. To date, we know that Eddie Siricco demanded money from Van Dyke in exchange for his silence. He threatened to spread it around that Van Dyke set the house on fire. Unfortunately, we don't know whether Eddie was spreading a rumor or whether he actually witnessed this. Now, look in the upper right of the screen. Here is a photo of Phillip Edelstein. We also suspect that Phillip Edelstein wrote the anonymous note hoping to destroy the Van Dykes and that Siricco knew about Edelstein's plans. Siricco must have attempted to extort money from Edelstein." Adam directed the officers to the bottom center photo. "Here is Ben Sheppard. Eddie had nothing good to say about Sheppard, if you recall. Anyway, Sheppard strutted in here yesterday announcing that Edelstein bragged to him about setting the fire."

"Any truth to that?" asked the officer on Adam's left.

"I wish it were true, but an undercover asset of ours overheard Sheppard conspiring with Myrna Van Dyke to frame and name, none other than, Phillip Edelstein."

"So you're telling us that Sheppard is turning on his fixer?" another officer asked.

"It seems that way. Edelstein put up a lot of money and Sheppard doesn't want to have to pay him back. They're both a couple of backstabbing swindlers." Adam leaned forward on his elbows. "Van Dyke and Edelstein each have flimsy alibis and a motive for silencing Siricco permanently."

Sergeant O'Riley tiptoed into the room and whispered, "Detective Jacobson, the Greens are here and say it's important. Could you step into the hallway for a moment?"

"Officers, I'll be right back. One moment." Adam left the room and saw Ellen and Charlie waiting right outside the conference room door. "What is it?" he asked.

Charlie presented him with a crumpled up piece of paper. "This." Adam looked quizzically as Charlie continued, "I picked it up in Ben Sheppard's driveway yesterday." Shrugging his shoulders Charlie explained, "Couldn't stand to see litter and not pick it up."

Adam read aloud, "'*Peek-a-boo. Shame on you! For my silence, 5 grand should do.'* So Eddie Siricco was demanding hush money from Ben, too! Charlie, this is a valuable piece of trash. Thanks," he grinned for the very first time today. "Gotta get back in the room and share this with the team."

Adam walked back into the conference room and moved the cursor on his laptop. "Let's go back to Ben Sheppard, once more. I was just given this piece of evidence by our undercover agents. It was found in Ben Sheppard's driveway. I'll pass it around."

After each officer had read the paper, one officer asked, "And this looks like Eddie Siricco's handwriting. Correct?"

Adam smiled, "Yes, New Paltz' very own poet laureate was busily at work extorting money."

"Does Ben have a solid alibi for the evening of September 25?"

"No. Nothing. But, now we have three people who wanted to get rid of Eddie Siricco."

"If we have to pick one, I say we go with Van Dyke," one officer reasoned. "Naming him can't do much to destroy his reputation. It's already in the toilet." A few rumbles of laughter circulated around the table.

"This is one hell of a way to name a person of interest." Adam found this very disturbing.

"Yeah. We might as well put the names in a hat and pick one out," another officer complained.

Adam listened as every officer ventured an opinion. Finally, he stood up. "Okay. Here's what we're going to do. We'll name Van Dyke as a person of interest, but not release his name to the press. That should shut the Mayor up."

Phillip was told to report to the police station to speak with Detective Sergeant Jacobson. He was not in any mood to play nice. The postponement of the planning board vote left him edgy. Phillip wanted this land sale to be done. Fortunately, he was not kept waiting. Sergeant O'Riley sent him right in to Jacobson's office.

Adam stood up to greet him. "Come in Phillip. Please sit down."

"I'm a very busy man, Detective. Please make this quick."

"I'm a very busy man, too, Phillip. I'll make it quick. You've been accused of setting the fire on Beekman Road."

Phillip's eyes would have popped out if they were not securely embedded in his skull. "You're full of shit!"

"Ben Sheppard ratted you out. He said that you bragged to him about it, pleased with the way you had destroyed the Van Dykes." Adam sat back and watched Phillip's face. "Is that quick enough for you?"

Phillip was livid. "Sheppard said that? The miserable toad!" Phillip composed himself and lowered his voice. "Alright, I admit that I wrote the note. I wanted to screw the Van Dykes, but I never set the fire. Jacobson, I demand to speak to the Mayor about this. He'll set things straight." Edelstein banged his fist on the table, oozing an unpleasant air of entitlement.

"So, Edelstein, you've accused Joseph Van Dyke. Do you have any evidence to back up your accusation? Describe what you witnessed."

"I believe the note is self-explanatory. Other than that, I have no more evidence than Ben has to back up his accusation. I'd say it looks like we're at a stalemate, Detective," Phillip smirked, slowly crossing his legs and leaning back in his chair. He transformed from defendant to prosecutor in a nanosecond.

"How much did Eddie Siricco demand to keep his mouth shut about your nefarious activities?" Adam glared at Phillip.

"Well, well, Detective, I see you're not used to questioning attorneys," Edelstein replied glibly. "Before you throw around questions, you better know the answers," he winked. "Now, if you'll excuse me, I'm going to visit my good friend, the Mayor. Good-day, Detective." Phillip nodded politely and walked out of the room.

Adam clenched his teeth in fury knowing that Edelstein had assumed total command of their meeting even when caught completely off guard. He was the reason Adam hated attorneys. Edelstein managed to tap into Adam's insecurity, making him feel naive and incompetent. Yet, Edelstein also tapped into Adam's strength: his integrity and determination. From this moment on, Adam was more resolute than ever about finding Eddie Siricco's murderer and bringing him to justice.

Ben left Myrna a voicemail to meet him in the parking lot at Water Street Market at noon. He waved when he saw her arrive and slipped into the passenger seat, eager to tell her about his fiendish act. Myrna did not say one word. She sat in icy silence as Ben began, "This stupid detective was shocked when he asked how I knew Phillip had set fire to the Beekman Road house. I told him that Edelstein bragged to me about it," Ben cackled. "Thought that was a good touch," he winked, pleased with himself. "So, Myrna, I do believe that our problems will end as soon as Phillip is charged with arson and..."

Myrna could contain herself no longer. She burst out laughing. "You really must have had a lobotomy, Sheppard. You think the police will take your word over Phillip's? You're crazy. He may be a sniveling bastard just like you, but he's got connections and you don't."

"But until he can prove that he didn't do it, he'll be tied up with lawsuits, possibly, for years."

"Really? Is that what you think? You're a pea brain!"

"Now, Myrna, that's not very kind," Ben chided her.

"You're right. That wasn't kind. I should thank you for framing Edelstein and taking the focus off Joseph," Myrna replied sarcastically. "But now that you've framed Edelstein, your Milo Road project will never get approved."

Ben gloated, "Myrna, it got approved yesterday afternoon. The entire planning board went for it."

"Hah! Sheppard, don't you know that the vote never happened? They didn't have a quorum. It's been postponed for two weeks." Myrna threw back her head and laughed as Ben stormed out of her car and slammed the door.

Adam knocked on Liberti's door. "Come on in!" the Chief shouted, twirling in his chair to face Adam. "Did your team agree to name Van Dyke as a person of interest?"

"We did, Sir, but we're not going to release his name. Anyhow, I'm having second thoughts about this. The murderer could just as easily be Phillip Edelstein or, possibly even Ben Sheppard. I don't feel right naming anyone at this time."

Liberti chuckled, "That's what I like about you, Adam. You've got principles. But, you've got to learn that principles don't mean a damn thing to the public. They want a suspect and they want it now. And the Mayor wants whatever the public wants. So, you and I are about to meet with a reporter from the Daily Freeman. Let's go." Liberti gave Adam an affectionate slap on the back as they got up to leave his office.

Before they reached the door, Sergeant O'Riley buzzed-in to the Chief's phone, sounding frazzled. "Sir, Mayor Bradley is on the phone and insists on speaking with you at once!"

"Thanks, Sergeant. Put him through." Chief Liberti rolled his eyes at Adam and pressed 'speaker'. "Hi Greg. Liberti here. What's up?"

"Liberti, just heard from a buddy of mine, Phillip Edelstein. You may know him--a local attorney. Been around forever."

"Yes, Greg. What about him?"

"Well, he popped into my office a little while ago very distressed. It seems that a young, inexperienced detective of yours--um, let me see--aha-- Adam Jacobson is his name." Mayor Bradley chuckled, "Well, you won't believe this, but Jacobson said that Phillip has been accused of starting the fire on Beekman Road."

"Okay."

"Well, come on, Liberti, I've known Phillip since we played high school football together. He did not start that fire. I'm certain of that," Mayor Bradley stated emphatically.

"Why are you calling me about this, Greg?"

Bradley talked out of one side of his mouth, "Liberti, be reasonable. Look, I never ask you for favors, but I want you to squash this preposterous allegation immediately and quietly. You need to make it go away," Mayor Bradley demanded.

"I'll look into the matter. Good talking with you, Greg."

"Thanks, Liberti. I know I can count on you," Mayor Bradley said. "Hey, we need to get in a last round of golf before the snow flies. I'll have my secretary set something up for next week."

"Sure. Sounds good." Chief Liberti ended the call. "So Adam, see what I mean? Small-town politics often keeps the truth just out of reach. Come on, the reporter is waiting."

Chief Liberti and Detective Jacobson met with Maggie Wilson, a reporter from the Daily Freeman. After introductions, Chief Liberti began, "Ms. Wilson, my department has worked tirelessly to find a murderer and bring him to justice."

"Are you telling me that you have a suspect, Sir?"

Liberti gave a condescending smile. "I'm telling you my department has worked tirelessly. But, we do have a person of interest in this case."

"Who have you named?"

"I'm going to turn this over to Detective Sergeant Adam Jacobson who has been in charge of the investigation into the murder of Eddie Siricco. Detective?" Liberti left the room and deserted Adam.

Adam nodded and swallowed hard. "An impressive team has been investigating this murder and, while we have a person of interest identified, we are not at liberty to name the person at this time."

"And why not, Detective? The residents of New Paltz are fearful and concerned that someone murdered their beloved 'Town Crier'!"

"We are all concerned but, the privacy of this individual must be maintained in order for us not to violate anyone's civil rights and, possibly, compromise the integrity of our investigation." Adam gave Maggie Wilson his winning smile.

"Detective, the entire community knows that Joseph Van Dyke burned down his house in order to collect the insurance money. Did Eddie Siricco know this?"

"Ms. Wilson, this is a rumor not a fact."

"We know that an anonymous witness accused Joseph Van Dyke. Have you discovered who this witness was?"

Adam smiled amiably, "Ms. Wilson, we are looking for a murderer and not the writer of an anonymous note."

"The State Police are waiting to assist you. Why haven't they been allowed to help?"

"We have been working closely with outside agencies, Ms. Wilson. In fact, a top-level undercover team from Florida has been assisting us. Every possible resource available to us has been activated."

"Is Joseph Van Dyke the person of interest?"

"No comment. Residents of New Paltz, rest assured. We are close to finding Eddie Siricco's murderer and we will not stop until that person is brought to justice. Thank-you, Ms. Wilson. Good-day." Adam shook her hand and they both walked out of the conference room.

Phillip prided himself on being a vindictive son-of-a-bitch. Ben Sheppard was going to pay dearly for his betrayal.

Harris Landau was in overdrive this morning. Settling disputes between Dorothy Dawson and Leonard left him snapping at everyone. Initially, Harris had been thrilled by their explosive scenes. He managed to spin their battles into lively publicity for the show. However, with the show only a few days away, ticket sales for opening night were dismal. Harris was determined to fill the theatre one way or another. Pride outweighed profit. That was why he stopped in at the Antique Barn.

"Hi, Walter. The shop looks great!"

"Thanks, Harris. What's up?" Walter knew that a compliment from Harris meant that a favor was coming next.

Harris held up two tickets and smiled, "I'm giving you and Cosmo two complimentary tickets for opening night of 'Desdemona'. That's Wednesday."

"That's very generous of you, Harris, but I'm not sure we can make it."

Harris leaned over the counter and pleaded, "Walter, you *must* be there. I need you both to show up. Please do this for me."

Walter reluctantly agreed to attend. He grimaced, "Sure, Harris. We'll make sure to be there."

"Great! I'm counting on you," he winked. "You know, Walter, you really should replace your flag. It's looking a bit shabby." Harris left to hit up Michelle and James at the Mudd Puddle.

Adam Jacobson decided to make a house call to inform Joseph of the recent change in his status. He rang the bell and was greeted by Myrna. "Yes?" she snapped.

"Good morning, Myrna. May I come in?"

"You want to see Joseph? I'll get him," she scowled walking to the den. "Hey, Joseph, your new best friend is here to see you." Myrna motioned to Adam to have a seat.

"Thanks." Adam sat down on the couch.

Joseph shuffled into the living room to join Adam. Adam was struck by the noticeable change in Joseph's posture. He appeared to have shrunk since they last met. "Yes, Detective, what is it this time?"

Adam stated, "Joseph, why don't you sit down." He waited as Joseph took a seat across from him. "The police have named you as a person of interest in the murder of Eddie Siricco."

Joseph turned a pasty color and he opened his mouth to speak but no sound came out. Myrna was livid. "Are you here to arrest him?"

"No. Joseph is not considered a suspect. In fact, Joseph, I have not released your name to the press. It buys us a little time. But it means that your every move will be followed."

"You were already doing that, I imagine."

Adam nodded. "Please know that we are checking into other potential suspects as well. We do know that Eddie attempted to extort money from several people. You weren't his only target."

Myrna fired back, "Well then, why is Joseph the only one named a person of interest? Huh? Answer that!"

Ignoring her outburst, Adam put his forearms on his knees and leaned in closer to Joseph. "I know that Edelstein threatened you if you were to oppose his Milo Road investment. But, Joseph, why the hell didn't you tell me that he threatened you? I've asked you this many times. I had to find out from another source. This doesn't make any sense."

"Nothing about this makes sense!" Myrna barked. "You've delivered your message. Now, beat it, Detective!" Myrna ordered.

"Actually, Myrna, I'll need to speak with you, as well."

"Well, out with it already!" she yelled.

Adam cleared his throat and began, "Myrna, I have learned that you and Ben Sheppard teamed up to frame Phillip Edelstein with setting the fire." From the look of revulsion on Joseph's face, Adam knew that this was the first Joseph had heard of this.

"I would never have anything to do with that pond scum, Ben Sheppard! That's an absurd accusation, Detective."

"The accusation may be absurd, but it also happens to be true."

Joseph clenched his fists so tightly that his fingers cramped up. "Myrna, what's going on?" His eyes looked wild with fury as he faced his wife.

"This is a friggin' lie!" Myrna screeched.

Adam scratched his head. "I still don't get it. I already know that Edelstein threatened Joseph if he interfered with the Milo Road approval, but he must have threatened you, too, Myrna. You never said a word to me either, yet, you're trying to destroy him. I'd think you'd have wanted me to know that Edelstein threatened you." Adam frowned and looked into Myrna's eyes. "What are you hiding, Myrna Van Dyke? And what are you trying to hide, Joseph?" Adam stood up, shook his finger at Joseph and Myrna, and warned, "I'll find out the truth. I promise you."

Adam turned his back to Myrna and continued walking. When he reached the door, he abruptly turned around to face Joseph. "Now, if you're smart, you'll find yourself a good lawyer. And it better be an arrogant son-of-a-bitch like Edelstein because you're going to need it!"

Ellen and Charlie were meeting the Bird-Watchers for lunch at P&G's. This pub has been operating since 1947 when friends, Pat and George, purchased it. Today, it is still a gathering place for tourists, college students, and locals.

Back in her college days, Catherine had enjoyed many rowdy evenings at the very table at which they were seated. They were still eating their sandwiches when Charlie received a call from Adam. He excused himself and took the call. "What is it, Adam?"

"Just want to let you and Ellen know that Joseph Van Dyke was named a person of interest yesterday."

"Is his name splashed all over the Daily Freeman yet?"

"No, Charlie. I never identified him. For the moment, this may be enough to calm down Mayor Bradley. He only cares about the optics anyway."

"What about Ben? Any idea about what Eddie had on him?"

Adam let out a sigh. "I called him in for questioning this morning but got nowhere. He's a stubborn bastard. Wouldn't say a word."

"Really? Maybe I can help out."

"What do you mean? You're not about to pull another 'Ellen', are you?"

"You don't need to worry about that!" Charlie laughed. "Thanks for letting me know about Van Dyke. Gotta go." They ended the call. Charlie returned to the table.

"Bud, could you take Ellen home? I have an appointment and have to leave right away," Charlie fibbed.

"Sure thing, Charlie. No problem."

Ellen gave Charlie a suspicious look. "What appointment, Charlie?"

Charlie winked, "I'll tell you later. Gotta run!" He dashed out before Ellen could ask anything else. Charlie got in his car and drove directly to Ben Sheppard's house. He had some unfinished business to take care of. Charlie figured that he had a better chance than Jacobson of finding out what Eddie Siricco meant when he wrote the crumpled up note Charlie found in the driveway.

Charlie pulled in the driveway right behind a vintage Porsche. He walked to the front door but before he rang the bell he stopped to listen to a thunderous barrage of obscenities hurled at Ben by the owner of the Porsche. When there was a brief lull in the shouting, Charlie rang the bell.

Ben Sheppard opened the door and Charlie boldly entered. Ben snorted, "Charlie Green. Well, what do ya' know. Looks like we're having a party!"

Charlie looked over Ben's shoulder and immediately recognized Phillip Edelstein leaning up against the wall. Charlie, ever the gentleman, reached out to shake Phillip's hand. "Charlie Green and, gee, you look familiar. Do I know you?" he could not resist adding.

"Phillip Edelstein," he grunted shaking hands with Charlie. "What are you doing here?"

"Probably the same thing you're doing here. I intend to take care of some unfinished business with Ben. And you?"

"The same." Phillip shook his finger at Ben as he spoke to Charlie. "See, this little pissant tried to outsmart me. I loaned him half-a-mill and to make sure he didn't have to pay me back, he decided to double-cross me." Phillip gave a loud braying laugh. "Only problem with you, Ben, is that you're a freakin' idiot!"

Ben lunged at Phillip who grabbed him by the scruff of his collar and shoved him onto the kitchen floor. He pinned Ben down and held him there. "So now, you piece of crap, you're going to sign this amended contract that ensures that I get my entire share plus repayment of the loan when the sale is completed before you get a single penny. You will receive your share ninety days after the closing. Ninety days!"

"The hell I will! You're out of your mind, Edelstein! It's my land," the heap on the floor of the kitchen roared back.

Before this negotiation escalated any further, Charlie wanted some information out of Ben. Looming over Sheppard, Charlie growled, "What did Siricco have on you that was worth five grand? Tell me!"

Ben cackled, "I wasn't about to tell the police. What makes you think I'll tell you?"

"Because now you're playing by my rules!" Charlie's eyes narrowed and his jaw tightened. As soon as he saw Edelstein loosen his grip on Sheppard, Charlie yanked Ben up and plunked him down at the kitchen table.

"What business is this of yours, anyway? Hey, Edelstein. Charlie, here, I think he's working with the police."

Phillip eyed Charlie. "Is that true?"

"That's bullshit. Why would you believe anything he says?" Charlie shot back. "My beef with Sheppard is that he assaulted my wife. I'm looking for anything I can do to repay him."

Ben tried to stand up and Charlie shoved him back in the chair. Ben yelled, "Hey Edelstein, this guy is here to cause trouble. Right now we need each other. You and me. We get rid of him and we're back on track."

"And how do you think you're going to do that, Sheppard?" Charlie retorted. "You planning to kill me?" Charlie saw that Ben and Phillip made fleeting eye contact. He had to find out some information before those two aligned against him or this visit would be a total waste. "So Sheppard, did you pay Siricco the five grand or not?"

"Hah! Siricco was never gonna get a damn thing from me! I'm no stooge!" he glowered. "Edelstein, I'll sign the papers. Let's get this over with and be done."

"Not so fast, Sheppard. You tried to frame me, you stupid bastard," Edelstein snarled through his teeth. "See, Charlie, he told the police I set fire to the Beekman Road house. Now that wasn't nice, Sheppard."

Charlie nodded, "You really are a fool, Sheppard. And, did they fall for that?"

Edelstein glared. "If they fell for it, Sheppard, we both lose. Your timing really sucks."

Charlie knew he had to get them to turn on each other. "That land deal will never go through now. Doesn't matter if the police fall for your story, Sheppard. Suspicion is all it takes. So I'd say, you're both screwed." Charlie shot them both a nasty grin. "All thanks to you, Sheppard!"

"You're a worthless moron, Sheppard, but you're right about one thing. We need to get rid of Charlie." With a menacing look Phillip stated, "Too bad, Charlie. You're a hell of a lot smarter than Ben but that's the problem, I'm afraid."

"Edelstein, you don't need Sheppard. You destroyed the Van Dykes. Now you're free to buy up whatever you want. Sheppard is nothing but a brainless liability!" Charlie spit out.

At that comment, the brainless liability popped up out of the chair, grabbed the pickle jar on the table, and hurled it at Charlie's face. Charlie reacted by smacking his fist into Ben's nose. Phillip sided with Ben and tried to restrain Charlie as Ben wound up ready to punch him. Charlie ducked and, instead, Ben's fist slammed into Phillip's jaw. Phillip let out an ear-shattering howl and recoiled in pain. Charlie easily broke away. He reached out and grabbed the nearest weapon he could find: a can of olive oil sitting on the counter. He faced his two foes while backing up quickly towards the door, spilling the entire can of oil on the floor separating them. Charlie roared with laughter watching them flailing their arms around as they tried to run after him and remain upright. When he reached the door he could not resist one more look back. He saw Laurel and Hardy tumble down on the slick floor, marinating their butts in extra virgin olive oil.

When he returned home, Charlie desperately wished there were some way to avoid having Ellen see him. He turned and lowered his head as he walked into the house in a futile attempt to hide his black eye. "What the hell happened to you, Charlie Green?" Ellen blasted him.

Charlie gave her a sheepish grin. "You think I look bad, you should see the other guys." He sat down and bravely faced her wrath.

Sunday, October 16

The Bird-Watchers planned to spend a crisp, fall day at, nearby, Minnewaska State Park, located in the Shawangunk Ridge. The park spreads out across twenty-two thousand acres and features waterfalls, three lakes, and rugged cliffs. Karen and Catherine decided to take a gentle walk around the lake while Bud agreed to join Ted on the trail to Gertrude's Nose.

Ted and Bud had barely begun their trek when Ted put his finger to his mouth, aimed his binoculars up into an oak tree, and whispered a loud "Shh! I've spotted a pileated woodpecker. See, Bud? Look on the northern side of that tree." Bud looked but could not see a damn thing. Ted was stoked. Today was the day he might even have a sighting of a peregrine falcon.

Catherine and Karen were enjoying their walk when Catherine's phone beeped. "Hey Charlie. What's going on?"

"I'm going to need you Bird-Watchers to tail Ellen. She's up to something and all I could get out of her was that she wanted to make amends with Myrna Van Dyke."

"I think Myrna Van Dyke made herself quite clear the last time. Your wife is out of her friggin' mind, Charlie!"

"We are in total agreement. Look, let me text you Myrna's address. I'm sure that's where Ellen is headed."

"Karen and I are on it. No worries!" Catherine ended the call. She explained the situation to Karen.

"Well, what are we waiting for?" Karen asked. "Let's get hold of the guys and get going. Duty calls."

"We never brought our radios with us and the guys left their phones in the car. There's only one thing to do."

"What?" Karen asked.

"We need to get in the car and find Ellen. I'll drive. The guys won't be back for hours."

Chief Liberti's head was pounding as he read the editorial in today's Daily Freeman. *"The New Paltz police are stumbling around like the three stooges except this is no slapstick comedy, folks. This is a murder investigation of our beloved Town Crier! Hey, Chief Liberti, do you think we fell for your naming a person of interest without publicly naming the person? Residents of New Paltz, there is no person of interest! Come on Mayor Bradley. Get the police some decent help! Maybe you need to call in the Cub Scouts!"*

Water Street Market was bustling, as usual. Matthew and Pablo were enjoying lattes at a table in the courtyard when they were accosted by Dorothy Dawson. "Yoo-hoo, my poor, little weekend refugees!" she warbled and waved.

Matthew cringed. Pablo politely stood up to give her a hug. "How are you doing, Dorothy? Rehearsals going well?"

"If Leonard would butt out and the little harebrained playwright would disappear, I'd be feeling a lot better." She chirped, "Anyhow, opening night is Wednesday. Don't forget."

"Dorothy, I don't think we can make it during the week," Matthew explained.

"Pfft, you guys are young and healthy. Drive up after work. Curtain time isn't until eight. Remember, I'm leaving your tickets for you at the box office. No excuses!" She shook her finger at them and tottered back to the theatre.

Matthew and Pablo were trapped and they, begrudgingly, accepted their fate. "Hey, Ellen!" Matthew waved.

Ellen heard Matthew and detoured over to greet them. "How are you?"

"We were fine until Dorothy came along," he answered.

Pablo continued, "She's trapped us into attending the grand opening of 'Desdemona' on Wednesday."

"Charlie and I will be there, too. It'll be fun."

"As much fun as a root canal," Matthew grumbled.

"I'm going to stop at the Antique Barn and buy our tickets from Walter right now. I'm sure Harris left him plenty." Ellen was delighted. Now she knew the perfect peace offering to give to Myrna. "See you guys on Wednesday," she winked.

Ellen marched to the counter to see Walter. She waited for him to complete a sale. "Hi Walter. Wanted to buy a few tickets for the opening of 'Desdemona'."

"You really are crazy. Why go if you don't have to?"

"Walter, this will be a hoot! Now, let's see, I'll need, hmm, six, no. Walter, eight tickets please, and don't even bother to ask. We all qualify for the senior discount."

"That comes to ninety-six dollars." Walter handed Ellen her change and tickets as he smirked, "Too bad Harris doesn't offer a super-senior discount."

Karen turned over the keys to Catherine. They arrived at a townhouse complex and parked past Myrna's house to avoid being seen. The two women donned their traditional Bird-Watcher camouflage: oversized sunglasses, wide-brimmed, floppy hats, and binoculars.

"Do you see any sign of Ellen's car?" Catherine asked.

Karen peered out the window aiming her binoculars at Myrna's driveway. "No sign of her. Let's wait." Karen took out her emery board and began filing her nails. She had not had a proper manicure since they left Cape Coral over a week ago.

Catherine was losing her patience when she heard a car pull up. She looked out her rearview mirror and saw it was Ellen. "Little Package has arrived," she stated.

"What do we do now?" Karen asked.

"We wait until she goes in and then we can slip around to the side of Myrna's townhouse. No one will ever know we're there."

"Dragon Lady is ready for action," Karen declared.

Myrna answered the door and saw Ellen standing in front of her. "You better have more than pepper spray with you this time!" Myrna warned.

"Myrna, I came to apologize. May I come in?" Ellen asked.

As soon as Ellen walked inside, Karen and Catherine slipped out of the car and hid behind a leafy viburnum planted between Myrna's townhouse and the one next door. "This is perfect! We can see right into the kitchen," Catherine smiled, "without being seen."

Myrna nodded indifferently and allowed Ellen to enter. She pointed to a chair in the living room. "Make this quick."

"I'm sorry about the other day when you were here with Ben Sheppard. I really wanted to check up on you, Myrna," Ellen dishonestly gushed.

Myrna sat across from Ellen and angrily replied, "You're full of it! In fact, I know you were snooping around and reporting everything you heard to the police."

"Oh, Myrna, I would never do that!" Ellen vehemently disagreed.

Myrna placed her hands on her hips. "I know you did. That Boy Scout detective was here yesterday and accused me and Ben Sheppard of framing Edelstein."

"No! But why do you blame me for that?"

"Because he's too stupid to think of that himself. That's why!"

"Myrna, I'm one of the few people who believe that Joseph did not set fire to his house or kill Eddie. I'm not your enemy."

Myrna returned Ellen's comment with a snooty upward turn of her head. "You have absolutely no idea what I've been through! Do you realize that Joseph is the person of interest the police have named in the murder?"

Ellen's performance was Oscar-worthy. "Oh, my God! They wouldn't do that! That's terrible, Myrna! Does he have a solid alibi?"

Myrna straightened her shoulders and retorted, "Yes. He was with me right here all evening."

"Myrna, the police need more than your statement in order to verify his whereabouts. What about neighbors? Could they have seen the two of you?"

Catherine and Karen were becoming bored spying on Myrna and Ellen. "And to think we gave up a walk around the lake for this!" Catherine snapped impatiently. "Watch, they'll be exchanging recipes any minute now!"

"Damnit, I wish we had something to eat," Karen moaned.

Catherine rummaged around in her purse and pulled out a couple of Hershey bars. "Tada! I always carry a couple of these for emergencies. Here, take one." They lowered themselves onto the grass and munched away, hidden behind the viburnum.

Myrna was becoming unhinged. Between Joseph's gambling away their life's savings, Edelstein's threats, the fire, Joseph being named, losing her earring, it was all becoming too much to bear. She was overwrought and began to hyperventilate. She held up her fists and vigorously shook them in front of her. "This is all too much for me!" Myrna's voice escalated to a strident shrill. "If the police ever find out that I wasn't home Sunday night, it'll..."

Ellen rushed in, "You weren't home? Where were you?"

Myrna quickly backed off. "Forget it. Forget I ever said that. I was just supposing."

"Myrna, you have to tell me. An honest alibi is stronger than a false one."

Myrna spewed, "No! Even Joseph doesn't know where I was."

"And was Joseph home all evening?"

"How the hell would I know, Ellen! I just told you I WASN'T THERE!" Myrna shrieked in hysteria. This Ellen Green person was the tipping point for her and she needed to do something or she would implode.

Ellen knew she had to lower the temperature in the room. "Look, Myrna, I'm giving you and Joseph a couple of tickets to the opening of 'Desdemona' at the Denizen. Show up and stop hiding from everyone. Stop running away and stand up for yourselves! If you want people to think you did nothing wrong, then you need to act like it!"

Instead of lowering the temperature, Ellen's comments caused the room temperature to instantly shoot up to a rolling boil. Myrna thought, "How dare she tell me what to do! Running away? Never!" She was bold. She was a fighter. And she had heard more than enough from Ellen Green. Myrna stood up and stomped into the kitchen. She grabbed a pitcher and shouted, "Be right back."

Catherine and Karen had finished their Hershey bars and were on tiptoes peeking through the window, their eyeballs barely making it above the sill. Catherine ordered, "Karen, boost me up so I can get a better look."

"Are you crazy? You should have thought of that before you ate that candy bar!" Karen griped.

Catherine shot Karen a snooty look. "Forget it then."

Perched on tiptoes, they could see Myrna's malicious grin as she picked up the pitcher. If Myrna had not been so intent on watching the pitcher fill with water, she would have spotted four eyes only inches away from the faucet.

"Dragon Lady, storm the castle!" Catherine yelled as she made an ungainly sprint to Myrna's front door. Catherine pressed the palm of her hand on the doorbell and held it there.

Unfortunately, Ellen was seated with her back to the kitchen and saw none of what Myrna was up to. Myrna returned to the living room. She raised the pitcher over her head and was about to pour it down on top of an unsuspecting Ellen when the doorbell startled her. The pitcher slipped from her hands and crashed to the floor.

Catherine turned the handle on the door. It was unlocked. She marched purposefully inside and trilled, "Why, Ellen Green! I thought that was your car. You need to come with us right away."

Karen placed her hands over her heart, "My deepest apologies for barging in on you like this! Please forgive us. We have spa treatments scheduled at Mohonk Mountain House today and we couldn't go without Ellen."

Ellen fumbled in her purse and pulled out the two theatre tickets. "Myrna, in case you change your mind." She threw them onto the coffee table as Catherine firmly grabbed her hand and dragged her out the door.

Myrna ignored the mess on her floor and sloshed over to the coffee table. She picked up the tickets and thought, "Maybe. Who knows?"

Ted and Bud returned to the parking lot at Minnewaska by mid afternoon. They had demolished all the Pringles, chips, and beef jerky that Bud stuffed into his backpack and were ready to meet up with Catherine and Karen. Ted was euphoric. Today he had a sighting of a peregrine falcon and a bald eagle. And, he had the photos to prove it.

Charlie spent the day icing his swollen eye in hopes that by tomorrow no one would notice.

During yesterday's scuffle, Phillip landed on his tailbone when he lost his balance. The pain from his swollen jaw was nothing compared to the excruciating pain he experienced when he tried to sit. Therefore, he ordered a rubber donut from Amazon that was expected to arrive this afternoon. Until it was delivered, Phillip popped half a dozen Advil and remained seated on his cushioned toilet seat.

Ben placed a call to Kevin, the assistant brokering the deal for the buyer. Ben explained, to a skeptical party, that the necessary land use approvals would be delayed another two weeks. Next, Ben reluctantly emailed the amended contract that Phillip had insisted upon. Kevin made his displeasure exceedingly clear, regarding these delays and changes. Ben spent the rest of his day wrapping his swollen nose in a cold compress and trying to mop up the olive oil that was still pooling on his laminate floor.

Adam Jacobson was disgusted when he read the scathing editorial in the Daily Freeman. He did not want to speak to anyone and ignored his calls and voicemails, even the ones from his mother. Once again, he took out all the photos of Eddie Siricco's personal notes. He rearranged the scribbles and words to try to uncover a pattern or meaning. Eventually, he fell into an agitated sleep, dreaming of random words and Eddie Siricco and his mother's bridge ladies.

Monday, October 17

Chief Liberti's frustration was all hurled at Adam this morning. "And, I've had it! Right now we issue a statement to the press and reveal Joseph Van Dyke's identity. No more discussion! I told you this secrecy would backfire!"

"Yes, Sir." Adam had expected this blowup.

"And, be sure that Mayor Bradley's office is notified at once!"

Adam returned to his office and made his first call to Mayor Bradley. He asked to be put through directly to the Mayor.

"Detective Jacobson," the Mayor began, "if you're not calling to publicly name someone in Siricco's murder, I'm hanging up." He added with a warning, "And it better not be Phillip Edelstein!"

"Sir, Mayor Bradley, the department has named Joseph Van Dyke as a person of interest."

"Now that's more like it," Mayor Bradley smiled, leaning back in his swivel chair. "Have you reported this to the Daily Freeman yet?"

"I wanted you to be the first to hear it."

"Good. Give me one hour and I'll come to the station. Be sure to have a reporter and camera crew waiting," Mayor Bradley ordered.

"Yes, Mayor." Adam sent a quick memo about this development to his team, texted Ellen and Charlie, and then, contacted the Daily

Freeman to tell them that an announcement would be made from the police station in one hour.

At the Mudd Puddle, Michelle was singing 'Fly Me to the Moon' as she retrieved the next batch of lemon-ricotta pancakes from the oven. "Ah! Perfection!" This new recipe had become a big hit with her regular customers. She walked over to take another order. "Hi Leonard. What can I get for you today?"

"A couple of Xanax, over easy," he groaned.

"That bad?"

"Worse, Michelle! Much worse! Dorothy is a total disaster and I'm a walking casualty," he wailed.

"I know what will be even better than Xanax. Try one of these," she suggested handing Leonard a lemon-ricotta pancake.

"Oh, my God! This is ambrosia!" he swooned as he tasted it. "What do I owe you for this and a large coffee?"

Michelle smiled and shook her head. "Leonard, it's on the house today. Enjoy!" She handed him his coffee.

Leonard reached across the counter and gave Michelle the two-cheek, continental kiss. "You're an angel! Thanks." He was about to find a courtyard table when he stopped. "Michelle, are you and James coming to opening night? Please say yes. I'll need the moral support," he begged.

"Harris cornered us about that last week. Besides, we wouldn't think of missing this! Are you kidding?"

"Tada, Michelle!"

Michelle called to James who was sautéing bacon, "Hey, Honey. I'll be right back." Michelle grabbed a couple of coffees and sat down across from Ellen, who was staring at the text from Adam. "Hi, Ellen. You okay?"

"I'm fine. Thanks, Michelle. You seem to be in good spirits."

"I am. We've hired someone to help out on weekends and, I want to thank you. The lemon-ricotta pancakes are a winner."

"That's great news!"

"I never realized how much I needed a change. Same-old, same-old wasn't doing it for me. Eddie would have loved this. It would even have earned me a shout-out from the Town Crier!" she winked. "Hey, have you heard anything new in Eddie's murder investigation?"

"Well, you might as well hear this from me. It'll be on the news in another hour."

"What?"

"Joseph Van Dyke will be named as a person of interest in his murder," Ellen disclosed.

"Really? I have a hard time buying that. He's always so calm and, well, courtly, in an old-fashioned way."

"Thanks, Michelle. I feel the same way."

"Ellen, don't turn around, but Ben Sheppard and Phillip Edelstein are huddled together in the corner behind you. Those two snake oil salesmen look like they're plotting and scheming. Can't stand them!"

"Michelle, please come with me. I'm going over to say hello to them."

"Why would you want to?" Michelle asked with disdain.

Ellen got up and was already heading to their table. Michelle was, quickly, at her side and ready to see what Ellen was up to. "Hello, guys. Can I get you anything?" Michelle asked.

Phillip picked his head up and said, "A black coffee, Michelle. Thanks."

"And the same for me. Extra milk, no sugar," Ben added, looking at Michelle.

As Ben looked up, Michelle guffawed, "Ben, your nose looks like a neon sign." She looked from Ben to Phillip. "What the hell happened to you, two? A barroom brawl?"

Ben muttered, "It's not funny, Michelle." He paused long enough to scowl at Ellen. "You again?" Raising his bushy eyebrows at Phillip he sniveled, "Let me introduce you to Ellen Green."

"And you are?" Ellen asked, despite immediately recognizing Phillip from his appearance in 'The Closet'.

"Phillip Edelstein," he replied with a smarmy grin. Ellen took pleasure in noting the way his purple jaw protruded with exaggerated prominence.

"Well, I hope you boys can learn to play nice," Michelle teased, shaking her finger at them playfully. "I'll grab your coffees."

Ellen triumphantly followed Michelle. Her Charlie was absolutely right. "Now I *have* seen the other guys," she giggled to herself.

Michelle laughed, "Those two look hilarious! I'm sure they deserved what they got. But what's with that red inner tube Phillip was sitting on?" Both women began laughing all over again.

Ellen shrugged her shoulders and strutted away, forgetting, for a moment, Joseph Van Dyke's dire predicament.

Charlie was on his way to the New Paltz Police Department to meet up with Ellen. They planned to brief Adam about their weekend escapades. Charlie parked and walked to the front lobby. Much of the lobby was roped off with signs saying, "Press only". Camera crews were assembled. The Daily Freeman reporter had been sidelined by the local TV affiliate. The media were poised to capture this breaking news story. Charlie obediently waited on his side of the rope as he watched.

Mayor Bradley took center stage, puffed out his chest and proudly awaited the cue. *"This is 'Live with Lauren' and I'm here with New Paltz Mayor Bradley."*

"Hello, Lauren. Ahem, I am proud to announce breaking news in the Eddie Siricco murder investigation. New Paltz' finest have been working hard. Let me turn this over to Chief Liberti."

"Thank-you, Mayor Bradley. I will keep this brief and to the point. The New Paltz Police Department has named Joseph Van Dyke as a person of interest."

"Chief Liberti, has he been arrested?" Lauren asked.

"Mr. Van Dyke has not been arrested. My team of detectives, led by Detective Sergeant Adam Jacobson, is proceeding in a judicious manner. Mr. Van Dyke will be arrested when it is appropriate," he gave Lauren a patronizing smile. *"A premature arrest could jeopardize this entire investigation."*

Lauren continued, *"One last question, Chief Liberti. Is there a connection between the house fire on Beekman Road and the murder of Eddie Siricco?"*

"At this time, no possibility is being ruled out. Thank-you, Lauren. Mayor Bradley. I must get back to work." Chief Liberti stepped away from the cameras and microphone. He knew this was a P.R. move to appease the Mayor rather than a solid piece of detective work. Ignoring questions shouted at him by the reporters, he walked to his office and shut the door.

Dorothy Dawson saw Harris in the courtyard, sitting with two men. She gracefully breezed over to them. "Well, hello there, Harris. Gentlemen, I'm Dorothy Dawson, starring in the one-woman show 'Desdemona'. And you are?" Paying no attention to Ben, Dorothy reached out to shake Phillip's hand. Despite his rather spectacular jaw, he was dressed head-to-toe in designer attire: an important detail that Dorothy found most attractive.

"Pleased to meet you, Dorothy," Phillip replied, well aware of his appeal.

Harris looked down at his phone. "Interesting. I just got a newsflash. Joseph Van Dyke has been named a person of interest in Eddie Siricco's murder. Can't believe it!"

Upon hearing this announcement, Dorothy dropped her purse. Ben snorted and regretted it immediately as he stifled a wave of pain. Phillip winced in agony, forgetting not to spontaneously move his derriere.

Harris continued, "Dorothy, please excuse us. We're in the middle of a meeting, but you're looking positively radiant today."

"Thanks, Harris. Two more days. I must keep Leonard calm. You know how he is!" She flitted away.

"Where were we?" Harris asked.

"Two weeks from an approval," Ben grunted.

"Ah, yes. Now, if you still want to count on my support, I demand something in return."

"What now, Landau?" Phillip asked with annoyance.

Harris pulled out two tickets and smiled. "You, two, will show up for the opening night of 'Desdemona' and you will stay for the entire performance." He folded his arms, pleased that he could fill two more seats.

Ellen arrived at the police station as the camera crews were packing their gear and heading to the next breaking news story. Charlie was waiting for her in the lobby. "Well, that was nothing but a P.R. move for Mayor Bradley," Charlie complained. "'Live with Lauren' loved it."

"Too bad for the Van Dykes," Ellen said. "Wait till Myrna sees that! She's going to freak out."

Charlie shrugged. "Come on, Ellen. Let's brief Adam on our quiet, relaxing weekend."

Sergeant O'Riley greeted them and motioned for them to go right to Detective Jacobson's office.

Adam did not bother to get out of his chair. He put his hands behind his head and groaned, "I take it you saw the media circus in the lobby?"

Charlie nodded, "'Fraid so, Adam."

Adam sat up straight in his chair. "Charlie, what happened to your eye?"

"It had nothing to do with a golf ball. I can tell you that! But this is one of the reasons we wanted to meet with you."

"Go on."

Charlie described the less-than-cordial rendezvous with Ben and Phillip. After a few good laughs, Adam asked, "So Ben admitted that he never paid off Siricco?"

"Yeah. That's not much to go on. He refused to tell me what Siricco had on him. I guess I didn't get any further than you did, Adam."

"Actually, you did. Ben has admitted to having a motive for keeping Siricco permanently silenced. That's important. Now Ellen, I imagine while Charlie was pretending he was Superman, you were probably on the edge of disaster, as well." Adam gave Ellen a sardonic look.

Ellen shrugged with indifference. "I paid Myrna an apology visit."

"You did what? Ellen, the last time you saw her she was ready to hold you hostage!"

"That's why I tried a totally new approach, Adam. It was necessary to come at her from a different perspective. And, if you must know, it worked," she stated with an upward tilt of her head. "Sometimes you just have to, well, turn the paper ninety degrees to the left," she added glibly.

"Okay, Ellen. So tell me about your ninety degree approach."

She cleared her throat and summed up her lively visit with Myrna. "Bottom line is that Myrna admitted that she was not at home the entire evening on the night of Eddie Siricco's murder. She regretted saying that, but you can't unsay something. Right?" Wearing a smug expression, Ellen sat staring at Adam.

"Did she tell you where she was?"

"Look, Adam, you expect me to do all your work for you? No, she wouldn't say."

"Did she say whether Joseph was home all evening?"

"I asked her the same question and she rather forcefully reminded me that if she wasn't at home, how could she possibly know whether Joseph was home all evening."

Adam was dumbfounded. This was an alarming development. He frowned as he tapped his head with his pen. "What do you think is going on with Joseph and Myrna?"

Charlie spoke up matter-of-factly. "I'll tell you what I think. If Joseph has been reluctant to say much of anything, even about Phillip, I think he's doing that to protect Myrna."

"Or could he be protecting himself?" Ellen wondered.

Tuesday, October 18

Myrna shuffled along in her Minnie Mouse slippers, opened the front door, and picked up the Daily Freeman. She and Joseph had stopped watching the local news on TV ever since Eddie's murder, fearful that Joseph would be the featured story. However, they continued to receive delivery of the local paper.

Myrna glanced at the front page headline. "*Local Activist Named in Town Crier Murder*". She steadied herself as she made her way to the kitchen table, opened up the paper, and began reading. With every line she took a big gulp of coffee from her BLM mug, wishing it were something much stronger.

"Joseph, you better come in and take a look at this!" she yelled. Myrna began to wonder if it was time to tell Joseph where she was on the night that Eddie Siricco was murdered. She sighed as she mulled over her options: what to tell and how much to tell.

Myrna placed a mug of coffee on the table for Joseph. He sat down as Myrna slid the paper over to him.

"Myrna, what happens now?" Joseph asked sounding defeated. "What do we do?"

"Joseph, we need to talk."

Adam rode his bicycle to Water Street Market. Maybe hanging out at the Market would 'turn the paper ninety degrees' as Ellen suggested. He needed to change things up. Besides, the police station was beginning to close in on him. Chief Liberti was expecting the state troopers to invade any day now. Mayor Bradley was demanding an immediate arrest. Half of his team of detectives wanted to arrest Van Dyke and the other half were chasing their tails. As Adam parked his bicycle, he saw Harris coming over to greet him. "Detective, wait up! Do you really think that Joseph Van Dyke murdered Siricco?"

"Mr. Landau, Joseph is not considered a suspect at this time. He is someone the department is following closely in this matter."

"I certainly hope you make an arrest soon. We're all getting worried, you know." Harris reached in his pocket to retrieve something. Ordinarily, Adam would have gone for his weapon but in Harris' case he decided it was not necessary. With a gleam in his eyes Harris pulled out two tickets. "I didn't forget about you, Detective! Remember I promised to save you tickets to the opening of 'Desdemona'. Here they are. Tomorrow evening at eight."

Adam was genuinely speechless. "I really don't think I can make it, Harris. That's a generous offer, but I am not permitted to accept gifts." Adam winked, "It could be construed as a bribe."

Harris thought Adam's comment was hysterically funny. "That's fantastic! Do you know what publicity that could generate? Please. I insist. You must attend." Harris handed Adam the two tickets.

"Harris, thank-you, but I can't accept." Adam felt like he was dealing with his mother. "Harris, wait a minute. I've changed my mind. I'll take the tickets. I'm going to take my mother with me. I think she'll love it!" Harris handed him the tickets. "But, Harris, I insist on paying you for them."

Ellen and Charlie were having lunch on the porch when Ellen's phone 'can-canned.' "Oh, hi Myrna. How are you doing?"

"How do you think I'm doing! Did you see the article in the Daily Freeman?" she snapped.

"No, I didn't."

"Joseph was the lead story. That little twerp of a reporter twisted it to look like Joseph is some kind of monster."

"Myrna, what can I do to help?"

"Well, I'm calling because I remember that you said Joseph and I should stop hiding if we have nothing to hide."

"Yes, I meant that."

"We've decided that we're going to attend the opening of 'Desdemona' tomorrow."

"Great! I'm glad you're doing that."

"Could you meet us outside the theatre and walk in with us?"

"I'll be happy to do that. A show of support. I'll meet you at the Denizen at 7:45. Now, try to relax today if you can."

"Yeah. See you tomorrow." Myrna ended the call.

Harris was about to check in with Leonard to see how things were going at the theatre when he received a text from Cosmo. He read it and, instead, stomped directly to the Antique Barn to confront Cosmo in person. "Cosmo," he yelled. "Hey, Cosmo, what the hell is this all about?" Harris marched behind the counter where Cosmo was listening to Cris, one of the antique dealers, tell him how to create a faux finish on a chest of drawers.

"Hi Harris. Calm down and tell me why there's fire coming out of your ears." Cosmo pointed to another stool. "Have a seat."

"No, I prefer to stand," Harris insisted. "Take a look at this text you sent me!"

Cosmo howled with laughter and almost fell off the stool as he read, "*Desdemona will be my cure for insomnia. If I start to snore, do not disturb! Hah, hah!! Lovu, Honey!*"

When Cosmo was able to stop laughing he turned to Harris, "I am so sorry, Harris. I meant to send that to Walter, not to you! Your text reminding us about tomorrow came just when I was about to text Walter. What can I say? I sent it to you by mistake."

"A cure for insomnia!" Harris was not feeling much better.

"Look, Harris, I really do apologize," Cosmo said unsuccessfully stifling a laugh. "I was just kidding with Walter. I'm usually in bed by eight. That's why I said it." Cosmo attempted to cover up his errant text.

Harris shook his finger at Cosmo as he walked to the door, "I'm going to be watching you tomorrow. You start to fall asleep and I'm coming over to wake you up! And that's a promise!" He opened the door and turned back to grin at Cosmo. "Honey," he winked.

Ellen was finishing her call with Ginger. "Sure, I don't blame you, Ginger. I'm only going because I promised Dorothy."

"You do realize that if I dragged Hugh to see 'Desdemona', I'd be expected to cook dinner for an entire week in return," Ginger groaned. "One whole week, Ellen! No way! Sorry. I couldn't possibly!"

Ellen laughed, "No problem. I'll let you know what you missed!" Ellen placed one more call to Pat.

"Hi, Ellen. What's up?"

"Wondered if you and Bill wanted to attend the opening of 'Desdemona' tomorrow night."

Pat roared with laughter. "Oh yeah, Ellen. You can only imagine how Bill has been begging me to take him." She spewed, "If I roped him into going to see 'Desdemona', do you have any idea what the payback would be? Do you?"

"Tell me. Come on!" Ellen giggled.

"Oh, I'll tell you, alright. He'd strut around the house like Popeye and expect me to play Olive Oyl. Popeye and Olive Oyl! 'I yam what I yam?' Sorry, Ellen. Not happening!" Pat ended the call.

Adam returned to the office and spent a frustrating hour with Joseph and Myrna Van Dyke. They both stuck to their alibi; they were home together the entire evening on Sunday, September 25.

By early evening, he picked up a small pizza from Rocco's and returned to his office. Adam vowed to sleep at his desk, if necessary, but he was not leaving the office until he deciphered Eddie's clues buried deep in his notepad. He whipped through page after page of scribbles, hoping to find themes and patterns in order to connect the dots. 'douse, house, louse'. Nothing. Many illegible scribbles were probably written in an inebriated state. Adam began to drift in and out of sleep as the night turned into the early morning hours. He forced himself to stay awake.

Adam remembered Ellen's words and, literally, turned the paper ninety degrees to the left. He rubbed his eyes, staring at the page in front of him. "Shit! Why didn't I see that before?" Adam was overtired but euphoric. He locked up and drove home to get a couple of hours sleep and a shower. He was absolutely certain who started the fire on Beekman Road. "Thank-you, Eddie Siricco!" he shouted, not sure whether to look up or down.

Wednesday, October 19

Chief Liberti sat at one end of the conference table with Adam at the head. The rest of the team of detectives filled in the sides. Adam began the meeting with a smile, for once. "Officers, I would like to show you who started the fire at the house on Beekman Road." Murmurs traveled around the entire table as Adam flashed a page from Eddie Siricco's notepad onto the large screen behind him.

Adam stood to the side and pointed with his finger. "Look here. We've seen these pages before." Adam read aloud a few random words. "Here Eddie wrote, *'liar-liar-house on fire'* and over on this page," Adam scrolled to the next photo, "*'douse, louse, house'* and see this one: *baa-baa-Beekman house.'*" Adam scrolled to the next photo. "Check this out." The officers were not impressed. They shrugged and looked from one to the other, clueless. Adam grinned. "It looks like some drunken doodling. Right?" Everyone nodded. "But watch what happens when I turn the paper ninety degrees." Adam scrolled to the next photo to demonstrate. He looked from one officer to the next as they deciphered Eddie's cryptic message.

Adam patiently waited for each officer to figure it out. Finally, he explained what had become obvious. The message was a rebus: a drawing of an eye plus a drawing of a handsaw plus a couple of squiggles that resembled a sheep. "Yes, officers. I plus SAW plus SHEEP--as in Sheppard. When this is combined with the other seemingly random words, we have the identity of the arsonist who set out to destroy the Van Dykes." Adam sat down. "Questions?"

Liberti ruminated, "Well, done, Jacobson. So, Ben Sheppard burned down the house. The crumpled note tells us that he knew Siricco caught him in the act and Sheppard admitted that he refused to pay off Siricco. Quite possibly, Eddie Siricco may have solved his own murder."

Another officer at the table said, "But, without evidence that Sheppard murdered Siricco, we've got nothing on him besides arson."

Adam replied, "You're right. But let's face it. A solar eclipse is brighter than Ben Sheppard. I think we can get him to trip over himself and provide the evidence we need. We have to set the trap and then be patient."

Adam had invited Ellen and Charlie to the police station. Sergeant O'Riley waved them on to Adam's office.

"Good morning, Ellen and Charlie," Adam grinned.

"Well, aren't you Mr. Congeniality this morning," Ellen remarked. "Someone had one heck of a wild night, I see!"

"You're right, Ellen and I'm completely worn out from it," Adam bantered back. "Look at this and tell me what you think this says." Adam placed two four by six photos of Eddie's scribbles in front of them.

Ellen and Charlie shrugged. Charlie said, "Looks like Eddie was doodling. That's all I see." Ellen nodded in agreement.

"Now, what happens when I turn the photo ninety degrees? What do you see?"

"My God! A rebus!" Ellen exclaimed. "Adam, you took my metaphor seriously!"

"Ellen, you and my mother are the two women I always take seriously."

"And those random words aren't really random after all: *'douse, house, baa-baa-Beekman house'*." Charlie rubbed his chin as he stared at the two photos in front of him. "So Ben Sheppard burned down the house and framed the Van Dykes. What do you know!"

"It certainly looks that way," Adam concurred. "But, you can't say a word about this. I want to find out if Sheppard murdered Siricco in order to silence him. You both have to promise to let my people take over. I want Sheppard to think he's in the clear and trap him into incriminating himself."

"Well, that shouldn't be hard. A cuckoo is brighter than Sheppard," Ellen retorted.

"A toad is brighter than Sheppard," Charlie added, punctuating it with several guttural 'ribbits'.

Ellen began to giggle. "My spider plant is brighter than Sheppard."

"A sloth is brighter," Charlie chimed in. "Hell, the Geico gecko is brighter than..."

"Okay, you guys." Adam rolled his eyes. "Enough."

Adam's scolding was too much for Ellen. She could not contain her giggles and, simply, kicked back and enjoyed the next round. While she struggled to compose herself, Charlie asked, "Will we see you at the grand opening of 'Desdemona' this evening?"

"I'll be there," Adam replied. "And I'll be escorting a very special woman."

That comment abruptly ended Ellen's fit of laughter. "Hah! I knew it!" Ellen gloated.

Adam said, "Ellen, I'm bringing my mother with me. See you this evening!"

Today Leonard had scheduled an abbreviated rehearsal to go over last minute technical issues (lighting, sound, placement of props). With only a couple of hours until she became Desdemona, Dorothy was in her dressing room, staring at herself in the mirror. Ever since Monday, when she heard that Joseph Van Dyke had been named a person of interest in poor Eddie's murder, Dorothy felt giddy. The New Paltz Police Department had apprehended the murderer and forever lifted a weight from her shoulders. Never again would she need to hear the name Eddie Siricco.

"Dorothy Dawson," she addressed her image in the third person, "you have the power to create your own future. You are free to rise from the grave and begin anew--just as Desdemona begins anew." She arose, placed a "Do Not Disturb" sign on her door, fell onto her fainting couch, and closed her eyes for a refreshing power nap.

This was opening night and the Denizen Theatre was buzzing with a palpable energy. The unpredictable nature of live theatre only heightened the experience. Tonight, the theatre was spilling over with possibilities. But no one at the Denizen Theatre could ever have anticipated the way the evening was about to unfold.

Excitement and apprehension surrounded this event. Harris and Judith arrived an hour before curtain time. Harris looked dapper in his dinner jacket and Judith was positively elegant in a classic Vera Wang dress. Judith insisted on bringing an extravagant bouquet to Dorothy. She knocked on the dressing room door and was greeted by an effusive Dorothy Dawson. A student intern cradled the bouquet in her arms and left to find a suitable vase for them.

Leonard was on stage giving last minute instructions to the stage crew. He made a striking appearance in his burgundy, velvet Gothic jacket. The cropped front and elongated tail gave it a retro look. Leonard waved to Harris and Judith. "Well, well. The impresario and his beautiful lady!"

They all exchanged the continental, two-cheek peck. Harris beamed, "And, Leonard, I think you'll have a full house tonight!"

"Marvelous, Harris! The audience won't be disappointed!" he promised, crossing his fingers behind his back. He took out a handkerchief and wiped the perspiration from his furrowed brow.

Matthew and Pablo stopped to grab a sandwich from the Mudd Puddle before the theatre. They sat at a table in the courtyard and wondered why they had allowed themselves to be bullied by Dorothy. They decided they would be firm and forgo the after-party. Six A.M. would come all too soon. Pablo was taking a bite of his veggie wrap when Matthew whispered, "Hey, Pablo. Look! It's Myrna and Joseph!" He waved to them as they walked in their direction.

Myrna appeared to drag Joseph over to their table as if he were a recalcitrant four-year-old. With forced cheerfulness she greeted them. "You boys came all the way from the City for the opening?"

Matthew groaned, "Dorothy strong-armed us into this, I'm afraid. It's really good to see you both. I know this has been a rough time."

"Thanks, Matthew. We have nothing to hide so we've decided to stop hiding," she nonchalantly replied.

Pablo smiled and asked, "Joseph, how are you holding up?"

Joseph shrugged but did not say anything. Showing up tonight did not appear to be something he fully embraced.

Ellen and Charlie parked the car and headed to the Denizen. Ellen carried a bouquet of, aptly named, Desdemona roses for Dorothy. They were carefully wrapped and preserved to last through the entire performance. She and Charlie walked inside, placing their jackets on a couple of seats. Ellen became edgy and tried to calm herself down. She could not manage to shake the uneasy feeling as she and Charlie waited for Myrna and Joseph. A couple of minutes later, Ellen saw them walk in with Matthew and Pablo. Myrna thrust back her shoulders and, Birkenstocks leading the way, marched into the Denizen Theatre ready to face the hostile world.

"Myrna, Joseph. Good to see you," Ellen greeted them.

Turning to Matthew and Pablo, Charlie added incredulously, "And you guys came from Manhattan for this?"

Matthew mischievously winked, "Wouldn't think of missing this, Charlie. Are you kidding!"

They chatted with Ellen and Charlie, while Pablo went over to the desk to pick up the tickets Dorothy had left for them. However, Myrna's eyes turned to daggers as soon as she saw Adam enter the theatre. Myrna abruptly turned her back to Adam and dragged Joseph in to find some seats. Matthew and Pablo followed close behind.

"Mom, I'd like you to meet Ellen and Charlie Green. This is the couple I've told you about," Adam graciously announced.

"Delighted to meet you both. Please call me Ruth," Mrs. Jacobson said. "And, Ellen, Adam's told me that you and I are very much alike," she whispered in confidence.

"I'm flattered, Ruth. Adam speaks very highly of you."

Adam exchanged an amused look with Charlie. "Mom, we need to find some seats."

"Sure, dear. See you later, Ellen and Charlie!"

Seated at a desk in the lobby, the young woman selling tickets announced that the show would start in five minutes. Ellen and Charlie went in to find their seats. People began filing into the theatre as curtain time approached. Harris delivered his promise. Opening night was filled to capacity.

The Bird-Watchers arrived at precisely the same time Phillip Edelstein made his entrance. He needed to make sure that Harris saw him arrive on time, so he blew by everyone to enter and find a seat.

"Hey, Charlie, look who just walked in!" Ellen elbowed him. "What is he doing here?"

"Whatever it is, it's not because he wanted to be here. I'm sure of that!"

The lights blinked twice, ushering everyone to their seats.

Walter and Cosmo dashed inside in time to nab two seats on the aisle in the back row. Walter was relieved that they had the perfect escape route.

Moments before the doors to the lobby closed, Michelle and James made it into the theatre. After cleaning and locking up the Mudd Puddle, they threw off their aprons, raced across the courtyard, and flew up the stairs to the theatre. Exhausted and sleep-deprived, they were each counting on closing their eyes as soon as the house lights were lowered.

Tension spread from the stage into the audience as the theatre was suddenly cloaked in darkness. Seconds later, a spotlight on the stage featured Leonard. "Good evening, ladies and gentlemen. Welcome to the Denizen Theatre and the premiere of 'Desdemona'. Before we begin our one-woman show, I'd like to give a shout-out to Harris and Judith Landau, our producers, our cheerleaders, our promoters." The audience gave a round of applause as Judith and Harris stood up to acknowledge everyone. "As owners of the Denizen, their creative spirit has become reality. And now, their reality has become a creative spirit." He paused. "Before we begin, I would like to remind you to look at the paperless credits projected at stage right. Two names deserve special mention: our playwright, Allyssa McPherson and our leading lady, Dorothy Dawson." Leonard gestured to the credits and waited until the applause died down. "I'd like to remind you to turn off all electronic devices. There will be one brief intermission during this performance. Now, without further ado, please sit back and take in the world premiere of 'Desdemona'!" The theatre became completely black.

Next, the stage was dimly lit showing a graveyard scene obscured by a dry-ice fog. Offstage, a musician played the bongo drums.

That was the moment that Ben Sheppard skulked into the theatre and slid into a seat, followed by an undercover officer who sat right behind him. Ted recognized Ben instantly and nudged Bud. "Look who walked in."

Bud glanced over his shoulder. "Would never have taken him for a theatre buff." Baffled, they both shrugged.

Ellen whispered to Charlie, "What's the arsonist doing here?" A sudden shiver traveled down her spine.

Charlie held his palms upward and shook his head in disbelief.

Adam, ever-vigilant, noted Ben's arrival but kept his head facing the stage.

All eyes were fixed on the stage as Desdemona dramatically arose from one of the graves. She was shrouded in black as she mournfully invoked Othello, "*You have wronged me with your jealousy and turned my passion for you into hatred!*" Dorothy slowly walked to the front of the stage. "*But, my spirit has returned and I will be avenged!*" She emitted an ear-shattering cackle as she whirled around the entire perimeter of the stage.

By the end of this soliloquy, Michelle and James were sleeping like babies. Cosmo was snoring loudly in the back of the theatre. When Walter poked him a couple of times, Cosmo responded with three loud snorts. Muffled titters circulated through the audience as heads turned to stare.

For the next forty-five minutes, Dorothy drifted in and out of the script. Leonard was pacing backstage the entire time. He was furious. Dorothy was veering off in random directions. Her orations were spontaneous discourses having nothing to do with the play. With intermission still several minutes away, Alyssa was futilely flipping through her script trying to find some way to reconcile Dorothy's words with her play.

The audience was befuddled. Catherine grumbled to Karen, "My nightmares make more sense than this foolishness."

Mrs. Jacobson leaned in close to her son and chuckled, "Desdemona reminds me of old Mrs. Mc Gruder who swore she was descended from Cleopatra."

Phillip never bothered to look up from his phone. He was texting clients and billing them at the rate of five hundred an hour. He fulfilled his end of the bargain with Landau; he showed up on time and planned to stay until it ended.

Ben was becoming very agitated. He had a feverish need to escape and began frantically turning around to check for the exits as the sweat dripped down his hairline.

A couple of people slithered out, not really caring whether they were noticed.

The scene was becoming more intense. Dorothy exited the stage and the bongo drummer moved onto the stage. He was joined by another drummer. Their hypnotic beat was getting louder and faster. This musical interlude gave Leonard a chance to talk to Dorothy who had a rare moment offstage. Dorothy got a thirty-second dressing down from Leonard. Alyssa sweetly refocused Dorothy on the script.

Dorothy appeared to have regrouped. She made a dramatic entrance as the drums simulated a thunderstorm. Dorothy swept onto center stage, raising her head and her arms upward. Leonard's breathing returned to normal as the scene appropriately played out. Dorothy waved the white handkerchief in her hand. *"This gift from you was a symbol of my fidelity, Othello. Alas, it weighs me down as a symbol of relinquishing my soul to a mad, cruel lover!"*

Sighing with relief, Leonard smiled at Alyssa who gave him a thumbs-up sign. Dorothy was back and she was brilliant! Intermission was only one brief monologue away. Unfortunately, that was one monologue too many.

Dorothy's voice rose menacingly above the bongo drums. *"You have mocked me. You have threatened to expose me. You know my demons."* Dorothy moved down stage, closer to the audience.

Leonard was ready to take a hook and drag her off the stage. "Where the hell was she going with this stream of consciousness?" he wondered. He warned the stage crew to stand by and be ready to stop her.

Dorothy stretched her arms out in front, beckoning to the audience. *"With the weight of your gift you smothered the life out of this defenseless body. And with the weight of my powerful spirit, arisen from the grave, I will smother the life out of you. Hand to mouth. Fingers to nose."* Waving the white handkerchief, she ended with, *"I am free!"* and exited stage left.

The spellbound audience burst into a thunderous applause as the house lights came on and intermission began. Charlie looked over at Ellen's seat and assumed that she had already gone to the ladies' room, trying to beat the crowd of women lining up.

Adam kept a close watch on Ben who never moved from his seat or made contact with Phillip. Adam excused himself. "Mom, would you like me to get you anything to drink?"

"No, dear. I'm fine," she smiled.

Adam decided to pay a friendly visit to Ben Sheppard. He walked to the far corner where Ben was slumped down, arms crossed as if he were wearing a straight jacket. "Enjoying the show, Ben?" Adam greeted him pleasantly.

"It's pure garbage, Jacobson. What did you expect? This is Landau's joke on all of us." As soon as Adam returned to his seat, Ben charged for the exit.

Ellen was aghast as she listened to Dorothy's words. She grabbed the bouquet of flowers and kept muttering Dorothy's shocking lines as she navigated her way backstage to Dorothy's dressing room. Ellen saw a glittery star on a door, knocked, and barged in. Leonard was holding Dorothy's hand and forcing himself not to scream at her for her off-script tirades. He wisely decided that calm and comfort might prove more effective.

Ellen did not give a damn about Dorothy's performance. She ordered Leonard to leave them alone. He was so stunned by the intrusion, he never questioned who she was. He accepted her authority, left the room, and closed the door.

"Dorothy, your performance was extraordinary. I brought you some flowers: Desdemona roses, as a matter of fact." Ellen smiled tentatively as she presented the flowers to Dorothy.

"Why, thank-you, Ellen, my cell mate," she tittered. "However, I don't think Leonard appreciated it very much. He, foolishly, wanted me to parrot the little playwright." Dorothy rolled her eyes at the mere thought.

"You have a special talent, Dorothy. You would have made an excellent playwright, yourself."

"You really think so?"

"I do. Your final words were haunting." Ellen repeated, "*With the weight of my powerful spirit, arisen from the grave, I will smother the life out of you. Hand to mouth. Fingers to nose.'* Do you realize that you described, in perfect detail, Eddie Siricco's murder, Dorothy?" Ellen stated accusingly.

Dorothy laughed a shrill, venomous laugh. "That's preposterous, Ellen. I never said those words," she emphatically denied. "Look, here's the script, the part right before intermission. See, that's what I said. *'Othello, my one and only love. We loved too much and trusted too little."* She gave Ellen a condescending smile, "See, dear, those were my lines. I never said those other terrible words."

"You described your murder of Eddie Siricco."

A gentle knock at the door said, "Five minutes, Ms. Dawson."

Dorothy's eyes became feral, her breathing came in short, staccato gasps.

"But why, Dorothy? Why did you kill Eddie?"

Dorothy invoked a stirring cadence. "*He mocked me. He threatened to expose me. He knew my demons!"* She brayed: a

302

hideous sound that emanated from deep within her core. Closing her eyes, Dorothy summoned up the distant past. "Annie Sullivan in the Miracle Worker. Without me, the play would have been a catastrophic failure. That razor blade. Poor dear. How was I to know there would be so much blood?" The braying grew louder and more strident. "She was sacrificed for the art of the theatre. A pity, really. I had no choice."

Suddenly, Dorothy grabbed the cut glass vase filled with Judith and Harris' extravagant floral bouquet. With all her might, Dorothy flung the vase and charged at Ellen. Ellen braced herself, ready to duck.

Ellen side-stepped to avoid getting smashed in the head. The vase shattered all around her. Dorothy kept charging at Ellen, ignoring the shards of glass. Dorothy's features became distorted in a grotesque simulation of Desdemona. Ellen grabbed Dorothy's arm and whipped it behind her back causing Dorothy to let out blood-curdling shrieks. Hearing the sounds emerging from Dorothy's dressing room, Leonard banged on the door as Dorothy continued to shriek.

Pushing Leonard out of the way, Adam exploded into the room with Charlie right beside him. They witnessed Ellen restraining a screaming, tempestuous Dorothy. She was trying to pull Ellen's hair with her left arm as her right arm was securely pinned behind her back. Both women were sprawled out on the floor amid the shattered crystal.

Charlie slammed the door shut while Adam took over and sat Dorothy down on her fainting couch. Charlie rushed to Ellen's side and helped her up. She limped her way to a chair and sat down.

Adam said, "Charlie, do not let Ms. Dawson move until I return." He opened the door to find Leonard and the stage crew all huddled together. "I am Detective Sergeant Jacobson. Leonard, please announce that there has been an emergency. Everyone must leave the premises immediately." Adam called the station for back-up.

Leonard stuttered, "Yes, Sir. Okay, Sir. Is Dorothy alright?"

"Dorothy is in capable hands," Adam replied. "Oh, Leonard, please ask Mrs. Jacobson to wait for me in the lobby." He whispered softly, "She's my mother."

Two police officers arrived and hand-cuffed Dorothy. Adam read her her rights. As the officers discreetly led Dorothy out a side exit, she seemed to be channeling Desdemona, wailing loudly, "*We loved too much and trusted too little*" as she was hauled off to the New Paltz Police Department to be charged with murder.

As soon as Ellen's superficial cuts were cleaned, she and Charlie slowly made their way out of the theatre. In one hour, they were due at the New Paltz Police Department to be debriefed. They reached the courtyard and saw that the Mudd Puddle had opened up and was serving coffee and pastries to a small gathering. As Ellen and Charlie got closer, they were greeted with a standing ovation from a crowd of Bird-Watchers, Walter and Cosmo, Harris and

Judith, Matthew and Pablo. Hooting and hollering was unrestrained. Even Myrna and Joseph got in on the action. Mrs. Jacobson stood proudly among the crowd. Conspicuously absent were Phillip Edelstein and Ben Sheppard.

Chief Liberti assembled the entire team of detectives in the conference room where Adam led the debriefing. Every detective was curious to finally meet the hot-shot undercover agents who played a critical role in solving Eddie Siricco's murder. Expecting the Avengers to march into the room, the investigative team was properly humbled when Ellen and Charlie were introduced as the top-secret assets.

Hours later, after a grueling and celebratory debriefing, Ellen and Charlie were free to return home. Chief Liberti asked Ellen one final question. "How did you know what the motive was?"

Ellen replied, "Dorothy's own words said it best. '*You have mocked me. You have threatened to expose me. You know my demons.*'"

Thursday, October 20

Even after a late night, Chief Liberti faced a jubilant team of detectives early this morning. "Detective Jacobson, I turn the meeting over to you."

"Good morning, officers. We should all be proud of this collaborative effort but we have one more matter to take care of: Ben Sheppard." The other officers nodded in agreement. "Now, here's what we're going to do." By the time Adam finished explaining the plan, the other officers were ready to roll. "Now remember, Sheppard still thinks Van Dyke is about to be charged with arson. Not a word to anyone about this!" Adam warned with a glint in his eyes. "But first, Detective Liberti and I have to step outside. 'Live with Lauren' is setting up the cameras."

This morning, Mrs. Jacobson was enjoying her coffee. She turned on the local news, just as Adam had told her to do. 'Live with Lauren' was on the scene with a breaking news story. "*Good morning, folks. I'm here with Mayor Bradley, Chief Liberti, and Detective Sergeant Adam Jacobson of the New Paltz Police Department.*" Turning the microphone towards Mayor Bradley, Lauren asked, "*Mayor Bradley, tell us about the breaking news story.*"

Mayor Bradley stood blocking the Chief as he boasted, "*Well Lauren, Eddie Siricco's murderer has been arrested. Our beloved Town Crier was murdered by Dorothy Dawson, actor and ex-wife of the deceased.*"

306

"This is a shocking revelation, Sir! What else can you tell us about the case?"

Mayor Bradley did not know another damn thing about the case nor did he care. He turned the matter over to Chief Liberti who spoke quite eloquently. *"Lauren, this was an outstanding example of teamwork by a tireless and talented group of detectives, led by Detective Sergeant Adam Jacobson."* Liberti stepped to the side and motioned for Adam to come forward. *"Detective Jacobson has shown intelligence and determination. He has used every possible resource available, including a top-level undercover team. Through this multi-faceted approach, justice was served. Residents of New Paltz, you can feel safe. You are our number one priority. Our only priority."*

Tilting the microphone in Adam's direction Lauren asked, *"Detective Jacobson, why did Dorothy Dawson murder Eddie Siricco?"*

Adam answered succinctly, *"He knew too much."*

"What about Joseph Van Dyke? Is he still suspected of arson?"

Adam looked directly at the camera with his charming smile. *"I really can't comment on an ongoing investigation, Lauren. Now, if you'll excuse me, we all have a lot of work ahead of us. Thank-you, Lauren."* Adam smiled into the camera. He and the Chief briskly walked inside the building, leaving the Mayor to fumble for answers to questions he could not possibly answer.

Mrs. Jacobson was bursting with pride. She could not wait to tell her bridge ladies that her Adam was a hero. She called Midge first. Midge's daughter, Rhoda, is single and moved to New Paltz last month. Mrs. Jacobson insisted that Midge and Rhoda come to dinner tomorrow to help them celebrate. Mrs. Jacobson was making her brisket. Midge agreed to come for dinner and she would see to it that Rhoda showed up. Midge proudly explained that Rhoda was a doctor. Not a dentist. A real doctor.

Mrs. Jacobson was ecstatic. She called Adam and left him a voicemail. "Adam, come for dinner tomorrow: brisket, your favorite! Oh, by the way, Midge and her daughter, Rhoda, will be joining us. Rhoda is a doctor." She positively tingled with excitement. "I figure it this way. So what if you're not a doctor, Adam. Big deal. You can always marry one! Be here at six. No excuses!"

Adam was about to leave to arrest Ben Sheppard, but, first, he made a call to Detective Sergeant Raul Swann in Cape Coral, Florida. Raul answered, "Hello, Adam. Things heating up in New Paltz?"

"Raul, Ellen and Charlie are everything you said they would be. That's the good news and the bad news."

Raul asked, "Nothing's happened to them. Right?"

"Believe me. They're fine! That's why I'm calling you. Thanks to Ellen and Charlie, Eddie Siricco's murderer has been apprehended."

"I'm not surprised. Please congratulate them for me!"

"I sure will, Raul."

"And, one more thing. Please tell them to do me a favor and stay up North for a while. There's no need to rush down to Cape Coral any time soon. Since they left, we have not had one single murder."

Next, Adam got in his cruiser and drove to Ben Sheppard's home. He had arranged for a back-up squad car to meet him there. Adam rang the bell and Ben answered, taking his time to get to the door.

"Well, Detective Jacobson. What's up?"

Adam reached out to shake Ben's hand. "Just wanted to bring you up to speed, Ben. May I come in?"

"Sure. Have a seat." Ben pointed to a chair with coffee-stained upholstery.

"Thanks," Adam replied as he sat down.

"So, that was really something about that actress, Dorothy what's-her-name! She sure is a nutcase!"

Adam shook his head. "I guess it's not safe having an ex-wife around. You ever been married?"

"Naw. That's not for me. And you, Detective? You have an ex hunting you down?" Ben sneered.

Adam smiled, "Thank God, no!"

"So, has Van Dyke been arrested yet?"

Adam smiled, "Not yet. We have to gather more evidence before we can make an arrest."

"Of course. But, I guess his motive was pretty convincing," Ben grinned as he sat on the couch across from Adam.

"Yeah. I agree. I'm trying to rule out any other motive someone might have."

"Do you think it might have actually been a hate crime? Is that what you're saying?"

"Probably not. After all, this is New Paltz. But, I'm still figuring someone really had it in for Joseph." Adam shrugged indifferently.

"I'd try to stick with the evidence if I were you, Detective." Ben was the genial host, confident that no one would ever connect him with the arson. "I still wouldn't even rule out Phillip Edelstein."

"Really?"

Leaning with his elbows on his thighs, Ben spoke confidentially, "Stick with the evidence. That's what I would do. In this case, the evidence isn't easy to hide. How the hell do you hide a bunch of five-gallon, neon yellow gas cans?" Ben chuckled. "No way to dispose of them either."

Adam was overwhelmed at Ben Sheppard's utter stupidity. "Hmm. You have a point there, Ben. Neon yellow gas cans, you say," Adam pondered thoughtfully. "But I'm curious. How did you know that Van Dyke used neon yellow gasoline cans for the fire?" Adam gave Ben a quizzical stare.

Ben stood up and sputtered, "Of course I don't know that. I, um, I, well. Just a wild guess, Detective."

"Let's go to the garage and see how wild your guess is," Adam suggested amiably.

"Wait a minute! You have no right to search my garage. Get the hell out of here! Now!"

Adam stood and pulled a search warrant out of his pocket to show a flabbergasted Ben Sheppard. "Two officers are searching your garage as we speak. Let's see what they've found." He gave Ben a couple of shoves towards the door to the garage.

They entered the garage and saw two police officers, surrounded by seven or eight five-gallon, neon yellow gasoline cans. Ben sat down on his trash can, put his head in his hands, and gave himself up.

Friday, October 21

The news of Ben Sheppard's arrest spread far and wide: from Harris to Phillip to the real estate company handling the sale of Ben's land on Milo Road. Phillip Edelstein's phone call to Kevin, the assistant brokering the land sale, was a brief one.

"Hey, there, Phillip. I learned about Ben Sheppard's arrest for arson," Kevin began in a jovial tone. He might as well have been talking about his golf game.

"Yeah, I just heard the news, also. Sheppard still owns the property and I'm confident that the planning board will be eager to..."

"Right, right, Phillip. But, my client has withdrawn the purchase offer." Kevin jauntily added, "No hard feelings, I hope."

"No. I understand." Phillip ended the call.

Dorothy Dawson was arraigned in court and charged with second degree murder. She basked in the histrionics of appearing before a judge, embracing the moment as a perfect opportunity for her to flaunt her dubious acting abilities.

The Bird-Watchers were meeting Ellen and Charlie for lunch at The Parish at Water Street Market. Today was the peak foliage week and The Parish offered a breath-taking view of the Shawangunk Ridge. They were joined by Myrna and Joseph. Adam promised to try to make it. Catherine had organized this luncheon as their send-off. The Bird-Watchers were going to begin their migration back South to Cape Coral later today.

As soon as this gregarious group placed their orders, everyone began talking at once. Their high-spirited conversations were a cathartic release from the tension of the previous month. The four women became hysterical as they replayed Ellen's notorious visit to Myrna. However, when Myrna mimicked Catherine and Karen's 'storming the castle', uninhibited hilarity erupted. The women all had tears streaming down their faces as they shrieked with laughter.

Even Joseph managed to relax and loosen up a bit. However, Myrna bounced back from the abyss more quickly than her husband. She found herself seated next to Adam and, for once, did not sneer and glare at him. "Adam, I've been wondering. How did you ever figure out that Ben was the arsonist?"

Adam gave her an inscrutable smile. "You know, Myrna, sometimes it's just a matter of turning the paper ninety degrees to the left." He winked at Ellen.

"Well, I always believe in heading left!" Everyone raised their glasses in agreement. "Here, here!"

"Myrna, I've been dying to know something."

"What, Ellen?"

"You weren't at home the evening of Eddie Siricco's murder. Where were you that was such a closely guarded secret?"

Myrna and Joseph made eye contact and did not answer Ellen's question. Myrna was delighted that the server chose that moment to deliver their lunch orders. However, Ellen was not about to be brushed off. "Myrna? Where were you?"

"Alright, alright!" She exhaled deeply. "I'll tell you what happened, Ellen." Myrna reluctantly explained, "That was the day of the rally. Remember, you were admiring my earrings the day before the rally? The peace earrings that Joseph had given me?" Ellen nodded. "Well, I wore them, again, to the rally the next day. Later that day when I threw the posters from the rally into a dumpster, I think one of my earrings fell off. I went to look for it. That's all," Myrna shrugged dismissively. "Now, let's eat!"

Karen blurted out, "Myrna, oh my God! You were dumpster-diving?" The hysteria broke out all over again.

The food was great and the repartee even better as their animated conversations flowed effortlessly. However, the gathering had a bittersweet tinge to it knowing the Bird-Watchers were preparing to take flight. Catherine summed it up perfectly. "The next time we get together, Ellen and Charlie, you're on your own. Chasing around after you two lunatics is way too stressful!" They all knew that Catherine would never let that happen. Her heart was bigger than her mouth.

Towards the end of their lunch, Adam had a few loose ends to tie up. "But, Joseph, why didn't you ever say anything? You both stuck with those phony alibis even though you knew I didn't believe you."

Joseph and Myrna, again, made eye contact before Joseph confessed. "It turns out that the entire time, we each thought the other one might have started the fire."

Ted found this all quite puzzling. "You mean that you both covered up for the other one and never told each other?"

They both nodded in unison. Myrna admitted, "Besides, I didn't want Joseph to know that I lost the earring. It was a birthday gift from him."

"That's so romantic!" Karen swooned, elbowing Bud. "Isn't it, Bud?" He grunted.

Adam spoke candidly. "You could have been arrested--either one of you! In fact, if it weren't for Ellen and Charlie..."

"Wait." Pointing to Ellen, Myrna lashed out, "You were working for the police? You lied to me and I fell for it!"

Ellen gave Myrna a noncommittal shrug in response.

Myrna let out a hearty laugh. "Ellen Green, you're one hell of a good liar! You got me!"

Adam looked at his phone to check the time. "I hate to leave but I've got to get back to the station." He flagged down the server. "I'll take the check." The server brought the check to the table as nine hands all started grabbing for it. Suddenly, Adam ordered them all to be quiet. "Now," he smiled, "this luncheon is compliments of Chief Liberti. He insisted. His way of saying thank-you."

The entire table raised their glasses to thank Chief Liberti.

Ellen got up to give Adam a hug. "Please give my best to your mother. I really enjoyed meeting her."

Charlie added, "One of these days, I want to try her brisket!"

Adam moaned, "Yeah well, I'll be sure to let her know when I see her tonight. I have to be there at six. And," he raised his hand to stop Ellen from making a snippy comment, "Don't you dare say one word, Ellen Green! Yes, another daughter of one of her bridge ladies." He waved and headed back to work.

Adam was on his way to his mother's for brisket tonight. He dreaded having to meet Midge's daughter, Rhoda, the doctor. Therefore, he was grateful when he saw a car pulled over on the side of the road, only a block from his mother's house. This was the perfect excuse for being late. Adam approached the car. "Hi, I'm a police officer. Are you okay?"

The attractive woman in the car explained, "I'm fine. Thanks for stopping. The truth is, I'm supposed to meet my mother for dinner and, well, I know she's playing matchmaker again," the woman grimaced. "If you don't mind, I'd much prefer spending the next two hours in my car. It's better than another awkward and forgettable evening."

Adam laughed, "Believe me. I know exactly how you feel. In fact, that's why I stopped. I'm avoiding my mother's dinner tonight." He rolled his eyes. "She's set me up with some overbearing, predatory hyena!"

They both laughed and chattered away, happy to delay the unpleasant experience that awaited each of them. Finally, Adam remembered his manners. "By the way, I'm Adam Jacobson and you are?"

A look of amusement danced in her big brown eyes. "Are you Adam Jacobson, the police detective who was on the news yesterday?" She paused, attempting to choose her words carefully. "I don't know how to say this any other way. I am Rhoda, the overbearing, predatory hyena."

Adam could not take his eyes off her bold, beautiful smile. Adam Jacobson was smitten.

Two months later

December 21

The trial of Dorothy Dawson was surprisingly speedy, much to her disappointment. She greedily sopped up the attention from the press as she vacillated between being Dorothy Dawson and Desdemona. Alas, by now, the two personas have become interchangeable. Dorothy née Dubinsky Dawson was convicted of second degree murder. She received a life sentence and was remanded to a residential facility for the criminally insane. She has begun offering acting workshops for the inmates. Dorothy is finding her stay profoundly rewarding.

Detective Sergeant Adam Jacobson and Chief Liberti were honored at a recent meeting of the board of trustees. Mayor Bradley praised their swift actions. Chief Liberti credited the entire New Paltz Police Department and gave a shout-out to the undercover team for their vital role in apprehending the murderer. Adam Jacobson is still smitten.

Mrs. Jacobson has chosen to end her career as matchmaker on a high note with what she considers to be her crowning achievement.

Phillip Edelstein managed to avoid prosecution for his nefarious, but not criminal, actions. However, his reputation as a barracuda, that he so carefully cultivated, was shot to hell. Even Ben Sheppard dismissed him as his attorney. Desperate for money, Phillip grabs whatever cases he can get his hands on. His current clientele are the bottom-feeders: druggies, swindlers, and small-time crooks.

Ben Sheppard pleaded guilty to arson, a class-2 felony. He was sent to prison for seven years. His property on Milo Road was purchased, for a nominal price, by the Town of New Paltz.

Myrna and Joseph Van Dyke successfully petitioned the Town of New Paltz to designate the newly acquired property on Milo Road as a wildlife and nature preserve. The Van Dykes received a hefty insurance settlement for their Beekman Road house. They plan to sell their townhouse and rebuild their home on the Beekman Road property. It will include a separate wing for Matthew and Pablo to stay on as their weekend guests.

Harris Landau is over the moon. The publicity generated by Dorothy Dawson's notorious arrest, is, truly, the gift that keeps on giving. Every performance at the Denizen Theatre has been sold out since that fateful world premiere.

Leonard is thrilled. In January, he will begin scheduling auditions for the springtime production of--you guessed it: 'Desdemona'.

Cosmo continues to work diligently at developing his eavesdropping skills. He feels duty-bound to carry on the legacy of Eddie Siricco, Town Crier.

Today, Walter wanted to speak privately with Ellen and Charlie. Shaking his finger at them he could not resist teasing, "I've waited to say this to you, but back in October, your booth wasn't up to its usual standards."

Ellen was taken aback. "Are you serious? Do you have any idea...!"

Walter cut her off before Ellen's tirade hit high C. He whispered, "Thank-you for finding Eddie's murderer. And all along, you managed to fool everyone around here. Well, almost everyone, I should say. Everyone except me," he winked. "I knew what you were up to the entire time. But I'll never know how you two nutcases managed to pull it off!"

"Walter, police chiefs from Florida to New York to Massachusetts are all saying exactly the same thing," Charlie grinned.

Notes

This book is a work of fiction. Therefore, most of the characters are creations of the author. However, real people whose names, in many cases, have been changed have inspired several of the characters. They include the following:

Catherine and Ted

Karen and Bud

Matthew and Pablo

Harris and Judith Landau, owners of Water Street Market

Michelle and James, owners of the Mudd Puddle Cafe

Walter and Cosmo of the Antique Barn

Christopher, Wendy, Marc, Syd, Annie, Joan, Barbara, Paul, Paty, Cris (Antique Barn)

Pat and Bernie, owners of Ward's Bridge Inn

Tara, server, Marc and Barbara, bartenders (Ward's Bridge Inn)

Pat and Bill

Hugh and Ginger

Ellen and Charlie Green

The following, listed alphabetically, are favorite local restaurants and places of interest:

Antique Barn at Water Street Market, New Paltz

Antiques on Main, Water Street Market, New Paltz

Clemson Brewery, New Paltz

Denizen Theatre, Water Street Market, New Paltz

Huguenot Street, New Paltz

Jar'd, Water Street Market, New Paltz

Lola's Cafe, New Paltz

Maglyn's Dream, Water Street Market, New Paltz

Main Street Bistro, New Paltz

Minnewaska State Park, Kerhonkson

Mohonk Mountain House, New Paltz

Mohonk Preserve, New Paltz

Mudd Puddle Cafe, Water Street Market, New Paltz

Otterkill Country Club, Campbell Hall

P&G's, New Paltz

The Parish, Water Street Market, New Paltz

Rocco's Pizzeria, New Paltz

Wallkill Valley Rail Trail, New Paltz

Ward's Bridge Inn, Montgomery

Water Street Market, New Paltz

William Smith Inn, Geneva, NY

Carol and her husband Bill Freeman grew up in Gloversville, NY and, currently, reside in Montgomery, NY. They rent two booths in the Antique Barn at Water Street Market where they spend much of their time. Prior to retirement, Carol worked as a school psychologist. She is the author of two previous books about parenting. Bill had a long career in sales and marketing. Together, they owned and operated a successful bed and breakfast for ten years. They bring their combined professional work experience, energy, and can-do attitude to every new venture upon which they embark.

In collaboration with Bill, Carol is the author of four other cozy mysteries that can be read in any order. The Cape Coral series includes the following: *The Cape Coral Caper, The Cape Coral Casanova,* and *The Cape Coral Cameo.* For antique lovers, Carol has written *The Baron of Brimfield.*

Carol's books are all available in paperback and ebook format through www.amazon.com

Book Group Discussion Questions

1. Which is your favorite character? Least favorite character?

2. Who is the most eccentric character?

3. Which character(s) is(are) the most sensible? What purpose do these characters serve?

4. With which character do you most closely identify?

5. What are some of Charlie's strengths? Are there moments when his strengths also become his weaknesses?

6. What are some of Ellen's strengths? Are there moments when her strengths also become her weaknesses?

7. Is Eddie Siricco a villain or a good guy?

8. Does Ellen discover the murderer through luck or through skill?

9. The "Two Months Later" section is my attempt to tie up loose ends. Are there loose ends still dangling?

10. With which character would you most enjoy having dinner?

11. Which characters would you want to meet in any future books?

If you enjoyed this book, try one of Carol Freeman's other cozy mysteries. Available on www.amazon.com.